BLACKSTONE UNDERGROUND

BLACKSTONE UNDERGROUND

RICHARD FALKIRK

THISTLE
PUBLISHING

Thistle Publishing
36 Great Smith Street
London
SW1P 3BU

www.thistlepublishing.co.uk

To Matthew, my youngest son

ACKNOWLEDGEMENTS

I wish to express my debt to Anthony Babington for two of his books, *The Power to Silence* (Robert Maxwell) and *The English Bastille* (Macdonald). Also to John Deane Potter for his work *The Fatal Gallows Tree* (Elek). But, in particular, I should like to commend to the reader a pocket book entitled *Chambers Guide to London the Secret City* (Ocean Books). I know of no better condensation of London Folklore than this. As always, any mistakes are mine not theirs.

CHAPTER ONE

It was a perfect day for a hanging.

The dawn sky clear and pale, a cold blade of cruelty in the air; roof-tops smudged with frost, candles spinning haloes in garret bedrooms.

But few of the 20,000-strong crowd gathered in the streets around Newgate jail noticed the cold. It was 7.45 – a quarter of an hour before two prisoners were due to be turned off – and the spectators had been celebrating all night.

On balconies which afforded a view of the executioner, or of the victim's friends hastening death by hanging on his legs, the bucks drank champagne and tossed the bottles into the crowd. The broken glass was soon ground to powder underfoot as the mob swigged beer and gin, fought, sang, recited prisoner's confessions from the condemned cells bought for ½d, kicked stray dogs to death, fondled the harlots, and had their pockets picked.

One or two did feel the cold; one or two did cut their feet on the broken glass. One of them was a boy of fourteen, barefoot, wearing ragged clothes stiff with grease and a top-hat minus its crown. His thumbs were stuck in his braces and a clay pipe stuffed with tobacco from a discarded cigar butt was clenched between his teeth; his manner was arrogant and only the acutely perceptive would have discerned his agitation.

In fact the boy was almost as scared as if the stolen silk scarf knotted round his neck was a noose. As the cold fingered his body through his tattered shirt and patched trousers the fear expanded inside him, an abrupt and premature knowledge of mortality and human debasement.

As the law stood, the boy could easily himself have taken his place on the gallows. A child was only completely safe from the rope if he was under seven; between seven and fourteen he could be hanged if the evidence against him indicated malice; over fourteen there was no mitigation. And he could be executed for any of 223 offences, including picking pockets, damaging a fishpond, impersonating a pensioner from Greenwich Hospital, stealing a shilling or a pound of turnips, or appearing in a forest with a blackened face even if there was no game there to poach.

The boy had already served his apprenticeship in crime and had qualified for the gallows a hundred times over in this the last decade of the eighteenth century.

Now 7.50 a.m. From beneath the scaffold a hand emerged and placed a rope on the platform. The crowd sighed and the pickpockets' fingers worked nimbly. In front of the boy stood a man who looked like a farmer, bull-shouldered and full of ale, jacket flapping open to reveal a wallet fat with bank-notes.

A pickpocket with a thin, pockmarked face noticed the boy eyeing the wallet and thumped him in the ribs with his elbow. 'Keep your hands to yourself, culley,' whispered the pickpocket nodding towards the wallet. 'That's mine.'

The boy shivered. 'You take it, if you want to be scragged up there.' He nodded towards the scaffold.

The pickpocket peered more closely. 'Haven't I seen you around Hyde Park doing a little bit of tooling from the young gentlemen when they're otherwise engaged with their ladies?'

'Not me,' said the boy edging away from the thief because his instinct, sharp like his ribs and his starved features, told him that the wallet was a plant and that a constable or one of the feared Bow Street Runners was close by.

'Not so fast,' said the fine-wirer grabbing the boy's arm, fingers feeling the bone. 'There's a lot of blunt in there, culley. A lot of stiffs, my dear. Maybe a finny in it for a smart lad like you. All I wants is a little distraction, like a good butt in the belly with your napper.' The thief tapped his own head. 'Then I lift the wallet and we'll be off quicker than the hangman can turn a body off.'

The crowd was settling down now, the climax of the night's sojourn due in five minutes' time. Above them the wealthy rakes continued their banter, demonstrating their superiority of rank and birth, and champagne corks popped like distant gunfire. For the élite there were invitations from the hierarchy of Newgate to eat later – 'We hang at eight and breakfast at nine.'

The mob made do with fried fish, hot pies and baked potatoes from stalls with plumes of sparks spiralling from their ovens. But not now; not with the juices dry in your mouth, and horror and lust and God knows what primitive appetites twisting your bowels. Two women fainted and were manhandled to safety over the spectators' heads; one man was trampled to death when constables broke up a thimble-rigger's game.

Inside the jail, only a couple of feet from Newgate Street, the two doomed felons waited in condemned cells, their fear of imminent and ultimate retribution muddled with alcohol.

The sun rose but there was no warmth in its rays, and the blue of the sky had the quality of ice.

'So what about it, matey?' the pickpocket asked the boy.

'Do your own tooling,' said the boy, twisting and butting with his head. Then he was away, as he had been away a hundred times before with wallets and watches and silk handkerchieves in his hands, scrambling through legs, grazing his knees. But this time he didn't go far; the pickpocket wouldn't leave his prey and *he* didn't want to leave the area he had chosen, because from here you could see the scaffold clearly without being too close.

There were two reasons for the boy's presence, one of them a conviction that a strong stomach was proof of manhood and that its sternest test was the witnessing of violent, premeditated death. Revulsion was his strongest reaction, but it was complicated by that old mischief-maker bravado.

The bells of St Sepulchre began to chime … The hangman was waiting on the scaffold – by tradition he wasn't admitted to Newgate on execution days – and inside the jail the two criminals left the Large Room where they had bidden farewell to friends and spoken to newspaper reporters.

They were led to an anvil where a blacksmith struck off their fetters, then were handed over to the Yeoman of the Halter, who pinioned their arms. A clergyman, called the Ordinary, urged them to pray and repent. Then, with the Sheriffs holding their wands of office, they were escorted through dark, stonewalled passages to the Debtors' Gate.

The black doors opened; they mounted the scaffold.

'Hats off, hats off.' The cries of the mob sharp on the frosty air. And 'Down in the front' from those who feared their view would be obstructed. The pickpockets tensed themselves because this was the best distraction ever devised.

The criminals were hooded: the noose was put around their necks. The hangman pulled the bolt and they swung.

One, a highwayman, managed to kick off his shoes and curse his executioner, which was the way the heroes of the poor and oppressed were expected to depart the world.

The other managed no such heroics. But he was only twelve and not acquainted with the requirements of his audience.

At least one member of the mob failed to see the execution. The boy wasn't sure whether the distraction twenty yards away was the culprit, or whether he would in any case have averted his gaze. Anyway he was grateful to the pickpocket with the pockmarked face who provided the distraction.

The boy heard the scuffle and shout and turned to see the pickpocket held in a wrestler's grip by the man with the fat wallet. It was now plain that the man wasn't up from the country; his voice had London accents as acrid as a Thames fog and, when he had squeezed the breath from the pickpocket's narrow chest, he produced a baton bearing a gilt crown, the visiting card of the Bow Street Runners.

'Greedy weren't you, culley,' the Runner remarked. 'Your sort never learn, do you? Our greatest ally – greed.' He twisted the pickpocket's arm behind him and propelled him towards Ludgate Hill.

The boy followed, pushing his way through the mob which was still staring enthralled at the bodies jerking in the cold sunlight. The Runner was the law and therefore the enemy, but the boy found that he didn't wholly despise him: there was about him a piratical swagger; this was no sermonising lawman; he was a competitor in a game, not averse perhaps to letting a prisoner go free for a share of the spoils. The boy felt that he was not the sort who wanted to see his prey swinging from the gibbet.

When he reached Ludgate Hill the Runner pushed the pickpocket into a waiting carriage and told the driver to take them to the Brown Bear, the inn opposite numbers 3 and 4 Bow Street, the headquarters of the Runners. There were cells in the inn and it was there, with pots of ale in front of them, that the Runners conducted much of their business.

The driver whipped up the horses and off went the coach as though giving chase. And now at last the boy turned and stared at the bodies hanging outside the brooding prison.

The cold seemed to reach inside his skull. He leaned against the mullioned window of a coffee-house; there was sweat on his brow. Other mudlarks and urchins ran whooping through the mob's legs, unaffected by the execution, making the boy feel ashamed of his reaction. Life at that moment was a brief and pointless journey, mocked by public enjoyment of death.

On the scaffold the body of the twelve-year-old twitched, life not quite extinguished by slow strangulation. Hand to mouth, the boy outside the coffee-house ran away towards Snow Hill, the knowledge that he could have been hanging there beside his friend like a dagger of ice inside him.

That was the second reason for his presence.

They had been ambitious, the two boys from St Giles Rookery, rebelling against the thieves who employed them for a few pence, ale and food, to scale drainpipes, squeeze through tiny windows and descend chimneys. The twelve-year-old was the best snakes-man, skinny but as swift as a cockroach up or down smoke-blackened walls if an alarm was raised.

One night they planned to branch out on their own and burgle a fine house in Highgate Village; but there are no secrets in the rookeries and knowledge spreads like infection. The two young rebels had to be taught a lesson, otherwise all the snakesmen might get ideas above their station and before you knew it adult thieves would have to take the risks they delegated to their young assistants. Putting a child into a bolted and barred mansion was like putting a ferret into a burrow: it might emerge with a bloodied nose or it might not emerge at all. None of the cracksmen wanted to lose their ferrets, so the constables were tipped off to make an example of the rebels.

The two boys cased the house in Highgate, owned by a retired jeweller named Sweetman, and decided that the best method of entry was down the chimney. The obvious candidate was the smaller boy, elbows still skinned and soot in his hair from a previous job.

Down he went as the harvest moon slid behind a cloud. The older boy waited in the dew-covered bushes outside. Waited, waited … Suddenly oil-lamps flared, doors opened, men were shouting and swearing. And he was running, as the moon waited behind the cloud.

There were men at the gate, so he vaulted the low fence, wriggled through clutching hands and headed for the fields – and straight into the arms of a man with prize-fighter's muscles which gripped him like manacles.

A candle-lantern was lit and the boy found himself standing beside a coach.

An elderly man leaned out of the coach and the boy knew at once that this was Mr Sweetman. 'What have we here, Gifford?' he asked. 'What have you caught this time?' You could tell from his voice that he was plump and something of a comic.

'A boy, sir,' the man said. And you could tell from his voice that his nose was flattened and he probably was an old fighter put out to grass by a kindly patron.

'Bless my soul,' remarked Mr Sweetman. He climbed down laboriously and flashed the lantern in the boy's face. 'Bless my soul,' he repeated. 'A mere child. They told me to wait here because a notorious gang of cracksmen were going to break in. They said nothing about children.'

The boy kicked backwards at his captor's shins; it was like a blow from a mosquito to Gifford, once the pride of the Fancy. He tightened his grip on the boy's arms.

Mr Sweetman said: 'How old are you, boy?'

The boy didn't reply until Gifford gripped him harder, squeezing out the reply: 'Fourteen, sir.'

'And you were waiting outside keeping watch, I presume. A crow, I believe they call it.'

'No, sir,' the boy said.

'You were going to, ah, enter?'

The boy nodded.

'Bless my soul.' The old man pondered, candlelight shining on his white whiskers. 'And how many of you are there in this, ah, gang?'

'Two.' The boy felt the tears gathering, fought them and lost. 'My mate's in there.' Nodding towards the house. 'I've got to help him. Please…'

'And how old is he?'

'Twelve.'

'The devil take me!' The old man seemed transfixed. Then: 'Come, Gifford, we must save the other lad.'

But they couldn't. Not then or later as the twelve-year-old awaited trial. The deterrent was the thing and the boy must hang to set an example to all hardened criminals over the age of seven.

Mr Sweetman appealed, wrote letters to the *Morning Post* and *The Times,* organised demonstrations, petitioned the King.

Once the fourteen-year-old boy presented himself at Bow Street and confessed his own guilt. A runner named Townsend listened to his story, gave him a shilling and advised him to run away to sea. But the boy persisted and finally Townsend consulted the magistrate. The magistrate was a friend of Mr Sweetman: the boy was reprieved. And at 8 a.m. on that frosty Monday morning his accomplice was hanged.

The fourteen-year-old boy hurried away from Newgate, bare feet breaking tissues of ice on the muddy street. The old man had offered him a home – and made him promise to report to him once a week – but it was in the Rookery of St Giles, an oasis of squalor, a sanctuary of villains, a breeding ground of disease, a graveyard of paupers, that the boy found solace.

He trusted Mr Sweetman as much as it was possible in a world where kindness was eccentricity. But to him the house in Highgate was as unreal as a stage used by a band of strolling players.

He would have liked at that moment to return to a mother working, perhaps, as a cook, warm and flushed and smelling of spices. Instead he returned to a two-room lodging-house where men slept against a rope – and to a mother who was a whore.

The boy's name was Edmund Blackstone.

CHAPTER TWO

A good many years later Edmund Blackstone, the most feared, respected and hated Bow Street Runner in the force, walked past Newgate on his way to his headquarters.

A lot had changed, he reflected, since those days when children were regularly strung up and a diarist noted: 'I never saw children cry so much. It appeared they did not want to be hanged.'

In fact hanging offences were declining. You could no longer be topped for damaging Westminster Bridge or being found disguised in the Mint! More pertinently, you wouldn't be executed if you stole property worth less than £5. Stolen goods were frequently undervalued to save a prisoner from the gallows, and George IV, for all his defects, was a merciful man who frequently granted reprieves to the disgust of the hanging judges. 'Too gallows merciful,' the judges called him.

Ah yes, the wind of reform was in the air as the nineteenth century passed its first quarter. Women were no longer publicly flogged bare-breasted; the use of chains in jail was declining; prisoners were given separate beds; women were segregated; church services were obligatory; prisoners were given work; moves were afoot even to abolish the death penalty for forgery and sheep-stealing.

Blackstone hurried past the walls of Newgate because he knew of the degradation within. He fancied he could smell the stink of it as he turned into Newgate Street. If it hadn't been for the old gentleman who had taught him how to read and write and left him £50 on condition he joined Bow Street, he might now be inside those walls despite his escape from the gallows.

Now it was he who dispatched men to the cells and the scaffold. But Blackstone, born on the other side of the law, always made sure that those he arrested deserved what they got – if, that is, any man deserved to die.

It was a fine winter morning, with the sun polishing the dome of St Paul's. Blackstone breathed deeply of the sharp air and strode briskly towards the River Fleet. Soon the jail stink was behind him. He was dressed magnificently in a blue broadcloth topcoat and a tall grey hat; one hand grasped his baton in his coat pocket; his other arm swung with martial vigour. Beggars, gonophs and pickpockets got out of his way.

Occasionally Blackstone frowned and the petty crooks moved even faster. None of them understood Blackstone – fop or thug? – and that made him doubly dangerous. He had been known to give a sovereign to a woman caught stealing a loaf; he had also been known to beat up a lodging-house owner when a child had suffocated to death in an over-crowded room. Anyway, best get out of his way, especially when he's frowning!

But the cause of the frowns had nothing to do with the criminals scuttling away from him. Blackstone had been given an assignment which baffled him. In an hour's time he had to report to Sir Richard Birnie, the Chief Magistrate, a man with little liking for unsolved puzzles, particularly when he had been asked to provide the solution.

A pretty girl wearing a low-cut bodice appeared in the door of a bakery shop and shouted: 'Hallo, Blackie, you look as if you've caught a thief and lost a murderer.'

Blackstone grinned and pointed his baton at the foot-hills of her bosom. 'Mind you don't catch a cold in the chest.'

The frown reappeared as he neared the River Fleet. Who could smile in the proximity of this waterway now known as the Fleet Ditch? It was the receptacle for London's refuse and its waters had thickened into sludge. Only pigs thrived in the Fleet and it was said that they lived wild in its upper, underground reaches.

Blackstone hurried along the Strand, having decided to have a few grogs in the Brown Bear before facing the impla-cable Birnie. It was said that Birnie's face would crack like a pea-pod if he smiled; many Runners had tried unsuccess-fully to make him laugh.

Blackstone paused outside a coffee-shop and sniffed. The morning was heady with scents and sensations and evocations of childhood. He fancied he could smell snow in the air and glanced at the sky. Was it darkening or was it his imagination? Blackstone shook his head and slapped his thigh with his baton. Unquestionably a drink was what he needed.

Ruthven was there with a tankard of ale in one huge paw, Page the pale-faced Runner with the nervous hands assigned to pickpockets, and Bentley, a young newcomer to the force. They were sitting at a table by the window.

Ruthven greeted Blackstone. 'How's the puzzle, Blackie?'

'Unsolved.' Blackstone sat down and ordered a mulled ale and a 'dog's nose' from the serving girl.

'Birnie won't like that.'

'Birnie can go to hell.'

'Trouble is he always comes back.'

Blackstone knocked back the hot gin and nutmeg and washed it down with ale. 'Have you got an answer then?'

'Can't say I have.' Ruthven's battered features didn't reveal any deep concern.

'Perhaps I can help—' Bentley, the newcomer, began, before Page interrupted him: 'I doubt it.'

Blackstone, who had never conquered an instinctive distaste for Page, snapped: 'Have *you*?'

Don't know too much about it, Blackie,' Page said, hands fluttering at his own pockets like moths. 'Something to do with a plan to rob the Bank of England, isn't it?'

'Just the opposite,' Blackstone said.

But Bentley, whose erudition was the bane of the Runners' lives, couldn't be stopped. 'I know a bit about the Bank if you think it'll be of any help,' he said, staring at the table as though a book was open in front of him. 'As you probably know' – they didn't – 'it was founded in 1694 to help finance the war William III was waging in the Low Countries.'

Blackstone snapped his fingers to summon the girl and try to cut short the lecture; he liked Bentley, with his puppy-dog enthusiasm, but like any puppy he had to be trained. The girl came languidly up to the table; Blackstone had spent the night with her and she didn't think a snap of the fingers was particularly gallant. Blackstone patted her backside; she mellowed; he had shown respect.

'...the Old Lady of Threadneedle Street,' Bentley was saying. His face was fair and fresh, his mouth slightly disfigured by a scar, a legacy from a broken bottle pushed into his face by a barroom brawler bored by a lecture on fist-fighting.

Page said: 'I know the Bank because I've picked up a few fine-wirers in the Rotunda. Next to the Derby or a hanging match, it's the best place in London to pinch 'em.'

Blackstone undid his coat and put his feet on the table. 'Aren't you ever bothered you'll pick your own pockets?'

'And arrest yourself?' Ruthven said hopefully.

Page said: 'I get more pinches than the rest of you put together.'

'If you can call arresting a pickpocket a pinch,' Blackstone said. 'I reckon twenty flimps put away is just about equal to one normal pinch. What do you say, George?' he asked Ruthven.

The animosity between Blackstone and Page had blossomed since Page had temporarily displaced Blackstone as guardian to Princess Alexandrina Victoria, heir to the throne of England, and subsequently allowed the Princess to be kidnapped.*

'More like fifty, I should say,' Ruthven said. 'Me, I don't even reckon 'em as villains. Pest, more like.'

'You'd reckon them as villains if they'd just lifted your wages,' said Page who was used to all this and attributed it to professional jealousy.

Blackstone said: 'It's your round, Page.'

Page's long fingers dipped into his pocket and emerged with a shilling. 'Didn't even notice myself lift it,' he said, smiling at his own joke.

Ruthven said to Blackstone: 'Best not drink much more, Blackie. Least not till you've reported to the old bastard across the road.'

'Plenty of time,' Blackstone said. He stared out of the window. 'I think it's going to snow.'

'No.' Bentley shook his head emphatically.

'How the hell do you know?'

Bentley said cautiously: 'I don't really know, of course. But there are no indications that it's going to snow.'

---

* See *Blackstone* by Richard Falkirk

'It's bloody cold,' Ruthven said.

'That doesn't necessarily mean it's going to snow,' Bentley told him. 'You've got to have the right conditions—'

Blackstone interrupted him. 'I could smell the snow on my way here.'

Bentley didn't reply; olfactory sensation had nothing to do with meteorology in his book.

Page said: 'Doesn't feel like snow to me.'

'One for, two against,' Blackstone said. 'Where do you stand, George?'

'It'll snow,' Ruthven said. 'And for a couple of hours London will look clean.'

Page, who liked to gamble, asked: 'When?'

'Today,' Blackstone said promptly.

Bentley shook his head again and said respectfully: 'The wind and the cloud formations are all wrong.'

'My nose is all right,' Blackstone said.

'I'll tell you what I'll do,' Page said. 'I'll make it a proper wager. I'll bet you a sovereign it doesn't snow for a week.'

'Done.' Blackstone glanced at his gold Breguet pocket-watch. 'No snow between now and 10.48 next Monday morning and I owe you a sovereign.' He held up his pot of ale. 'Let's drink to it.'

They drank, then Blackstone buttoned up his coat, patted the girl's backside once more and crossed the bow-shaped street to the dignified four-storeyed building where Sir Richard Birnie presided.

He was sitting as usual at his desk, smoking a church-warden pipe. He was dressed as usual in black and his lined old face was stern. Blackstone guessed that, as usual, he was thinking about Robert Peel.

On his desk was a copy of the *Morning Post* and a plan of the Bank of England. He glanced from one to the other; neither afforded him relief. He pointed to a chair and Blackstone sat down.

'Well?'

'No luck, sir.'

Birnie didn't seem surprised. He stabbed his finger at the newspaper. 'They've repeated their challenge.'

Blackstone nodded. 'I thought they would. And they'll do it again, I'll wager.'

'Damned impudence.'

Birnie, Blackstone thought, was understating the case. A threat to break into the Bank of England was more than mere impudence, even if robbery wasn't the motive.

'And this time they've involved Peel with Bow Street.' Birnie blew out a jet of smoke which lost itself in the soot-laden smoke billowing from the coal fire.

Blackstone realised the depth of Birnie's anger. 'How have they done that, sir?'

'Written a letter informing the public that the directors of the Bank of England have called in the Bow Street Runners, and implying that Peel will regard it as a test case when he returns from Paris. If the Runners fail to stop them carrying out their threat, then he'll use their failure as ammunition to establish his damned police force.'

Blackstone picked up the newspaper. The letter was signed *The Diddiki* – cant for gypsies – and repeated the boast that three persons would present themselves to the directors of the Bank of England in the bullion vault 'at a dark and midnight hour' next Sunday.

Birnie stared hard at Blackstone, pipe held like a gun. 'Have you an idea how they heard that we were involved?'

Blackstone said he hadn't.

'Only you, me and two or three other Runners knew we had been called in.'

'I suppose no other magistrates or politicians knew anything about it,' Blackstone said cautiously, knowing how swiftly gossip spread through the network of rich men's clubs in St James's.

'Are you suggesting that it was my doing?'

'No, sir. I suppose …'

'Suppose what, Blackstone?'

'Nothing, sir.' The only Runner likely to blab in drink was Page.

'Whoever it was has played into Peel's hands.' Birnie – who was never sure about the motives of the man sitting in front of him – went on: 'You're something of an admirer of Peel, aren't you, Blackstone?'

'I didn't blab,' Blackstone said stiffly.

'You haven't answered my question. Do you admire Peel?' – as though the Home Secretary was a highwayman.

'I admire him as a reformer, sir.'

'Ah yes, soon you'll be able to murder your grandmother and get off with a caution.' Birnie stood up and walked across the room to warm his scrawny backside in front of the fire. 'How far do you think reform should go?' He paused. 'What would you say if he scrapped the Runners?'

Blackstone grinned for the first time since he'd entered the office. 'That wouldn't be a reform, sir. That would be a capital offence.'

Birnie almost smiled, but this austere office with its portraits of former magistrates, including the Runners' mentor, Henry Fielding, was no place for such miracles.

'The fact remains that Peel wants to get rid of us and there have been too many libellous reports about us in the newspapers lately.'

'We did save the life of the heir to the throne,' Blackstone said.

'But the public never heard about that.'

'Peel did.'

'All he remembers is that we were supposed to be protecting her when she was kidnapped.' Birnie massaged his buttocks, as tough as the saddles he once made before he started his social climb. He walked back to his desk, sat down and aimed the pipe at Blackstone's head again. 'If we fail to stop these men – these Diddiki – carrying out their threat we'll be the laughing stock of England.'

Blackstone said: 'I doubt if they are gypsies. That sounds like a red herring to me. They'd like to think I was touring every camp and fairground in the country.'

'Have you any idea who they might be?'

Blackstone shook his head. 'I've checked with the best cracksmen in town – at Ben Lewis's inn in Wych Street – and they don't know a thing. And I only spoke to men I trust not to blab,' Blackstone added, anticipating Birnie. 'I've examined all the plans of the Bank, searched the whole building and interviewed the staff. Nothing.' Blackstone took a pinch of snuff and leaned back in the chair.

'Perhaps I should assign another man to the case to help you. Page, perhaps?' Birnie suggested slyly.

'That's your prerogative, sir.'

'You really think you can handle it by yourself, Blackstone?'

'There's nothing more anyone else can do.'

Birnie knocked out his pipe. 'I'll take your word for it. And I'll leave you in sole charge of the case for the time being. But just remember this – if these men present themselves in the vaults of the Bank of England at this "dark and midnight hour" next Sunday, then the streets of London will ring with laughter every time a Runner produces his baton. In other words, Blackstone, the honour of Bow Street is in your hands.'

Birnie gestured with his pipe; the interview was over.

The girl from the Brown Bear, who was in her room lying across Blackstone's knee, squealed: 'It wasn't me, Blackie, I swear it.'

Blackstone raised her skirts higher. 'It wasn't a Runner. I don't really think even Page would blab. It wasn't Birnie or me, and it wasn't anyone at Sol's Tavern – I'll stake my life on that. The only other person who might have heard about the Runners being called in was you.'

'I wouldn't blab, Blackie. You know that.'

'You're so different from other women?'

'I might gossip. I don't blab.'

'I wish I could believe you.'

The girl lying across Blackstone's knee wriggled and kicked her legs as Blackstone made another adjustment to her clothing.

Blackstone said: 'Do you swear it wasn't you?'

'On my mother's grave.'

Blackstone gazed thoughtfully at the soft white flesh bared in front of him. 'But your mother's not dead,' he reminded her.

'I didn't blab.'

'I believe you,' he said, picking her up, laying her on the bed and turning her over, relieved that he could divert his energy from corporal punishment to more pleasurable activities.

The night was crisp and clear, the light from the moon and stars bestowing tranquillity on the slums of London. It even made them look pure, Blackstone thought, as he spurred his horse Poacher towards Paddington Village. And that, surely, was the ultimate illusion.

There were two different Londons, and he never knew which was his. Was that his territory, the sprawling Rookery of St Giles on his right, its battlements of leaning roof-tops and drunken chimneys sharp against the sky? Or was it the other London, the elegant twin, where life was grace and favour, palaces and patronage?

Blackstone skirted the Rookery.

When he reached his rooms in Paddington he noticed an outline blurring the portal of the house. Had someone from the Rookery come to exact revenge on a traitor?

Blackstone drew a horse pistol and dismounted.

But the figure leaning against the porch couldn't have exacted revenge on a lame dog. She was about eighteen, dirty, pretty and on the point of fainting.

CHAPTER THREE

She finished the game pie which should have lasted Blackstone for a week, drank some brandy and coughed.

'Better?' Blackstone poured himself some port and regarded her speculatively. The next step, he decided, was a bath.

She nodded.

'You're not a great talker, are you?'

'I'm sorry … I'm very grateful.'

'No need to be.' Blackstone sipped his port. 'Why did you come here?'

'Because I need help.'

'Ah.' Blackstone waited

'I was told you were the only man who could help me.' Her voice was sharp and cockney, her hair dishevelled, her muslin dress patched.

Blackstone tried to put her at ease. 'Where are you from?' He threw another log on the fire.

'From St Giles, same as you.'

'How did you know where I was born?'

'I was told,' she said.

'You haven't been sent here to poison me or put a knife in my back or compromise me?'

'What's that?' the girl asked.

'No matter. How did you get here?'

'Walked, of course.'

'You were lucky to get here alive, then.' Although, Blackstone thought, if she had survived in the Rookery until the age of eighteen or thereabouts she was tough, despite her fragile appearance.

He poured her some more brandy and suggested it was time she elaborated.

It wasn't really she who needed help, she told him.

Who was it then?

She began to cry, and Blackstone knew that further interrogation was hopeless if he wanted a coherent explanation. He glanced at the Breguet: 2 a.m. The bath would have to wait, because it would take an hour to heat the water. He would put her to bed – and have the bed-linen laundered in the morning.

He took her to the spare room and left her there staring in awe at the clean white sheets. Minutes later he heard her snoring, and as he climbed into bed after tucking a Manton pocket pistol beneath his pillow, he was assailed by the mixed emotions of a man who has acquired a stray dog. Affection and irritation.

He was woken at nine by the smell of frying bacon and coffee. And when he went into the kitchen he was met by another girl: hair combed and curling, face shining – though the eyes were still shadowed and the tiny premature lines were there, the indelible birthmarks of the Rookery.

'Your shaving water's ready,' she told him.

'Were you in service?'

She nodded. 'But I had to leave.'

'The master?'

'No, the mistress. It was my knees. You know, they got swollen and I couldn't kneel properly and she said I was lazy.'

'No reference?'

The girl shook her head.

'What's your name?'

'Bristow,' she said.

'Your other name.'

'Mercy,' she told him.

'Good grief,' he said and went to the bathroom.

Thoughtfully he ran the blade of his ivory-handled razor through the tough black stubble on his cheeks. He had an uneasy feeling that he was now the employer of a dollymop without references.

When they had eaten the thick rashers of bacon and eggs supplied by a Paddington farmer and were sipping the coffee, he said: 'And now, Mercy, you must tell me just what you're doing here.'

'It's my brother,' she said, tears gathering.

'Your brother?'

'Johnny. It's his birthday today; he's thirteen.'

'Then you should be celebrating.'

The tears trickled down her cheeks.

'Come on,' Blackstone said, 'dry them up.' He handed her his handkerchief. 'We can't carry on like this. Why can't you celebrate your brother's birthday?'

'Because he's in Newgate jail,' the girl said.

Blackstone sighed. 'Picking pockets?'

'No, he broke into a house and stole a pocket-watch.'

'And you want me to get him out of Newgate?'

'They said you were the only man who could do it.'

'There are a few others,' Blackstone said. 'The King for instance … Has he got a long sentence?'

'Not long,' the girl said softly. 'Less than a week. He's due to be hanged next Monday.'

Blackstone patrolled his rooms, restlessly touching the fine pieces of furniture he had bought or been given by clients for services rendered. Then he got out his collection of guns and began to clean and oil them while she watched him, hope and trust lodged firmly in her face. It was the trust that aggravated Blackstone. What right had she to trust him?

'You realise I'm supposed to represent the law?'

She said she did.

'And not to flout it?'

'I just want you to save my brother.'

'But the law has decided that he's guilty.'

'He *is* guilty,' Mercy Bristow said.

'And the law has decided on the punishment—'

'But they mustn't hang him,' she said. 'They mustn't…'

'You say you've appealed?'

'I haven't

'But someone has on your behalf?'

'Lots of people. They all signed a petition or something but no one seemed to care. They all said that justice would have to take its course.'

'The King would have understood,' Blackstone said. 'And Peel for that matter. Unfortunately they're both out of the country. Prinny's a humane man for all his faults.' But at the moment he was far away, and Blackstone had no doubt that the hanging judges would take the opportunity to indulge in an orgy of legalised slaughter. A deterrent – an example – the frightening thing was that most of them believed in these justifications.

'What was the value of the watch?' Blackstone asked.

'Five guineas,' she told him.

Blackstone sighed. They were determined to get this boy. Nowadays the prosecution often valued loot at less than the fateful sum of £5 to avoid the gallows. But someone had decided that Johnny Bristow, now aged thirteen, must pay his debt to society, and that debt meant death.

Blackstone examined a four-barrelled duck's-foot pistol designed to fire into mobs at close range. 'Where did he pinch the watch from?'

'Some old toff's house.'

'Which old toff was that?' Blackstone asked patiently.

'His name was Barrington.'

'Lord Barrington, the judge?'

'That was him,' Mercy Bristow confirmed.

'He could have done worse,' Blackstone said. 'He could have broken into St James's Palace. How did he get his paws on his lordship's gold watch?'

'He was put up to it.'

'You mean he was working for someone?'

'Someone in the Rookery as like as not. I asked Johnny but he wouldn't blab because he said all the other boys working for this bloke would be scragged.'

'Have you any idea who it might be? I mean there aren't many secrets in St Giles, are there?'

'I don't know,' she said. 'There's a lot of thieves employing snakesmen. You know that as well as I do, Mr Blackstone.' She thought about it. 'Someone pretty clever, I'll wager, because Johnny was told where to find the watch and a lot of blunt besides.'

'What happened to the money?' Blackstone asked.

'He was pinched before he got to it. Johnny thinks someone nosed on him.'

'Why should anyone do that?'

'I don't know.' The girl shrugged and continued to wait for the Blackstone Escape Plan.

'Who told you to come to me?'

'Everyone in St Giles knows about you.'

'And half of them would like to see me with a noose round my neck.'

'I was told … ' she hesitated.

'Told what? That I had betrayed them and gone on to the other side of the law?'

'I was told that, seeing as how you were on both sides – you know, up to a bit of villainy as well as catching thieves – then you'd be in a position to help.'

'And what did they suggest? Breaking into Newgate? Kidnapping the judge who sentenced Johnny to death and holding him to ransom? Who was the judge, by the way?' Blackstone asked.

The girl went to the window and gazed across the fields. 'I can't remember. Something like Hardy.'

'Hardinge?'

The girl nodded. 'That's him. Do you know him?'

Blackstone knew him, and thought the chances of saving the boy were nil. Hardinge was a hanging judge, a pillar of society, determined to lead the war on crime. Men like Hardinge saw nothing wrong in executing children. What was wrong with terminating a criminal career in its infancy?

'How did your brother effect entry? How did he break in?'

'Through a window. He's very small for his age.'

'Was he the only one there?'

'No, he says there was another boy outside but he won't say who.'

He stood up, tightened the belt on his dressing-gown and frowned. He told the girl to stay there while he got dressed. He put on breeches, black riding boots, and a new bottle-green coat made by his tailor in Bury Street, St James's.

What could he do? The appeals had been rejected; the judiciary was resolute. In any case, how could a Bow Street Runner take up arms against the system whose decisions he was supposed to implement? What ammunition for Peel I Blackstone imagined Birnie's reactions and smiled despite it all.

When he emerged from his bedroom the girl was washing the crockery in the kitchen. 'Lor',' she said looking at him, 'what a swell.'

'Is Johnny your only brother?' Blackstone asked.

'Yes,' she said.

'And who do you live with?'

'I live by myself,' she said. 'Least I did until yesterday.'

'But you haven't anywhere to go because you didn't pay the rent and you were thrown out?'

'How did you know?'

'I knew,' Blackstone said. He stuck his baton and a pistol in his belt. 'Well, you'd better stay here. But just for today. And have a proper bath while I'm away,' he said, noting the tide-mark round her neck.

'You mean you'll get Johnny off?'

'I didn't say that.'

The girl ignored his words, the trust on her face firmly established. It irritated Blackstone and he told her: 'There isn't much I can do. I'm only a Runner, not the Lord Chief Justice. I'll go and see your brother but, God knows, I can't do much more.'

Mercy Bristow smiled happily back at him. 'What would you like for dinner?' she asked.

'I shan't be in to dinner.'

'I'll have something hot waiting for you.'

'Don't wait up,' Blackstone snapped. He paused at the door. 'Was there one person in particular who told you to come to me?'

'Well,' she said, 'there was one fellow…'

'Who was he?'

'He told me not to tell you,' Mercy said. 'He said you might be angry.'

'He was right. Who was he?'

'I shouldn't—'

Blackstone reached her in two strides and grasped her thin arms. 'Who was he, Mercy?'

'His name was Lawler,' she said.

Lawler. Aged about thirty, sharp and dark, no known Christian name, living off his wits, considerable abilities as an impersonator, nothing proven against him – nothing proven, but a pile of suspicion as high as the castles of dung that proliferated in the less salubrious quarters of the great capital city of London.

Lawler lived in a basement room in the Rookery in Holborn. He shared it with a thrush which sang about spring and summer in a cage in the corner. The walls were covered with sporting prints of prize-fights, cock-fights, badger-baits, racehorses, and fighting dogs with furrowed faces; and the air smelled of sausages and gin, which comprised Lawler's staple diet.

But from this squalid burrow there had emerged lawyers, footmen, jockeys and cracksmen. Or rather Lawler in his various guises. He hardly altered his dress, he made no elaborate change of diction, but, if Lawler had decided at any given moment to become a Member of Parliament, he would have been admitted to the House without demur. After all, he wasn't the first MP to reek of gin and he wouldn't be the last.

On this cold afternoon, poised to give way to evening, Lawler was counting the profits from a book he had made on a prizefight in Sussex. An unrewarding affair that had been broken up by a posse of constables in the middle of

the thirty-eighth round. It was Lawler's contention that all
the bets were now his property because there had been no
result to the fight; others disagreed because, at the moment
the constables arrived, the favourite appeared to be uncon-
scious on his feet. In particular those who had backed the
other contestant disagreed with Lawler's logic.

In his basement Lawler locked the money in an old
leather bag and prepared to leave, to fade into the shadows
for a while. Then came a knock on the door. Lawler took a
pistol from his pocket and cautiously opened it.

'Good afternoon, Lawler,' Blackstone said, pushing his
way into the burrow.

Lawler appraised the Runner warily. It was always a pleasure to see Mr Blackstone, he said, but at the moment it was
a little inconvenient because he was just leaving for a business appointment.

Blackstone slammed the door. 'Sit down and shut up,'
he said.

Lawler sat on the edge of the bed; the thrush raised its
beak and sang. Blackstone took a seat opposite Lawler and
put his baton on the table between them; this, Lawler knew,
meant business.

Blackstone said: 'What the hell did you mean by send-
ing that girl to me?'

'What girl?' Lawler poured himself a finger of gin.

'You know bloody well what girl. The dollymop with the
brother who's going to be topped.'

'Ah, that girl.' Lawler sipped his gin. 'A sad case.'

'I can do without sad cases.'

'I thought you might be able to help. The poor little
bastard only stole a watch.'

'They've strung 'em up for less than that,' Blackstone
said.

'Doesn't make it any easier for the girl—'

'Which are you interested in,' Blackstone asked, 'the girl or the boy?' He stared suspiciously at Lawler. 'You haven't been dabbing it up with her, have you?'

'She lived next-door. I just felt sorry for her,' said Lawler, reflecting that it was a useless comment because likely Blackstone had never felt sorry for anyone in his life.

'What do you imagine I can do?'

'You're her last hope,' Lawler said. 'She's tried everything else. One of them reform societies got up a petition but it didn't do no good. Not with a bastard like Hardinge.'

'It's not up to him,' Blackstone said.

'Come off it, Mr Blackstone. He could stop the hanging, you know that. All the judges are in it together, aren't they? He could stop the scragging in his club tonight if he wanted to.'

The quality of mercy... Blackstone thought – Mercy Bristow! But Lawler was right: Hardinge *could* intervene.

Blackstone pointed at the bag. 'Going to the bank, Lawler?'

Lawler nodded because he couldn't think of a retort.

'Anything to do with that fight they broke up down at Arundel?'

'I made a bit of blunt out of it,' Lawler admitted.

'But you wouldn't if the fight had gone on another minute. I hear,' Blackstone said, examining the crown on his baton, 'that there are some coves who don't think you're entitled to all that blunt.' He paused. 'But I'll tell you this, Lawler, you *are* going to a bank. *The* bank. In fact, Lawler, you're taking up a new occupation. How does stockbroker appeal to you?'

It didn't, Lawler told him. 'I thought you said a bank.' He poured himself more gin to prepare himself for the shock that always accompanied Blackstone's visits.

'I did – the Bank of England. The Old Lady of Threadneedle Street, Lawler. Because that's where those who aren't quite up to Stock Exchange standards go about their business. In the Rotunda you'll find every swindler who tried to make a dishonest penny on the market. That,' Blackstone said, 'is why I think you'll fit in nicely.'

'Thank you,' Lawler said. 'And now perhaps you could tell me what this is all about?'

Blackstone told him about the Diddiki's bold promise to present themselves in the bullion vault. 'If anyone knows anything about it, they'll be in the Rotunda. That's why I want you there.'

Lawler said: 'I don't want to do it. Honest, I don't, Mr Blackstone. You can't force me,' he added without conviction.

'No,' Blackstone said, 'I can't and that's the truth. But this is what I can do. I can always find you, Lawler, and you know that. Now there are a lot of hard men after your blood. Men who seem to think you owe them some blunt. What if I were to tell them where you were? You know, in the interests of fair play. You remember what happened to that bookmaker at the Derby who tried to welsh on his bets? He looked as if the favourite had trampled over him by the time the mob had finished with him. He died next day as I recall it.'

Lawler said: 'You're threatening me with murder.'

Blackstone didn't reply and the thrush sang sadly.

After a while Lawler asked: 'Is there anything in it for me?'

'I can give you protection,' Blackstone said. 'I reckon you need it, culley.'

The timing was theatrical. As Blackstone finished speaking there was a hammering on the door and men's voices shouting. 'Open up, Lawler, else we'll blow the lock off.'

Lawler picked up his pistol but Blackstone said: 'Put the barker away and open up like they say.'

'But they'll do for me.'

'Like I said, I can give you protection.'

'But you don't know how many there are.'

'Two by the sound of it,' Blackstone said. 'And you've only got one ball in that flinty of yours.'

Now they were kicking the door. Any second now the lock might be blasted through the woodwork by a shot from a blunderbuss.

'Open up,' Blackstone said. 'And get out of the way when they come for you.'

Lawler turned the big key and took the chain off the latch. Blackstone stood beside the door, double-barrelled Manton in hand.

Then they were in the room, Lawler ducking away, Blackstone pointing his gun at their backs. Everything as planned – except that there were three of them. Big, bitter men with their own rules of justice – one with a black patch over one eye; all three wearing unkempt but flamboyant clothes, the uniform of the Fancy.

'Drop your guns,' Blackstone snapped.

They whirled round and faced him. Only one held a gun, a blunderbuss; but he didn't drop it. If he pulls the trigger, Blackstone thought, he'll blow my head off. Apart from the Manton he had only one weapon: the awe in which the Runners were held.

'And who might you be, me dear?' the man with the black patch said before he noticed the baton on the table and exclaimed: 'A Runner. God blind me, it's Blackstone.'

A second man said: 'Nice pickings, lads, a welsher and a Runner.' To the man with the blunderbuss he said: 'Let him have it and do the Fancy a favour.'

'I don't know,' said the man with the blunderbuss. 'Do for a Runner and we'll be on the run for the rest of our lives. I wasn't reckoning on a scragging job,' he added.

'Then give me the barker.'

Blackstone said: 'There's a foot-patrol on the way. Shoot me and you won't get farther than Seven Dials.' He jerked the Manton at them. 'Leave the little welsher to me.'

'Was that why you were here?' the man with the patch asked. 'To pinch Lawler?'

'What else would I be doing here?' Blackstone asked. 'Now get on your way and you'll hear no more of this.'

'What about our blunt?'

'Take what's yours,' Blackstone said.

It was then that Lawler spoiled everything. He hadn't discarded his ancient pistol, and the suggestion that the three men should rifle his leather bag enraged him. He pulled the trigger and the rusty flintlock exploded in his hand. Not with a lethal crack, more a roar of smoke and flame that stunned the senses. The ball jammed in the barrel, which split wide open, and the trigger guard crumpled like paper. But, such is the quirkish behaviour of explosive, Lawler wasn't badly hurt, just shocked like everyone else in the room.

Blackstone was the first to recover. He grabbed the blunderbuss and jerked it upwards so that the butt cracked its owner's jaw. Then he was away from them, blunderbuss levelled at their heads. 'One shot,' he said, 'should see both of you off.' He jerked the gun towards the man with the broken jaw lying on the floor. 'Pick him up.'

They bent down and picked up their colleague, who was spitting out teeth. 'Get out of here and take him with you.'

When they had gone Lawler said: 'They would have robbed me and thumped me to death. Why didn't you nib the bastards?' He rubbed his scorched hand.

'It was you who robbed them,' Blackstone reminded him. 'And they'll be back. Do you want me to let them know where you are? Or do you want to co-operate with me and have the protection of Bow Street?'

'That's what I like about you, Mr Blackstone,' Lawler said. 'You always give a man a choice.' He picked up his leather bag with dignity. He was now Lawler the City gent.

With a touch of bravado Blackstone had walked to Lawler's dungeon through St Giles Rookery, the triangle of human nests bounded by Bainbridge Street, George Street and High Street where he was born. He knew every blind alley, every court, every escape route. And now, as he made his way back, he kept his hand on his pistol as he passed windows stuffed with rags and paper, ducked beneath strings of washing, stepped over gutters choked with filth. When he reached Rat's Castle, the thieves' inn at the centre of the Rookery, he drew the pistol just in case; he felt eyes watching him from the windows and saw the hatred in the faces of the loungers outside, men in broken hats and ragged jackets, women with babies at the breast and clay pipes stuck in their mouths.

Blackstone passed the inn without incident and entered a lane where a few legitimate traders – the minority in the Rookery – plied their trade. Dog-dealers, costermongers, hawkers, watercress sellers, rat catchers ... Blackstone knew that in this short lane more than one thousand people lived, ten to a room and more, sleeping, eating, boozing, coupling and dying.

Blackstone knew of only one worse place to live in London, and that was Newgate Jail, and that was where he was going.

CHAPTER FOUR

R eform had come to Newgate prison, and visitors could only wonder how, before their advent, conditions could have been more degrading than they were now.

True, prisoners no longer paid fees for privileges, men and women were now kept in separate wards, prisoners were only manacled if they were trouble-makers, and sanitation was alleged to have been improved. But harlots were allowed into wards, booze flowed freely from a nearby hostelry, and men gambled and fought the days and nights away. A criminal's idea of heaven – if he could ignore the stink, jail fever, over-crowding, fetid air, corrupt turnkeys and wardsmen, pigswill for food, and the spectre of death which forever haunted the place.

One wing of the prison was reserved for debtors, another for felons. You entered by narrow steps into the turnkeys' office; this opened into one of the yards with walls so high that it was more like a well.

Of all the yards into which the prisoners poured from the wards for exercise the most chilling was the Press Yard where the scaffold was kept. Here fifty or sixty prisoners awaited execution or reprieve; at one end was a cistern of water, at the other a double grating through which the condemned spoke to visitors. At five in the evening they were locked up in the cells until seven next morning. There were fifteen condemned cells, boxes nine foot high and six foot wide, withfour-inch-tnick doors, tiny barred windows, a bench, a rug, a prayerbook, a candlestick and a Bible.

Blackstone was taken to the grating at the end of the Press Yard by a grumbling turnkey. Through the bars he saw the condemned sprawled around a wood fire; many were drunk, and thus they would remain until they died at the end of a rope. The smell of death reached him and he pressed a silk handkerchief to his nostrils.

Inside the long, narrow yard another turnkey kicked a boy lying on the fringe of the group of men and pointed towards the grating. The boy stood up and walked across the yard.

Blackstone turned to the turnkey. 'Now you get out of my sight.'

The turnkey, balding and sly-faced, shook his head. 'More than my job's worth.'

Blackstone gave him a shilling.

'Ten minutes then,' the turnkey said.

The boy stared through the grating at his visitor. He was thin, with the same shadowed eyes as his sister, hair so black that it seemed to have a bluish light to it, and a voice that hadn't yet broken. His clothes were rags.

Blackstone said quickly: 'I've come to help you.'

The boy stared at him suspiciously. 'Who are you?' he asked. 'Did Mercy send you?'

'She thinks I might be able to help. I can't promise anything but we Runners can get things done. Sometimes, anyway…'

'A Runner? Why would you help me' Blackstone recognised the distrust, the mockery; he knew it well because he had practised it once. Why should the law help a thief? Why should the hunter save his prey? Why should anyone with food in his belly feed the starving?

Blackstone tried to explain; but he knew the explanation was a mess – it always was. In any case, what could he do?

The boy listened, then turned on his heel.

Blackstone shouted to him to come back.

The boy turned and said: 'Leave me alone, mister. There's nothing you or anyone else can do. I'm going to be topped and the sooner they get it over the better.'

Blackstone jingled some coins in his hand. 'At least these will help you pass the time.'

The boy came back. 'Gently, mister, so's no one hears them.'

Blackstone wrapped the coins in his handkerchief and slipped them through the grating. 'If anyone asks what I've been doing here, tell 'em I'm making inquiries about a crime – any crime.'

'Then they'll think I'm a snout.'

'Tell 'em you didn't blab.'

The boy shrugged. 'Doesn't really matter, does it? I'm going to be turned off next Monday anyway.'

'Don't give up hope,' Blackstone said, thinking that he sounded like a visiting clergyman distributing crumbs of comfort before hurrying home to his wine and venison.

'Hope? What hope is there with toffs like Lord Hardinge rattling through the death sentence so's he can have an extra half hour in Windmill Street before returning to her ladyship?'

'Windmill Street?' A prickle of intuitive excitement that every lawman knows when he's about to make a pinch, when the curtains of a deception have suddenly been drawn, when a clue has suddenly surfaced like a gold nugget in the mud of the Thames.

'Yes, Windmill Street. Ain't you ever been down there? And you a bleeding Runner?'

'I've been down there,' Blackstone told him. 'How do you know Lord Hardinge has?'

'Bound to have, isn't he. All the nobs get down there.'

'But you don't really know.'

'No, I don't really know.' Johnny Bristow took a pipe from his pocket. 'Got any baccy, mister?'

'Sorry – I'll bring some next time.' Blackstone paused. 'What makes you think Hardinge is the sort of man who'd use the establishments down Windmill Street?'

'Got to be, hasn't he. So good, so bleeding noble. I know the sort all right; I've worked for them as boots. Sacking a footman 'cos he's caught dabbing it up with the pantry maid and then tearing off to the Haymarket to find himself a judy.' The boy sucked at his empty pipe. 'I know the sort, don't I just.'

Blackstone took some snuff to clear the stench of the prison from his nostrils. 'I wonder...' he said.

'Wonder what, mister?'

'It doesn't matter,' answered Blackstone, who was wondering what skeletons hung in Lord Hardinge's cupboards and if they would influence him in any way if they were taken out for an airing. But there was so little time. 'I'll call again tomorrow,' he told the boy.

'Shouldn't bother, mister. But if you do, don't forget the baccy.'

Blackstone turned – and found the turnkey standing behind him. 'I thought I told you to clear off.'

'I gave you ten minutes.' the turnkey said. 'Your time's up.'

The boy said: 'Tell me one thing, mister. Why should a Bow Street Runner do anything for me? I'm a thief, aren't I? It's your job to put the likes of me away, not save us from a scragging.'

The turnkey looked interested, too. Another shilling there, Blackstone decided, to keep his mouth shut.

Blackstone told the boy: 'Because the Bow Street Runners are concerned with justice.'

'Not the way I heard it,' the boy said.

For a moment Blackstone felt like reaching through the grating, shaking the boy and demanding: 'Don't you want to live?' But he knew you couldn't suddenly teach a boy of thirteen to respect the enemy, even if it could save him from the gallows.

The boy asked: 'What's your name, mister?'

'That doesn't matter.' Reveal his identity and he would be on Birnie's threadbare carpet by dawn tomorrow. 'And do me one favour. Don't tell any of that mob in there' – Blackstone pointed into the yard – 'that you've had a visit from a Runner.'

'I don't talk to them,' the boy said. 'Only to my mate.' Through the grating Blackstone saw another boy.

'What's he done?'

'Coining,' Johnny Bristow told him. 'Helping an old bit-faker in the Dials. Forging's always a topping job, you know that.'

Blackstone knew it. By tradition the forger was always brought to the scaffold on a sledge, God knows why.

'But they think he'll get off,' Johnny Bristow said. 'They'll string up the arch cove and let him off. Botany Bay for him, I shouldn't wonder.'

'I'll be back tomorrow,' Blackstone told him. 'Don't give up hope.'

He walked rapidly back through the dank corridors. When he reached the steps leading to freedom Blackstone slipped the turnkey another shilling and said: 'I'd be obliged if you said nothing about my interest in the boy.'

The turnkey said: 'Mr Blackstone, isn't it?'
Blackstone gave him a sovereign.

The night was cold and smoky and London was stirring. In the great mansions they were chalking the floors for balls, chilling the champagne for a soirée or two, laying out the cutlery for the dinners at which, after the ladies had retired, men would decide the political and commercial future of Britain; maids were laying out madam's gown, combing her hair and forcing her into her stays; while the master, who took only an hour to dress, drank his whisky and soda and pinched the housemaid's bottom. In the clubs – sporting, gaming, drinking, whoring – preparations were starting: rings erected for fist fights, packs of cards fixed for the unwary, brandy watered for the drunkards, ladies of the night bathed and perfumed for the fastidious. For the rich it would be a good night's sport – it always was.

In the stews of London preparations were also afoot: to make the most of nothing and, if nothing was not enough, to take something from the rich who had too much. Footpads, highwaymen, harlots, pickpockets, magsmen, macers and murderers laid out their tools and took a few nips of Geneva to fortify their nerves. Then out they went into the night in which they shared the stars and briefly it seemed that all men were equal.

Blackstone took a carriage to Sol's Tavern, the inn where the élite cracksmen drank, and ordered a tankard of ale. He valued the company of these men–knowing the sentiment wasn't necessarily reciprocated – because, in their way, they were straight; also he needed their company in the interval between his visit to Newgate and his impending visit to the sort of places where one of His Majesty's judges might debauch himself.

Jack Barclay, the master cracksman who drove a cab with a racehorse between the shafts, was there, drinking with Sammy Levy, the lawyer employed by those villains who could afford him.

Blackstone bought them drinks.

'What is it this time, Blackie?' Barclay asked. He was the best-dressed thief in London; he always wore dark blue jackets and trousers, with frilled white shirts and diamonds on his cuffs. His black hair was combed forward, his features were bold.

'A little deal maybe?' Sammy Levy asked. If a Runner was assigned to a robbery he sometimes did a deal with the thief; the victim got two-thirds of the loot back and the Runner took a percentage of what the thief kept. When dealing with the élite you had to approach Levy first.

'No,' Barclay said knowingly, 'Blackie wants something else. You can always tell – he bought the drinks. What is it, Blackie? The little snakesman?'

Blackstone, who thought he had lost the ability to be surprised, crashed his tankard of ale on to the table. 'How in the devil's name did you know that?'

'Seems someone's got their eye on you, Blackie. Up to anything at the moment that might cause certain people to keep an eye on you?'

'Like a certain party threatening to break into the Bank of England?' asked Peter Prince, the penman, who had joined them.

'Someone's been keeping their glims on you,' Barclay said. 'Word has it you had a caller, a little dollymop whose brother's due for the jump on Monday. Knowing what a kind heart you've got, Blackie, I put two and two together.'

Sammy Levy sipped his brandy and water. 'Wish I could help, Blackie. Jack here told me he thought you'd be interested and I made a few inquiries. It's hopeless, Blackie, the poor little devil will swing. The law has decided that he's got to be made an example of. I can't do anything, and if I can't no one can.'

'Ah, but you can,' Blackstone said, ordering another round of drinks. 'You know the judges; you make it your business to.'

'Maybe I do, maybe I don't.' Levy looked at him warily.

'If you wanted to find a bent judge tonight, where would you look?'

'Depends what bends him,' Levy said.

'I don't know,' Blackstone said.

'Then I can't help you, my dear. Does he like the tables, the sight of blood in the ring, a spot of ratting maybe? Cruel men, judges…'

Peter Prince, who forged banknotes and risked the gallows every day of his life, said: 'Which judge, Blackie, then we might be able to help you?'

Jack Barclay said: 'That's simple. Lord Hardinge.'

'You should have been a Runner,' Blackstone said.

'Not enough blunt in it, my dear.'

'Don't be too sure about that,' Sammy Levy said.

Peter Prince said: 'As Sammy says, a hanging judge must be a cruel man. My guess is that he retires to one of those gouty clubs in St James's where they use *The Times* as a shroud. Then he will go either to a high-class flash house where they cater for perverted old sadists, or to one of the select sporting establishments to watch some young kid beaten to death by a pickle-fisted thug from the rings.'

Sammy Levy said: 'Give me an hour, Blackie, and I'll find out.' He grinned, teeth very white in his dark, sleek features. 'It could be useful to me some day when I've got Barclay in the dock or Peter with one foot on the gallows.'

When he had gone Blackstone picked up a newspaper and stared at it with unseeing eyes. One day, he thought, when he had amassed enough blunt and worldly possessions he would leave this stage. As a Runner he had been able to peer into other theatres: homes in the suburbs where happiness was the family, villages where the rewards were in the land. Horizons beyond this twilight world. He had been saved from sneak-thief squalor but he could still be corrupted by the more sophisticated vices that touched his life every day. The danger was accepting the values of Sol's Tavern as the only ones; as the years passed the danger expanded. One day he must move into one of the new houses Cubitt was building in Belgravia, or a white farmhouse amid the red and green cushions of Devon . . .

While Barclay and Prince played dice Blackstone read the newspaper: *Catholic Emancipation; Some Observations on the Combination Act Which Would Allow Workers To Form Trade Unions…* Blackstone turned the page and came to a haunting.

According to the article, a ghost had returned to the Ship Tavern in Lincoln's Inn Fields, Holborn. In the sixteenth and seventeenth centuries Roman Catholics had held illegal services while a potman kept watch; when their persecutors were spotted the priest disappeared into a secret hiding place. In 1586 a Catholic named Anthony Babington was arraigned for his part in a plot to murder Queen Elizabeth and rescue Mary Queen of Scots, A wax effigy of Queen Elizabeth pierced with pins was found in Lincoln's Inn Fields, therefore the Fields were presumed to be the headquarters of the plotters. Babington and thirteen accomplices were arrested and Babington was hanged, drawn and quartered at Lincoln's Inn Fields on 20 September. The hanging, however, was brief so that Babington would still be conscious while he was cut to pieces. For years afterwards his screams of agony were said to have been heard in the area, and Babington was often seen wandering the rooms of the Ship. Then his ghost had disappeared, only to return, according to the article, two days ago.

Blackstone folded the newspaper. The story of the ghost had stirred some memory. A presentiment. A connection with the matters at hand. He closed his eyes and tried to reach it…

Sammy Levy strode into the tavern bringing a gust of cold night air with him. 'I think I know where you might be able to find his lordship,' he announced.

CHAPTER FIVE

The Rotunda is the elegant heart of the labyrinth of courtyards, hallways and corridors which comprise the Bank of England, known affectionately as the Old Lady of Threadneedle Street, a matron who hides demurely between high walls reconstructed between 1823 and 1825.

The Bank is the power and pinnacle of Britain's finance, the storehouse of her riches. But its foundations were trembling these troubled years of George IV's reign.

The financial crisis of 1825 had run the Bank's gold reserves down to a mere one and a quarter million pounds. Wild-cat mining schemes in South America were the main culprits; as a result there was a panic run on gold as company after company folded up.

And, as if this wasn't enough, the daily invasion of mobs of villainous 'financiers' was becoming increasingly difficult to control, not that the messengers in their pink coats and scarlet waistcoats really tried to control them: they preferred not to enrage customers who might easily have a pistol or a life-preserver in their battered leather cases.

These 'businessmen' who came to plunder the system concentrated in the Rotunda, but were already spilling over into the Bank stock office. They would have looked more at home in a bear- or cock-fighting pit.

The Rotunda was one of the principal hunting grounds of Daniel Page, the Bow Street Runner who specialised in pickpockets. When he was there he liked to pinch about half a dozen fine-wirers; he preferred to catch them in the act, but if they didn't collaborate he pinched them just the same. If they were willing to part with a few shillings he sometimes let them off with a caution; if they hadn't the foresight to carry a small consideration in their pockets, then he hauled them off to Bow Street.

On this cold morning Page, leaning against a wall beneath a portrait of the King, was looking for 'financiers' with their hands in their pockets. A pickpocket's fingers had to be nimble, and on bitter days like this he often carried a hot potato in his pocket, to stop them from freezing.

Page also had his ears open for any whisper about the challenge from the Diddiki which had enthralled London. The humiliation over the Princess Alexandrina Victoria affair still rankled and he would have given a month's bribes to thwart the Diddiki before Edmund Blackstone.

At this moment he had four men under surveillance. Three of them were swarthy-looking fellows with oiled hair and flamboyant clothing, carrying expensive leather bags embossed with gold initials. Italian or Spanish, Page decided; foreigners anyway, and therefore doubly suspect. Page, who was knowledgeable in these matters, had little doubt that their fine feathers clothed human magpies; that their claws were poised to steal.

The fourth man under observation was more insignificant. A dark and busy little man who might have belonged to any City calling: banker, stockbroker, swindler, thief… Page harboured no illusions about insignificance: it was as suspect as flamboyance.

After a while a pattern of movement became apparent in the raffish crowd: wherever the three foreigners went the small dark man followed. Intriguing. What if the little flimp – because he was already that in Page's book – tried to tool one of the three foreigners? Set a thief to catch a thief. Page grinned, fingers darting around his own pockets.

The three magpies stopped and conferred with two City gents in swallow-tail coats. The leather bags were opened; stocks and bonds changed hands; a seal was produced. Another rich find of fool's gold changing hands?

Page edged nearer; so, he noticed, did the small dark man. Page listened.

One of the City men was saying: 'We must have an address before we can go any further.'

His companion said: 'Absolutely essential. And a legitimate address at that.'

One of the magpies looked affronted and gave his views on gentlemen's agreements, trust and other such unlikely commodities in a torrent of broken English. Another of the foreigners rounded on him and told him to hold his tongue. Page's pallid features beamed. An old ploy which he and the other Runners often used: turn on one of your own kind and you gain the trust of your victim.

The third foreigner held up his hands, smiled radiantly at the two City men, the dupes, and told them not to worry. Of course they could have an address, a respectable address. He took a leather wallet from his pocket and extracted a visiting card; the card went into the wallet of one of the dupes, a wallet, Page noted, that was bulging with stiffs.

The small dark man edged closer. Page waited, one hand on the baton in his coat pocket.

Foreigners and financiers shook hands energetically, their word their bond. It was pathetic, Page thought. One born every minute.

As the gentleman with the fat wallet turned, swallow-tails whirling, a hand darted out. The wallet was lifted as swiftly and neatly as a snake takes its prey.

A pinch or a deal? Page debated the choice as he followed the small dark man through the throng. There were a lot of stiffs in that wallet, maybe £50 worth of them. Say £30 back to the dupes, £15 for himself and a finny for the pickpocket to keep him quiet.

Page hummed to himself as he gave chase. Best never to nib them inside the Rotunda; there was always the possibility of a scuffle and he would be recognised in the future. Page would have liked promotion from these shifty responsibilities; but deep down he knew he had found his niche. If he spoiled his prospects on his own territory, fouled his own doorstep, there was nothing left except a desk job under Birnie's nose, and that was as bad as a stretch in Newgate.

Fifty pounds. Perhaps £17 10s for himself and £2 10s for the fine-wirer. Just enough to keep him quiet.

The small dark man stopped at the entrance to the Rotunda, looked furtively around and thumbed through the contents of the wallet. Dear God, what was he doing? Page paused, hand on baton. Should he pinch him now? He continued to stare, mesmerised by the unexpected.

What the hell was he doing now? As far as Page could make out, the pickpocket had removed a slip of paper – a £5 note most probably – and slipped it into his trouser pocket. Surely he wasn't going to be content with a fifth of the swag?

Page's incredulity began to turn to anger. The little thief tucked the wallet into another pocket, turned on his heel and started back through the throng, catching Page by surprise. And now what the blazes! He was tapping one of the two City gentlemen on the arm and handing the wallet back to him!

Page watched the rest of the pantomime in a state of shock. The surprise, the gratitude – and the dupe handing the little bastard a bank-note. But why? – when he had almost got away with at least £50?

It was one of the worst examples of double-dealing Page had ever witnessed. The little man was worse than a fine-wirer: he was a confidence trickster.

Now where had he gone? The little man surfaced fifteen yards away and Page was after him, anger exploding inside him. But he was slippery and as fast as a sewer rat. Page manhandled his way through the mob, reaching the entrance a couple of seconds after his quarry.

But it wasn't until Page was outside the Bank that he spotted his quarry again, rounding Tivoli Corner. Page ran, flabby muscles burning with the effort. What should he do? He didn't normally engage in the indignity of pursuit; and last time he had shouted 'Stop thief!' someone had promptly tripped him up. But this little rodent mustn't be allowed to escape.

Page ran towards St Paul's, legs and lungs screaming at him to stop. As he slowed down he collided violently with the thief emerging from a coffee-house. Page grabbed his arm and twisted it behind his back. 'And now,' he said breathlessly, 'What the hell was all that about?'

'Let me go or I'll call a constable,' the thief hissed, wriggling.

Again the audacity of it took Page by surprise. But he hung on to the arm. 'I'm a Bow Street Runner,' he shouted into the thief's ear.

'And I'm the Duke of Wellington,' the thief said, kicking Page's shin with his heel.

'You're under arrest,' Page said.

'For what?'

'For picking pockets, pulling a confidence trick and assaulting an officer from Bow Street. In fact you're for the gallows, the hulks or, at the very least, Botany Bay.'

'You've got no proof,' said the thief.

'Of what?'

'Of anything. If I picked any pockets where's the swag?'

Triumphantly Page dipped his hand into the thief's trouser pocket and pulled out a £5 note. 'Where did you get that finny from then?'

'A gentleman gave it to me,' the thief told him.

'Can you prove it?'

'Of course I can.'

Page, who had already considered this possibility, said: 'You can prove it at Bow Street. Now tell me, why did you lift a wallet full of stiffs and hand it back?'

'I didn't lift it,' the thief said. 'I saw it was about to fall out of the gentleman's pocket, so I grabbed it and then gave it back to him. He was ever so grateful,' the thief said, 'and I've no doubt he will come forward and confirm it.'

'Maybe he will and maybe he won't,' Page said. 'Maybe he won't even hear that you've been charged. Meanwhile' – Page crackled the note in his hand – 'I'll look after this.' Page tightened his grip on the thief's arm. 'What's your name?'

'Lawler,' the thief said.

'You can't do it.' Page's voice rasped with fury.

'But I am doing it.' Blackstone's tone was aloof.

Flames flapped round the logs in the grate in the Brown Bear, and Ruthven and the novice Runner Bentley listened to the exchange between Page and Blackstone with interest.

In front of the fire, a glass of hot gin in his hand, stood the prisoner.

Page said: 'He's under arrest. He was tooling in the Bank of England and he's got to stand trial.'

'He goes free,' Blackstone said mildly, taking a pinch of snuff.

'Who says so?'

'I say so.'

'To hell with you, Edmund Blackstone. Pickpockets are my business and I'll see him in the dock across the road if it's the last thing I do.'

'Then say your prayers,' Blackstone said.

Lawler downed his gin and watched the two men as though he was watching a dog-fight in a tavern.

'I'll see Birnie about this.'

'Do so by all means,' Blackstone said. He lowered his voice and whispered across the table at which they were sitting: 'I rather think he'll be more interested in my plans to trap the Diddiki than he will be in the conviction of yet another flimp.' Blackstone ordered another round of drinks and, when the girl departed, went on: 'Nor do I think Birnie will take too kindly to your meddling. Lawler reckons he was on to something until you nibbed him.'

'What the hell can he have been on to? And what sort of colleague is he?' Page turned and nodded towards Lawler. 'I shouldn't think Birnie would approve of the Runners working with scum like that.'

Lawler stared at him impassively; he had been called worse.

Bentley, eagerly learning his trade from his seniors, asked: 'What exactly *was* this man Lawler doing in the Bank of England?'

Silence. There were questions you didn't ask. Bentley had learned another lesson.

'Anyway,' Page said, 'I'm taking him across the road and charging him.'

Blackstone shrugged his shoulders. He seemed to be peering intently down the street, past a woman selling rosemary and lavender from baskets slung over her shoulders. 'If you must, you must.'

Page was nonplussed. 'I thought you said ...'

'No,' Blackstone said, 'you go ahead. Right must be done.'

Ruthven and Bentley looked puzzled; Lawler looked pained.

'Why the sudden change?' asked Page who trusted no one, and Blackstone less than anyone.

The serving girl hovered in the background, sensing drama. Blackstone was still peering down the street. A man in a black cape and tall hat, carrying a cane, came into sight. Blackstone turned: 'Best take your prisoner across the road, Page.'

The door of the parlour opened. Sunlight burst in as the man in the cape entered.

Blackstone said: 'Ah, good morning Mr Jenkins. A fine morning. What will you be having to drink?'

Page stared at the financier, the dupe, whose pocket Lawler had picked and said: 'Just what the hell is all this about, Blackstone?'

'And what the hell was all that about?' Ruthven asked later as they walked down the Strand in the afternoon sunlight.

'A slight breakdown in communication,' Blackstone told him. 'I should have warned Lawler. I asked Jenkins – he's a friend of mine in the City – if he could get the address of those three foreign-looking merchants who've been hanging around the Rotunda for the past few days. Then Lawler arrives and immediately spots the same three gents. And what does he decide? Why, being the sharp little ferret he is, he sees the address change hands and decides to lift it from Jenkins's pocket.'

'The fifty pounds must have been a great temptation,' Ruthven said.

'Doubtless it was. But he knew that if I caught him thieving when he was working for me I'd have him on the treadmill for the rest of his life.'

Blackstone glanced up at the bright sky. 'Do you think it'll snow?' he asked.

'I think we're in for a heat-wave,' Ruthven answered.

CHAPTER SIX

Blackstone and Ruthven had been out together the previous night. Touring the brothels.

The address supplied by the crooks' lawyer, Sammy Levy, had proved to be an exclusive club where rich men could enjoy a little sport away from the brutalising influence of the Fancy.

The club was a couple of hundred yards from St James's Palace. A discreet entrance, a winding staircase leading to a gaslit chamber with expensive furnishings and brocade curtains. The only drink was champagne, no women allowed.

Usually the sport was fist-fighting, the sport being to gamble on how many rounds a slightly-built pugilist could last against a thug with fists of teak. The endurance of pain was held to be ennobling and the fallen combatant was always well paid.

Sometimes there was a whipping match with two men stripped to the waist slashing each other with rawhide whips. This test of endurance was also edifying – the spirit that sustained Britain against her enemies – and the sovereigns rained into the ring, provided the contest had been long enough.

Lord Hardinge always sat alone. He never drank too much champagne and only rewarded the contestants if they endured maximum punishment. He felt that these exhibitions of human courage purged him of the duplicity and cowardice he was forced to observe every day in court.

He was a man of sixty, his grey face lined by his responsibilities. His frame was spare, his dark hair only touched with grey, his clothes smelling faintly of mothballs. He had a country house near Windsor and a town-house in St James's. He was married with four sons, two at Eton and two studying law, three daughters learning how to become ladies, and he had passed sentence of death on fifty-two men, women and children.

Occasionally, after a visit to the club, Lord Hardinge retired to a small room upstairs and changed his clothes. Then he took a carriage to one of the many establishments around Leicester Fields where you could enjoy a little frivolous entertainment.

On the night that Blackstone and Ruthven called at the club he had already departed. The doorman opened up for the two Runners, then slammed the door when they identified themselves.

Ruthven, never renowned for subtlety, began to kick the door down. The door opened again.

'Look,' said the doorman, 'cause any trouble here and you'll be in Newgate by dawn. Judges, magistrates, lawyers – we've got the lot here, my dears. Bow Street Runners!' The doorman began to close the door again. 'They don't rank higher than second footmen here.'

'Really?' Ruthven shoved his foot in the door and spat on his broken knuckles.

'Don't you try anything,' the doorman said. He was a slender youth with golden hair combed into ringlets; probably as swift and vicious as an alley-cat, Blackstone decided. 'You touch me, culley, and you'll answer to Peel.'

'Who's that?' Ruthven asked.

Blackstone stepped forward. 'Look,' he said to the door-man, whose hand was sidling towards a bell, 'we haven't come here to make trouble.'

'Then hop it,' the doorman said.

'We want to ask you about one of your members.'

'All confidential. Sorry I can't help.' The youth tried to close the door again but Ruthven's foot was still there like a kerbstone.

Blackstone gave the youth a sovereign, which he pocketed in a single swift movement like a pelican swallowing a fish. 'There's more where that came from,' Blackstone told him as the youth ran his hand through his curls and looked speculatively at Ruthven.

'I should hope so,' the doorman said. 'I get that sort of tip for calling a cab.'

'And this sort for being too cocky,' Ruthven said, showing the doorman his clenched paw.

Blackstone took another sovereign from his pocket. An expensive dollymop, Mercy Bristow. He held it between thumb and forefinger and told the doorman: 'You don't even have to walk across the street for this. Just tell us about Lord Hardinge.'

'More than my life's worth,' the doorman said, pushing back an errant curl. 'More than my neck's worth. In any case,' he said, 'he isn't here.' He paused. 'What do you want to see him for? More clients for the scaffold?'

Blackstone said: 'You don't like him, eh?'

The hostility was evaporating. 'A miserable old bastard,' the doorman said. 'And holy with it.'

Ruthven said: 'There's a boy due to be hanged next Monday and we want to stop it.' He was being subtle.

The doorman began to understand; threats and black-mail were his currency. 'You're playing with fire,' he said.

'We always do,' Blackstone said. He gave the doorman another sovereign.

'How can I help?'

'When did he go?'

'About half an hour ago.'

'Where to?'

'I don't know.'

'But you can find out?'

'Maybe.'

Blackstone sighed and produced another sovereign. 'Find out.'

'I've just remembered,' the doorman said.

'Don't lose your memory like that again,' Ruthven said. 'I might have to jolt it back for you.'

'Listen,' the doorman said, 'I don't have to tell you anything.'

'Where?' Blackstone asked.

'Down Kate's, I expect.'

'Why you *expect*?'

'Because that's where he always goes when he puts his other clothes on.'

'What other clothes?'

'He arrives looking like a judge. You know, as colourful as a gravedigger at his mother's funeral. But when he leaves he's quite flash. Well, as flash as a beak can ever be. But he's got some nice frilly shirts. Quite dashing, really.' The doorman leaned forward. 'I hope you get something on him. I'd like to see him caught with his trousers down ...'

Blackstone said: 'Don't tell anyone we've been asking.'

'Come again,' the doorman said. 'I've got plenty of other customers for you.'

'Call us when Robert Peel joins,' Ruthven said.

Blackstone and Ruthven walked up the Haymarket
crowded with men of all classes, whores of all sizes, shapes
and ages. In the gaslight most of the women looked passable – the pox-ridden tarts had retired to the docks – and it
was only in the light of dawn that men questioned what they
had bought. The oldest were in their thirties, the youngest,
pulling at men's coat-tails, twelve and under.

They arrived at Kate's and marched down the long passage leading to the salon. The thugs who guarded the establishment stepped out belligerently, retired hastily when they
recognised their visitors.

Inside the salon the gas lighting flared with fierce
brilliance from wall-brackets hung with glass pendants.
Whores, professional and amateur, chatted together while
men in top hats and starched shirts, cigars in their mouths,
leisurely made their choice for the night like farmers ear-
marking cows before an auction. On a platform sat Kate,
all twenty-one stone of her, making sure the girls didn't
behave indecently and the men bought their champagne
at ten shillings a bottle. Kate's wasn't a true brothel: it
was a trading centre: the commodity was whores but the
revenue came from the booze.

Blackstone examined the clientele while Ruthven, a
firm believer in mixing pleasure with business, took a bottle
of champagne, omitting to pay for it.

After a while Blackstone said: 'The bastard's not here.'

'Picked his judy and moved on, I shouldn't wonder.'

'And to think he passes judgement on kids dragged up
in the stews. I shall look forward to meeting his lordship,'
Blackstone said, sipping champagne.

A couple of girls with dresses barely covering their
breasts made their approach. But Ruthven repelled them
with a wave of his paw.

Ruthven said: 'It's a dangerous game you're playing, Blackie.'

'More dangerous for that boy in Newgate.'

'He isn't the first to be hung and he won't be the last. In any case, what can you do if you find Hardinge? You know as well as I do that it's no crime for a gentleman to frequent places like this.'

'It's a crime to get caught,' Blackstone said.

Ruthven shrugged. 'Not really. Not when you're a judge. Nothing's a crime when you're a judge.'

'I wonder what his taste is,' Blackstone said. 'And I wonder why he comes here. You would have thought he'd have used Mott's or somewhere like that. There must be something special here for him,' he added. 'But how the hell can we find out? If we ask Kate the King himself will know what we're at by morning.'

'Ask a judy,' said Ruthven, grabbing a plump girl with a lace handkerchief stuffed in the valley of her bosom.

'Hey,' she said, 'who the hell do you think you're pulling about?'

They gave her some champagne and she told them where Hardinge might have gone to, and, as they prepared to leave, looked at them sadly and offered herself without much hope. Blackstone shook his head and she said 'Any time' and he smiled at her and they left, heading for Windmill Street where vice proliferated like spawn in a pond.

'Looks like we're going to visit every whore-house up West,' Blackstone said.

'Another bottle of champagne,' Ruthven said, 'and I could begin to fancy the goods.'

'You'd break their backs,' Blackstone told him as they turned into Windmill Street,

They called first at the Black Bull, for old time's sake, because it was one of the most vicious underworld taverns in London and they liked to remind customers of their existence. A few left hurriedly and the whole atmosphere changed during their brief stay.

Then on down the narrow street on the trail of the errant judge who seemed to have been dispensing money with less restraint than he dispensed mercy.

'He's got specialised tastes, this one,' Blackstone remarked as they left an establishment where virginity was faked to cater for men who still believed that defloration cured disease.

'But he didn't stay there,' Ruthven said. 'Seems he's only been making inquiries wherever he went.'

The trail ended at a tenement at the end of the street, where the lights grew dimmer, the penumbra of the world of vice. A door opened and Blackstone pushed Ruthven into a doorway.

Out came Hardinge. He looked up and down the street, then beckoned. A girl came out of the building and the two Runners watched Hardinge give her a coin. She giggled and ran off into the night.

Blackstone's hand flew involuntarily to his pocket pistol. Ruthven restrained him.

'How old do you think that girl was?' Blackstone asked.

'About ten,' Ruthven answered. 'Now we know his lordship's tastes.'

'Three years younger than the boy in Newgate,' Blackstone said. 'Tomorrow morning I'll pay a call on his lordship.'

CHAPTER SEVEN

Wednesday. Four days till the threatened appearance of the Diddiki in the bullion room of the Bank of England. Five days until Johnny Bristow was due to be hanged.

And still no snow.

Blackstone breakfasted off ham, eggs and muffins washed down with coffee. He was wearing a silk dressing-gown fashionably embroidered with Chinese dragons and was reading the *Morning Post*.

A coal fire was already lit; the coffee was good and hot. Firelight danced on freshly-polished brass and copperware. Blackstone looked like a country squire.

In the background hovered Mercy Bristow, trusting and happy.

With his mouth full of ham and eggs, Blackstone said: 'You mustn't have any false hopes, Mercy.'

'No, Mr Blackstone.' She began to hum to herself.

Blackstone glanced out of the window. Frost crusting the fields, ice patterns sliding down the glass, an orange sun dispersing the mist. He turned a page of the newspaper and there it was: another letter from the Diddiki.

Sir, We are taking this opportunity of keeping your readers up to date with the precautions taken by that illustrious band of law-keepers, the Bow Street Runners, to prevent our promised appearance in the bullion room of the Bank of England next Sunday. The seriousness with which Sir Richard Birnie, the Bow Street magistrate, is taking our promise is evinced by the fact that he has placed Mr Edmund Blackstone, one of the most famed of this élite body of thief-takers, in charge of the investigation.

How the hell did they know that?

The letter went on:

Mr Blackstone's activities came into the public eye when he took part in the raid on the infamous Cato Street conspirators. It will be recalled that all the conspirators bar one were apprehended and were duly hanged outside Newgate prison. It is not, of course, to Mr Blackstone's discredit that the only conspirator to escape was the wretch being pursued by the said Mr Blackstone.

Blackstone choked on his coffee.

We are confident however, that the zealous and vigilant Mr Blackstone will enjoy a similar lack of fortune in his efforts to prevent the undersigned from carrying out their plan, and we would ask Sir Richard Birnie not to chastise Mr Blackstone too harshly next Monday when it becomes apparent that he has failed in his assignment. We hereby reaffirm that we shall present ourselves to the esteemed directors of the Bank at a dark and midnight hour.

The Diddiki

Blackstone pushed his plate away. They were out not only to discredit the Bow Street Runners but to make him the laughing stock of London. But why? And who? There were hundreds of villains in the underworld who would like to humiliate him, but not many with sufficient ingenuity. One sprang to mind: Henry Challoner, the Cato Street conspirator who had escaped from him, the man with whom he had fought a private vendetta ever since. A man remarkably similar to Blackstone, except that he had stayed on the other side of the frail barrier separating law enforcement from law violation.

'Is anything the matter?'

'Nothing,' Blackstone told Mercy. 'Nothing at all.'

'Was the breakfast all right?'

He smiled at her. 'It was fine, Mercy.'

He examined the letter in the *Morning Post* again. It was far from illiterate, but that meant nothing. With two shillings in his hand a half-wit could employ a screever to write an articulate letter. Not that there were too many top-class screevers; that was a line of inquiry to pursue, Blackstone thought. And he should also visit the offices of the *Morning Post* to examine the original of the letter.

The only other lead to the Diddiki was the address that Lawler had lifted from Jenkins. Lawler could visit the address – if it existed. They could pick up the three foreigners and take them in for questioning, although Blackstone sensed a trap. Another letter in the *Morning Post* or *The Times*, inquiring: By what right has Edmund Blackstone, the eminent Bow Street Runner, held three innocent financiers from Rome for questioning?

What was his priority? Diddiki or Johnny Bristow?

Blackstone turned to the girl. 'Are you happy here?'

She nodded. Her neck was clean, her hair shiny; she looked as if she had been there for at least five years and intended to stay longer.

He gave her some coins. 'I want you to visit your brother today. Take him some food and some baccy.'

'What shall I tell him?'

'Tell him ... Tell him that I'm working on his case.'

'Nothing more?'

'Nothing more, Mercy.'

'When do you think he'll be allowed out, Mr Blackstone?'

'I don't know that he will be allowed out. The whole machinery of the law is against your brother,' Blackstone said, thinking it ironic that the Diddiki should command so much space in the newspapers whereas the fate of a thirteen-year-old boy had so far merited only a couple of paragraphs.

He went to his bedroom and began to dress, listening to the clatter of crockery as Mercy went to work, humming a testament of faith.

Blackstone arrived at Lord Hardinge's London home at 9 a.m. He was admitted to the hall by a butler with a face as long as a coffin.

'I don't think his lordship––' the butler began.

'I think he will,' Blackstone interrupted.

'Who shall I say is calling?'

'Edmund Blackstone.'

The coffin lid opened a fraction. 'I have just been read-ing about you, sir. Pray wait here for a few minutes. Shall I tell his lordship that your visit is, ah, in connection with anything in particular?'

'Tell him it's about a crime in Windmill Street,' Blackstone said.

The butler pondered. 'His lordship doesn't usually––'

'He will this time,' Blackstone said.

'Very well, sir, I'll see if his lordship can spare a few moments.'

Blackstone patrolled the lofty hall, heels clicking on Italian marble. Hardinge's ancestors peered down at him from the walls. Hanging judges! Blackstone grinned.

The butler returned. 'His lordship can spare you a few moments, sir.'

Lord Hardinge was sitting behind a mahogany desk with a green-leather top embossed with gold. The walls of his study were lined with books; the heads of stuffed animals gazed glassily at each other. On the desk was a miniature of a woman, presumably Lady Hardinge. Lord Hardinge, wearing a scarlet dressing-gown with velvet lapels, was toying with an ivory paper-knife.

'Good morning, Mr Blackstone,' he said. 'Please sit down. This is somewhat irregular but the butler implied that you wished to see me on a matter of some urgency. Something in Windmill Street, I believe.' He picked up a copy of the *Morning Post*. 'Is it anything to do with this strange affair at the Bank?'

'Nothing to do with it,' Blackstone said. He looked curiously at the features of the man with life and death in his hands. Grey skin, pale eyes and pale lips, going a little scraggy under the chin, but his face unlined apart from furrows forming a letter N between his eyes. Pale eyebrows, nostrils plucked, a small nick from a razor on his chin.

'Then what, pray, is on your mind?' Lord Hardinge consulted his watch. 'I haven't much time. Please be as quick as possible.'

'I will, sir.' Blackstone cleared his throat. 'It's about Bristow.'

'Bristow?' Hardinge looked puzzled.

'The boy due to be hanged on Monday.'

'Ah, that Bristow.'

'Yes,' Blackstone said, 'that Bristow.'

'What about him?'

'I've come to ask you to intervene and recommend a reprieve.'

'Quite impossible.' The N between Lord Hardinge's eyes narrowed. 'And what, pray, is a Bow Street Runner doing pleading for the life of a convicted felon.'

'A thirteen-year-old felon,' Blackstone said.

'Is the age relevant? The public must be protected. And that, surely, is your responsibility, Mr Blackstone.'

'I don't arrest children,' Blackstone said.

'Really?' Hardinge made a note on a piece of paper. 'Who do you arrest, Mr Blackstone?'

'The men who force children into crime.'

'There was no evidence that this boy was *forced* into crime.'

'Only his word for it,' Blackstone said. 'You would hardly expect the men responsible to step forward and put their heads in the noose.'

'I act only on the evidence before me,' Lord Hardinge said. 'That is the English way of implementing justice.' His voice had assumed a sonorous, courtroom tone. 'And it is the best in the world. benefiting both the innocent and the guilty. In this case there was no lack of evidence against the accused, a great absence of evidence for him.'

'Except his age,' Blackstone said. 'He was only twelve when you sentenced him to death.'

'Really,' Hardinge said, 'this is most improper. I must ask you to leave, Mr Blackstone, and you can rest assured that Sir Richard Birnie will be hearing from me.' He picked up the newspaper again. 'Wouldn't you be more meaning-fully employed in the bullion vault of the Bank of England?'

'I think the life of a thirteen-year-old boy is more impor-tant than gold.'

'Really?' Hardinge reached for the bell on his desk. 'I think, sir, that you are seeking to distract public attention from what has the hallmarks of a humiliating failure both for yourself and for the Bow Street Runners as a body.'

Blackstone said: 'I shouldn't ring that if I were you, sir.'

Hardinge's hand froze in mid-air. 'I beg your pardon?'

'I said I shouldn't ring that if I were you.'

Hardinge said: 'It is time for you to leave, sir. I shall report your conduct to Sir Richard and I have little doubt that we shall meet again in the very near future when you face me in the dock.'

Blackstone said: 'I went to your club last night.'

The pale eyebrows lifted. 'I shall instigate an inquiry into how you gained admittance. Now get out, sir, before I have you removed.'

Blackstone went on: 'And then we went to Kate's.' He named the other establishments visited by Hardinge, counting them off on his fingers.

'So you followed me, eh? I have a good mind to have you arrested here and now.' But Hardinge's voice had lost a little of its assurance.

'It seems you made the grand tour seeking a particular kind of diversion.'

'Is that so, Mr Blackstone?'

Blackstone nodded. 'And you finally found that diversion in Windmill Street. An odd locality for one of His Majesty's judges to besport himself in.'

'Has it occurred to you that I like to acquaint myself with the mode of life of those unfortunate members of society who are arraigned before me? It is only too easy for a judge to become aloof from the conditions which drive men and women into crime——'

'And children,' Blackstone said.

'Look, Mr Blackstone.' Hardinge leaned forward across the desk. 'There is nothing I can do to save that boy. There has already been a petition and it has been turned down. I do not have the prerogative to reprieve—'

'You could make recommendations,' Blackstone said.

'To whom? Neither His Majesty nor the Home Secretary is in this country.'

'You could grant a stay of execution.'

'That is not my responsibility. And now, sir, please leave.'

'I believe,' Blackstone said softly, 'that cohabiting with a girl less than twelve years of age is a criminal offence.'

Hardinge stared at him, one hand tugging at the drooping flesh beneath his jaw. 'I believe that is so. Do you mind explaining the relevance of the observation?'

'I believe, sir, that you understand the relevance. There are some very youthful occupants of the houses in Windmill Street.'

'Indeed there are,' Hardinge said, fingers tapping on the desk. 'And I have made it my business to study the degrading practices into which these poor little mites are forced.' Hardinge placed his hand on a pile of writing paper beside the miniature. 'In fact, Mr Blackstone, I am currently engaged in writing a treatise on the subject with a view to promulgating reforms in that area.'

They stared at each other across the desk and Blackstone thought: You corrupt old bastard. Corrupt but as tough as winter, and as unrelenting.

Hardinge broke the silence. 'You may not be aware of it, Mr Blackstone, but I am also something of an authority on blackmail.'

'But you would need evidence.' Blackstone was aware that he was being forced on to the defensive.

'I think my word would suffice.' Hardinge's hand rapped the bell. 'And I have found from my research that it is extremely difficult to persuade the, ah, denizens of areas such as Windmill Street to give evidence ...'

The butler entered and stood like a mourner beside Blackstone.

Hardinge said: 'Mr Blackstone is leaving now. Please see him to the door.' To Blackstone he said: 'Rest assured that I shall be in contact with Sir Richard.'

I wonder, Blackstone thought. To Hardinge he said: 'Rest assured, your lordship, that I shall continue the line of investigation we have been discussing.'

Blackstone decided to give Bow Street a wide berth this diamondbright morning. If Hardinge reported him, then the outcome was simple: he would be thrown out of the force and might well be prosecuted.

He mounted his horse and rode towards Soho, where most of the screevers carried out their trade. Foreigners seemed to gravitate to Soho, so the screevers gathered there to write their letters for them. For an ordinary letter a screever charged sixpence, for a legal document complete with forged signatures of clergymen, doctors, magistrates, he might charge as much as two shillings.

The letters in the newspapers had all the hallmarks of a top-class screever, a disbarred lawyer or an unfrocked priest. But Blackstone had bargained without the latest letter in the *Morning Post*. It had captured the imagination of London. Blackstone *v.* the Diddiki – as if he was in the prizefighting ring, every blow being watched by an enraptured audience. And Blackstone was left in no doubt who the populace wanted to win. He couldn't blame them: the appeal of a challenge to law and order was irresistible. If he hadn't been personally involved he, too, would have put his money on the Diddiki!

A one-eyed pieman, one of his principal contacts, was the first to apprise Blackstone of public opinion. Blackstone reined his horse and dismounted beside the pieman's stall.

Before he could speak the pieman said: 'Don't bother to ask me, Blackie. It's more than my life's worth.'

'Ask you what?'

'About the Diddiki, of course. That's why you're here, ain't it?'

Blackstone tried to stare between the good eye, as bright as a blackbird's, and the empty socket, which he found distracting.

The pieman said: 'How about a steak and kidney, Blackie? Warm the cockles of your heart this cold morning.'

'I haven't come here to eat pies,' Blackstone said.

As usual there was a collection of urchins at the pieman's feet begging and fighting for scraps of pastry. One of them shouted: 'See you at the Bank, Mr Blackstone.'

'At a dark and midnight hour,' another shouted.

They laughed uproariously, hugging each other with delight.

The pieman said: 'I can't help you, Blackie. In any case I don't know anything. No one knows anything. No one even knows who the Diddiki are.'

'Someone does,' Blackstone said.

'Certainly someone does. The Diddiki knows who they are. Bold, ain't they, Blackie? As bold as brass – and every bird in the Rookery on their side.' The pieman looked at Blackstone apologetically with his good eye. 'How about a pie then, Blackie – on the house.'

Blackstone bought a pie, but he wasn't hungry. He gave it to the urchins. The urchins looked repentent, but not very.

'Keep a weather eye open for me,' Blackstone said without hope. 'Don't turn the blind one ...'

He mounted the Poacher and rode on, stopping occasionally to talk to the people of the streets who had helped him in the past: an old sailor selling cockles, a pale girl with a cough selling vinegar, an actor who had lost his voice selling week-old Newgate confessions two for a halfpenny and ballads for a penny, ratcatchers, road sweepers, child beggars with chilblained fingers and sharp frozen faces, tarts, tinkers and gonophs.

They greeted him warily and Blackstone heard their laughter as he rode away.

He called at half a dozen taverns without success. At one a badger-bait was in progress: a tough old badger imprisoned in a small ring with three starving dogs snapping at him. They would snap and bite until the badger died, and that was the fun.

It sickened Blackstone, and on another day he might have found reason to take the innkeeper to Bow Street and find something in the charge book to throw at his head. But he knew he would make a fool of himself in front of the customers. Diddiki. Diddiki, Diddiki – the whisper that followed him like a shadow.

Finally he called at the Red Lion, the tavern from which Peter Prince, the penman, had graduated. Here the screevers sat at the tables round the fire waiting for business. They were the best in the business and they could afford to wait, warming their inkstained fingers in front of the blaze.

Blackstone joined them, a pot of mulled ale in his hand. He asked if any of them had penned the letter in the *Morning Post*. They looked at him derisively and shook their heads. Did the big, bristling Runner really imagine they would tell him?

For all Blackstone knew the Diddiki were in the tavern now, enjoying the show. Enjoying their revenge. For what?

He called at the offices of the *Morning Post* and examined the letter. But it was printed in capital letters and, according to the editor, it had been pushed under the door overnight.

Blackstone galloped away, stopping at the Ship in Lincoln's Inn Fields on his way to Bow Street to drink a measure of hot gin and to see if the ghost was walking.

The landlord recognised him and tactfully talked about the haunting.

'Saw him plain as a pikestaff,' the landlord said with relish. 'Walking out of the pot-room with a Bible in his hand. He walked down the corridor, then vanished. Then,' said the landlord in a theatrical voice, 'I heard the groans and shouts of misery and agony.'

'Perhaps he'd just supped some of your gin,' Blackstone suggested.

'Ain't nothing wrong with my gin,' said the landlord, a rosy-cheeked man with sly eyes. 'You know that, Blackie.'

'I know there's one bottle for the sober and another for the drunk. Which did he have?'

'The same as you're drinking.'

'No doubt he appreciated a good spirit,' Blackstone said.

The landlord stared at him incredulously.

Sir Richard Birnie was pacing his smut-filled office like a man possessed. Occasionally one of his old knees would click with a noise like two billiard balls colliding.

'How the hell did they know *you* were in charge of the investigation?'

Birnie had asked the question several times and Blackstone didn't bother to reply. He wondered if Birnie might suffer a collapse; not that he had ever shown any evidence of mortality.

'Did you–?'

'No, sir, I didn't.'

'The Diddiki' – Birnie pronounced the word with profound distaste – 'seem to be very well informed. Has it occurred to you, Blackstone, that they may be working in collaboration with one of the directors of the Bank?'

Blackstone said it had and took a pinch of snuff.

'Do you have to take that disgusting stuff?'

'It clears the cavities, sir.' Blackstone looked meaningfully at the smoke pouring from the fire and from the bowl of Birnie's churchwarden.

'Smoke a pipe, man. A masculine habit.' He paused and looked through the window at the Brown Bear opposite, and, after a few moments' contemplation of his Runners' second headquarters, said: 'It's no use, Blackstone, I shall have to put other men on the case. I can't afford to have the Runners made the laughing-stock of London. I can just hear Peel in the House...'

Blackstone said: 'Just as you please, sir.'

'You don't seem too bothered, Blackstone.'

Blackstone, who was thinking that reinforcements would give him more time to attend to Lord Hardinge and Johnny Bristow, said: 'I understand your position, sir.'

'It will seem as though we're beginning to accept defeat. You know, one Runner not being enough for three gypsies...'

'It would seem that I'm not, sir.'

'That remains to be proved.'

Blackstone shrugged.

'Then you agree to me calling in other Runners?'

'It's not for me to say, sir. But I realise your dilemma.'

Birnie looked at him suspiciously. 'Is anything wrong, Blackstone?'

'No, sir.'

'You seem, ah, preoccupied.'

'Just thinking about the gypsies, sir.'

Birnie remained unconvinced. He had always feared that Blackstone's criminal tendencies would one day reassert themselves, and he was never sure whether or not to be grateful to old Mr Sweetman who had presented him with the brawling, swaggering recruit who was to develop into one of his most unorthodox and successful Runners. The challenge of the Diddiki was so outrageous that it wasn't inconceivable that Blackstone was involved. Birnie was a little ashamed of the theory.

He re-lit his pipe with a taper before saying: 'I presume there are no developments?'

'Not really, sir.'

'Perhaps you would be good enough to tell me what moves you have made since our last meeting.'

Blackstone told him. As *moves* they seemed pathetic.

'No leads?'

'None, sir. We've got the whole underworld against us.' He took his silver snuff-box from his pocket, looked at Birnie and put it away again. 'In fact we've got the whole damned country against us. The gypsies have become Robin Hood and his Merry Men.'

'And I'm the Sheriff of Nottingham?'

'I think we share the distinction,' Blackstone said.

Birnie took a list of the Runners from a drawer in his desk. 'I can't spare anyone but I'll have to. I'm putting Ruthven, Bentley and Page on to the case.'

'Very well, sir.'

'Does the choice meet with your approval, Blackstone?'
'Perfectly, sir.'

That night Blackstone returned to Windmill Street – without much optimism. The word of a child against a judge! If, that was, he could find the girl and persuade her to make a statement.

First he would have to confront the child's keeper. Probably a baby-farmer who had bought her from an unmarried mother for a few pounds. And he-or-she, would hardly be likely to confess that he was living off the immoral earnings of a minor.

The night sky had lost its polish and rain was beginning to fall. He went straight to the lodging-house from which Hardinge had emerged. He pounded on the door and listened to the echoes within. Rain bounced on the brim of his hat and trickled down his neck.

He went into the Black Bull and saw a copy of the letter in the *Morning Post* nailed to the wall. The faces of the customers cracked into broken-toothed grins.

Blackstone drank up and went outside again. Windmill Street was a dark canal with a few lights pulled across it like ships' lights on a harbour. A few women lurked in doorways but they had lost their initiative because rain is a great dampener of ardour.

Blackstone spoke to a few of them. No, they knew nothing of any young girls working at the empty lodging-house. They recited their own accomplishments but their words were soon drowned and they stood with Blackstone listening to the rain.

Blackstone made a last sortie down the street, and it was when he was passing the Black Bull that the three masked men took him.

One rammed a pistol into his back, whispering: 'One move, culley, and you'll join every poor bastard you've sent to the gallows.'

Another searched him expertly, removing the Manton from his coat pocket and the French stiletto from inside his boot.

Lord Hardinge, Blackstone thought, had some strange bedfellows. He looked up and down the street; but you couldn't expect help in enemy territory.

His arms were jerked behind his back, cord was knotted around his wrists, his eyes were bandaged and he was marched to a carriage.

'What do you want?' Blackstone asked, as the carriage moved off.

The answer was a rag stuffed into his mouth.

Ten minutes later the carriage stopped. The barrel of the pistol was shoved into his ribs. 'Out, my covey. You're moving lodgings.'

They pushed him out of the carriage. A door opened. He climbed two steps and was out of the wet. Another door opening, a smell of damp and whitewash.

Then he was stumbling down a winding staircase. A man pushed past him. Another door opened. Damp, stale air, a cobweb brushing his face.

'There, culley, that'll keep you out of trouble for a while. You'll find bread and water in the corner.'

The cord on his wrists was deftly severed. He was pushed forward. The door closed with a thud.

Blackstone tore the bandage from his eyes, pulled the rag from his mouth. After a while he began to see a little. High above him a small grating. He felt his way round the walls, encountered a jug of water and a wooden plate.

Just like a condemned cell, Blackstone thought.

CHAPTER EIGHT

Later that night the rain stopped, the temperature dropped, and, when Lawler set out from his basement in St Giles, London was sheathed in ice.

Shivering and cursing, Lawler headed for the boundaries of the Rookery. Urchins skated on hobnailed boots, old nags trotted carefully and daintily like circus horses, old gentlemen thumped to the ground to the intense pleasure of the urchins.

Conditions were not ideal for the composure of a dignified financier on his way to work; and Lawler was grateful that this morning he was not bound for the city. This morning Lawler was a sleuth; although, he conceded, streets paved with ice were hardly ideal for detective work: if you were following a suspect the chances were you might catch him up on your backside.

Lawler was bound for Kilburn, to the address unwittingly supplied by Mr Jenkins. Blackstone, thought Lawler, might have told him about Jenkins, might have shared his suspicions about the three flash foreigners operating in the Rotunda.

But Lawler no longer expected consideration – or gratitude – from Blackstone. In fact Lawler now accepted that both commodities were in short supply anywhere in his world. What you didn't expect, you didn't miss. At least he had the promise of Blackstone's protection.

Lawler stopped and looked around. What worried him at the moment was the strength of that protection. Instinctively Lawler knew that Blackstone's power would diminish with loss of respect, and the respect he enjoyed was waning with every fresh taunt from the Diddiki. It was therefore in Lawler's interests to help Blackstone beat the gypsies. Although he couldn't help admiring their audacity, wishing that he had been born with such swashbuckling tendencies.

Once outside the Rookery, Lawler hailed a cab and, as the cabby flicked at the horse with a whip held in numbed fingers, reflected on the limits of his aspirations. If the Diddiki could carry out a scheme like this, why not Lawler? Why confine yourself to miserable crimes with a minimum of profit and a maximum possibility of getting a bullet in the back? In the back of the cab, swaying and sliding northwards, Lawler became the Master Criminal.

A coup, perhaps, at the Derby; another stunt like that when the winner was later found to have been disguised with brown paint. Or a robbery that would be the talk of every flash tavern in London. Had anyone ever tried to rob St James's Palace? Or a confidence trick that would send the Stock Exchange reeling with its professionalism, its audacity. Why should he continue to be a lackey to Edmund Blackstone, who paid him in shillings, when he could be commanding crisp white notes for his services? To hell with Blackstone!

The driver rapped on the side of the cab. Lawler leaned out. 'What's the matter?'

The cabby pointed behind him. 'Another cab been following us for the past mile or so. Thought you might like to know. Friends of yours?'

Lawler, who had no friends, moaned and asked: 'Can you get rid of them?'

'Depends,' the cabby said, wiping tears of cold from his eyes.

'Double fare,' Lawler shouted.

The cabby whipped up the horse; the cab took a corner in a long slide before the horse regained its footing and they were away into a maze of small streets on the outskirts of Kilburn.

No need for any rash decisions about the future, Lawler decided. Blackstone and he needed each other.

The address was a lodging-house and it was owned by a woman with dyed red hair and rouged cheeks and several rings biting into her fleshy fingers. She was a widow. Her husband had been a seafaring man whose hobby was making model ships and putting them in bottles; the bottles were now anchored among the ferns in the parlour.

Lawler told her that he wasn't looking for lodgings. She seemed disappointed but made him sit down beside a tall sailing ship inside a whisky bottle; then she asked the serving girl to bring them tea and seed-cake.

'What can I do for you, then?' she asked, gazing at Lawler with a maternal affection that sounded alarm bells inside his skull. Women often wanted to mother Lawler; worse still they wanted to reform him, put him on the straight and narrow, a contortion that would have crippled Lawler.

Lawler told her that he was trying to find three foreign-looking gentlemen who did business at the Bank of England.

'Ah,' she exclaimed, 'my Italian gentlemen.'

'You mean they lodge with you?'

'Of course. Quite nice gentlemen but, you know, a little on the, ah, colourful side. I prefer English gentlemen. So much more reliable ...

Lawler accepted a cup of tea and a large slice of cake from the girl. 'Where are they now?' he asked, mouth full of cake.

'It's funny you should ask that...'

'Yes?'

'I haven't seen them for two days.'

'How long have they been here?' Lawler asked.

'About two weeks now. They landed at Gravesend and my little establishment was recommended to them. I have some wonderful references from my lodgers. Are you sure you wouldn't like to stay Mr...'

'Lawler.'

'Mr Lawler. I have a very nice room vacant and it's not expensive.'

'No, thank you,' Lawler said as she refilled his cup.

'A little something extra in that?'

'I beg your pardon?'

'A little something to give your tea an extra bite. It's such a cold morning and you look frozen, Mr Lawler.'

Yes, he thought, I am cold. Bloody cold. 'Very well,' he said.

'A little brandy?'

'That would be nice,' Lawler said as she uncorked a bottle and poured a generous slug into his cup – and into her own.

'There,' she said, 'that's better, isn't it?' She drank from her cup. 'Have you come far, Mr Lawler?'

'From Belgravia,' Lawler lied.

'A lovely part. But Kilburn is so handy for both City and country.'

'I'm sure it is,' Lawler said. 'Did these foreigners say where they were going?'

'I didn't ask, Mr Lawler. I'm sure it's no business of mine. I presumed they were going to work.'

'And what sort of work was that Mrs…'

'Mrs Rawlinson. Emily Rawlinson.'

'What sort of work, Mrs Rawlinson?'

'Something in the City,' she answered vaguely.

'Did they pay in advance?'

She cut Lawler another slice of cake and asked: 'Why all these questions, Mr Lawler?'

'It's something to do with a business deal,' Lawler said indistinctly. 'You know, we have to be very careful.'

'Well, they paid a month in advance,' Mrs Rawlinson said.

So they had money. Which partially explained the aspect of the Diddiki's threat that had been puzzling everyone. If you knew how to break into the Bank and get your hands on the bullion why advertise your intentions? Why not make an appearance at a dark and midnight hour without telling anyone and clear off with a few gold bars tucked in your vest? Unless, of course, money was no object and the whole elaborate charade was merely to show what daring fellows you were – and discredit the Bow Street Runners at the same time.

'Did they talk about their business at all?'

'Not that I remember.' Mrs Rawlinson's face was flushed by the fire and her beverage. 'Another little drop, Mr Lawler?'

'Just a drop,' Lawler said. 'Not too much tea.'

'Are you … something in the City, Mr Lawler?'

'Something,' Lawler said – thinking: But not very much. 'I was wondering … ' he said.

'Yes, Mr Lawler?'

'I was wondering if I could have a look at their room.'

'I don't think that would be quite—'

'I just may decide to lodge here, Mrs Rawlinson,' Lawler said. Blackstane, what greater sacrifice can a man make?

'Well

'It would give me an idea what a room looks like when it's been … lived in.'

'I suppose it won't do any harm.'

The room was cheerless, the grate filled with ash, curtains faded, bunches of heather in two vases. It contained three single beds, two ships in bottles, and it smelled faintly of pomade.

'Of course you must remember that they are bachelors' rooms.' Mrs Rawlinson said, standing behind Lawler, very close to him. 'They need a woman's touch.'

Lawler edged away. 'I suppose—'

'Yes, Mr Lawler?'

'No, I suppose I shouldn't ask…But I do like the…the feel of this place. I think maybe I just might take a room here.'

'What is it you want, Mr Lawler?'

He turned and faced her. 'I should like to look through their bags,' he said.

Nothing much there.

Clothes – lots of silk handkerchiefs and colourful waistcoats, some correspondence in Italian – at least it didn't look like English to Lawler – shaving gear, legal documents, nothing that looked like a plan of the Bank.

He went downstairs to be met by an expectant Mrs Rawlinson.

'Did you find what you wanted?' she asked, settling him down in an armchair.

'Not really,' Lawler said.

'What exactly were you looking for?'

'Plans,' Lawler told her. He felt a little muzzy from the brandy. 'Did they ever…did they ever say anything about the Bank of England?'

'They may have done but they were speaking in Italian most of the time.' She sat opposite Lawler. 'What about a spot of lunch?' She paused. 'Perhaps I could call you by your first name.'

'I haven't got one.' Lawler said.

'But that's terrible. I mean … didn't you ever have one?'

'Never,' said Lawler defiantly.

'And people just call you Lawler?'

'First names are unnecessary.'

'Yes … yes, I suppose they are. But they're nice, aren't they?' She leaned forward. 'I'm going to give you a first name, Mr Lawler. I'm going to call you Frank.'

'Frank?'

'Yes, Frank Lawler. What do you think?'

'I don't know,' Lawler said.

'My husband was called Jack. He was a seafaring man.'

'I gathered that,' Lawler said.

'He died at sea, did Jack. He was on the smallish side like you, Frank. But tough, as tough as a walnut. I prefer smaller men …'

Lawler tried to rise but the room was beginning to spin.

Mrs Rawlinson said: 'Have you made up your mind, Frank?'

'Made up my mind?'

'About staying here.'

'I'll have to think it over,' Lawler said.

'Plenty of time,' Mrs Rawlinson said. 'You can make your mind up over lunch.'

'Lunch?'

'I've got a nice piece of pork in the oven. You look as if you need fattening up,' she said playfully.

'I really must get back to the City.'

'No hurry,' she said, pushing him gently back into the chair. 'Plenty of time.' She looked at him fondly. 'You dear little man,' she said.

Lawler wondered if she was going to try and put him in a bottle.

Lawler left at three in the afternoon. The streets were still thickly glazed with ice and fog was beginning to gather.

He found a cab and told the driver to take him to Paddington Village. He was not a man who experienced intense emotion, and the best description of his feelings towards Blackstone at the moment was deep indignation. So far Blackstone had guided him into situations where he had been arrested for picking pockets and imprisoned with a man-eating widow. It wasn't good enough, especially when he had been followed to Kilburn and Blackstone's side of the bargain had been protection.

The fog was thickening – all week seemed to have been a rehearsal for deep winter – and the ice gleamed in the lights from cosy parlours. But Lawler didn't feel the cold: his belly was stuffed with roast pork, and brandy still flowed in his veins.

Lawler knocked at Blackstone's door and waited. Mercy opened the door. She told him that Blackstone wasn't in and said: 'You were right about him, Lawler. He's a good man.'

Lawler went into Blackstone's drawing-room where a fire burned brightly. Mercy had been cleaning the cutlery and the spoons lay on the table, each reflecting a tiny fire. She picked up a fork and began to polish it. 'When do you expect him back?' Lawler asked, refraining from giving his views on Blackstone.

'I don't know. He didn't come back last night and I had a meal waiting for him. I hope nothing's happened to him,

Lawler. He's been very kind and I hope nothing's happened because of what I asked him to do.'

'He agreed to help?'

'Of course.' She looked at Lawler in surprise. 'He's going to get a reprieve for Johnny just like you said.'

He said: 'Did Mr Blackstone say where he was going yesterday?'

She shook her head. A tear fell on to one of the spoons and she wiped it off with a black-stained rag.

'Don't worry,' Lawler said awkwardly. 'Blackstone can look after himself.'

'Can you find him, Lawler?'

'I'll do my best,' Lawler said.

She stood there, waiting for him to charge into the night in search of a Bow Street Runner, of all people. She was decidedly pretty – those big, sad eyes – and Lawler wondered … No, she wasn't Blackstone's type.

'I'll see what I can do,' he said, thinking that Blackstone was probably in bed with the girl from the Brown Bear.

'Thank you, Lawler,' she said.

'You can call me Frank,' he said.

He went first to the Brown Bear, but the girl was there chatting to George Ruthven so that was one possibility dispensed with.

He approached Ruthven cautiously. Lawler was Blackstone's man and the other Runners were notoriously contemptuous of their colleagues' underworld contacts.

Ruthven looked at him without interest. 'Well?' he asked, tankard in a hand that reduced it to a wine-glass.

Lawler asked if he had seen Blackstone lately. Ruthven replied that he hadn't and asked what business it was of Lawler's.

Lawler told him.

'How the hell did you know about the scragging?'

I sent the girl to Mr Blackstone. I've just returned from his rooms.'

'What were you doing there?'

'Looking for Mr Blackstone.' Some of the spirit which had enabled Lawler to survive in the Rookery returned. Why should this great ape treat him like dirt? 'I work for him and there's nothing to say I shouldn't call at his place.'

Ruthven drained his tankard and ordered another. 'Well, I suppose the likes of you have their uses.' Ruthven took his arm. 'Come over here where there's no ears flapping and tell me what you know.'

He led Lawler across the parlour to a table at the window.

Lawler told him all he knew; it didn't take long.

'Any luck with this Bank business, eh?'

Lawler shook his head, making a private bet with himself that Ruthven wouldn't buy him a drink. 'None.'

'Well, keep your mouth shut about this scragging business.'

'I do work with Mr Blackstone, not against him,' Lawler said.

'I know your sort,' Ruthven said, without elaborating.

And I know yours, Lawler thought.

'As a matter of fact,' Ruthven said, lowering himself into a seat opposite Lawler, 'everyone's looking for Blackstone. Birnie in particular. I thought he was just keeping out of the way. I wonder...'

Lawler waited to hear what he was wondering but Ruthven didn't enlighten him.

Ruthven continued to stare at, and through, Lawler and eventually said: 'Seeing as you know already I don't see that it can do any harm...'

'No?' Lawler said.

'Me taking you with me.'

Apprehension stirred inside Lawler. It aggravated the pork and brandy and he belched. 'Taking me with you where?'

'Doesn't matter,' Ruthven said, making a decision. 'Just remember you know nothing about any boy due to be turned off. Just remember that and you won't come to any harm.' He stood up and grabbed Lawler's arm with fingers like handcuffs. 'Come on, culley, there's work to be done.'

Ruthven put on his thick grey coat and his hat and they went out together into the night, Lawler reflecting that he had won his bet about the drink.

They walked to Windmill Street in the fog which footpads greet as others welcome spring sunshine. Outside the tenement from which Hardinge and the little girl had emerged Ruthven said to Lawler: 'Go on, knock.'

'What the hell for?' Lawler coughed as the fog found his lungs.

'Do as I tell you.'

'Why can't you knock? You're big enough.'

'They'll have a spy-hole,' Ruthven said. 'A judas eye. If they see me they won't open the door.'

'Hey,' Lawler demanded, 'what's this all about?'

'Knock and you'll find out,' Ruthven said, pushing him towards the door and standing back.

Lawler knocked.

After a while the door creaked open and a woman's voice said: 'Yes?' She was carrying a lantern.

Lawler had begun to mumble some meaningless reply when Ruthven passed him at speed, thumping the door with his shoulder and knocking the owner of the voice to the floor. He stooped, picking up the lantern with one hand and the woman with the other. 'Come on,' he said, 'upstairs.' And to Lawler: 'Close the door and follow me.'

The woman was too stunned to speak. She stumbled up the stairs with Ruthven directly behind her. At the top of the stairs Ruthven kicked a half-open door and they were in a seedy room furnished with a double bed covered with surprisingly clean sheets, a couple of chairs, two long mirrors, a wash-stand with a marble basin and a jug decorated with roses, and a chest of drawers with a flint-lock pistol lying on top of it.

As they came in a man reached for the pistol. He had got his hand round the butt when Ruthven chopped at his arm with the side of his hand. The man yelped and dropped the pistol. Ruthven kicked it into the corner of the room. 'Time for a little chat,' he said pleasantly.

'Who the hell are you?' the man demanded. He was thick-set, unshaven, with a curl of hair greased over his forehead. Lawler could see that he knew perfectly well who Ruthven was.

Ruthven showed him his baton.

The man said. 'Why don't you get over to the Bank of England?'

Ruthven hit him across the face with the back of his hand, drawing blood. Then he pushed the woman on to the bed and told Lawler to keep an eye on her.

To the man touching his bloodied mouth Ruthven said: 'I want to know where Blackstone is.'

'Who?'

'Edmund Blackstone. Don't tell me you haven't heard of him.'

'I've heard of him,' the man said warily. 'Who hasn't? But I don't know–'

'Yes, you do, my dear,' Ruthven said in his most amiable manner. 'Do you want me to, ah, question you?'

'Do what the hell you like. I don't know where Mister bloody Blackstone is.'

'Very well.' And Ruthven began the sort of interrogation in which he had no equal. There were several schools of thought about Ruthven's interrogations but everyone agreed that they cut through a lot of protocol, that they were brief, and that they usually produced results if there were any to be produced.

Ruthven started with a couple more slaps, then slammed the man against the wall, holding him by the lapels of his greasy jacket. Then he released him and, as the man fell forward, hit him in the stomach. The man slumped to the ground groaning.

The woman on the bed was shouting and moaning. 'We don't know where Blackstone is. Why the hell should we? Leave him alone…'

Ruthven glanced at the man lying on the floor and said: 'Get up.'

When he got up Ruthven knocked him down again.

The man spat out a tooth and sat on the floor, back against the wall. 'You big stupid bastard,' he said. 'I've got friends. You wait till Hardinge hears about this.'

'Ah,' Ruthven said, 'now you're talking.'

Fear flickered in the man's eyes.

Ruthven asked: 'What would Lord Hardinge do if he heard about this?'

'Nothing,' said the man.

'Then why bring his name up?'

'Why not?'

'He comes here, doesn't he?'

The man didn't answer so Ruthven picked him up and hit him in the mouth.

'All right he comes here,' the man said in a thick voice. 'So do a lot of other toffs. They ain't committing any crime, are they?'

'Depends,' Ruthven said. 'Depends on the age of the girls.'

'They're all over twelve,' the woman on the bed said.

'There ain't nothing wrong in that,' the man said.

'What age does his lordship like 'em?'

'Over the age of consent,' the man replied. He dislodged another tooth with his tongue. 'And I don't know nothing about Blackstone.'

Lawler said: 'I think he's telling the truth.'

Ruthven turned and said: 'No one was asking you.'

But he seemed to agree. He gave the man another couple of punches, then said: 'If you go blabbing to Hardinge I'll give you such a beating you'll feel like you were fifty years over the age of consent.'

They retired to the Black Bull. Customers disappeared into the fog and the landlord spoke wearily. 'You lot again? If you keep coming here I'll have to close down.'

'Then I'll have achieved something,' Ruthven said. 'Two tankards of mulled ale, landlord, and chalk it up.'

Lawler looked at him in surprise.

'I'm going to make some more calls,' Ruthven said. 'You stay here and keep your ears flapping. If Blackstone was brought here, then someone may have heard something. And they may be more willing to talk to you than me,' he said grudgingly.

Lawler shrugged. It was also possible that he might have his throat cut for consorting with a Bow Street Runner; but there was no arguing with Ruthven. He took up a position near the door.

A few minutes after Ruthven had left, a little man whom Lawler recognised as a bookmaker's runner who visited the coffee-houses, tobacco-shops and taverns of Holborn joined him. He was very dirty and he had a hare-lip.

'Who's he after?' the bet collector asked, nodding towards the door.

'What's it to you?' Lawler felt socially superior to the runner; it was an experience to be savoured.

'There was a bit of milling outside last night. I thought it might be to do with that?'

'What sort of milling?' Lawler asked.

'A fellow was taken right outside this place. I was just coming in and I saw it all.'

'What did the fellow look like?'

'Big, hefty bastard.' The runner looked sly. 'Looked a bit like that Blackstone everyone's talking about.'

'And the others?'

'All masked. But I did hear–'

'What?'

'I did hear talk of where they were taking him.'

Lawler felt in his pockets and gave the runner a shilling. 'Where?'

'The Rookery,' the runner said.

'What part?'

'I'm a bit hard of hearing.'

Lawler gave him his last shilling.

'Rats' Castle, of course,' the runner said.

When Ruthven returned he asked Lawler if he'd learned anything. Lawler said he hadn't.

CHAPTER NINE

R ats' Castle was the core of the abscess called St Giles Rookery, also known sardonically as the Holy Land.

It was a block, a huddle, a despair of buildings containing a tavern, lodging-rooms, hideouts, passages, kitchens, escape routes. Its ramparts were leaning chimneys and roof-tops that looked like a scattered pack of soiled playing-cards; its dungeons were deep and dank, but healthier perhaps than its living rooms. The élite of London's underworld apart, almost any type of criminal could be found in the Castle: coiners, rampsmen, gonophs, kidsmen, magsmen, cash carriers and others. Could be found, that is, by their fellows, not by lawmen whose heavy footsteps triggered an alarm system and sent the 'rats' scurrying through passages, across roof-tops, over walls, into their holes.

Not that there wasn't vibrant life in the Castle's chambers – in the kitchens, for instance, where men, women and children, dogs and the occasional mangy cat gathered around an open fire on which sausages, potatoes and chest-nuts sizzled; and beer and gin flowed free; songs were sung to the accompaniment of a squeeze-box; the dice tumbled; boys and dogs fought; in the flickering shadows men and women fornicated, and the general atmosphere was convivial.

Blackstone suspected his whereabouts. The smells and muted sounds reaching him through the aperture in the ceiling of his cell were unmistakable to anyone reared in London's stews. The only question was: which of the many stews? St Giles was the nearest to Soho, and Blackstone assumed he was somewhere in the bowels of his birthplace.

One thing in particular puzzled Blackstone: the attitude of his captors. Since his arrival they had given him a blanket and two bowls of hot soup. This indicated that they didn't want him to die, an unusual attitude towards a Bow Street Runner.

But, Christ, he was cold!

The aperture was like an inverted chimney, with fog pouring through it and settling; the slime on the walls had frozen into sheets of ice. Blackstone exercised, ran on the spot, thrashed his arms round his sides, but he had been there a long time and the cold was taking over his body. Night had faded to day and come back again; time was running out for the directors of the Bank of England, for Johnny Bristow – and for Blackstone.

He had tried to reach the aperture but the effort was hopeless. He recalled how a seaman had once climbed the high walls of Newgate, back to the wall, finding the footholds with his heels. But the ice defeated Blackstone. He had tried to rush his warders but they came mob-handed. As he drank his third bowl of soup he thought about Lord Hardinge, imagining him on the gallows, hanging from the gibbet... But the solace was feeble: I have taken on the majesty of the law and lost, he thought.

It had been dark for about six hours when he heard a voice at the aperture. An undistinguished voice to most people but unmistakable to Blackstone.

'Are you there, Mr Blackstone?'

'Of course I'm here,' Blackstone said. 'What kept you, Lawler?'

Why, Lawler had reasoned, should a bullying oaf like George Ruthven take charge of Blackstone's rescue? Furthermore, what chance did a hulking great Bow Street Runner have of approaching Rats' Castle unnoticed?

In Blackstone's interest – and his own because, surely, he would be rewarded – Lawler set out through the fog in the direction of Seven Dials and St Giles. His main fears were that word might have spread that he was a Bow Street nose and that the punters hunting him for their stake money might be in the vicinity of the Castle.

But he entered the Rookery without attracting attention; chameleon-like he had reverted to type and he was now just another member of the riff-raff wandering its alleyways.

He circled Rats' Castle warily, grateful for the fog. If Blackstone was a prisoner here, then he was in one of the cellars. At the first grating there was no reply to his call, just a verminous scuffling in the black depths. At the second he heard the sort of response he might have expected. 'What kept you?' Why, Lawler thought, did I bother? Why did I risk my life?

He called through the grating: 'Nothing kept me. You're bloody lucky I found you.'

Blackstone said: 'Try those bars – they may have rusted away.'

Lawler tried them: they hadn't.

'What shall I do?' he called down.

'Go and get a barker,' Blackstone told him. 'And be quick about it.'

Swearing to himself, Lawler crept away. At least guns weren't in short supply in the Rookery – if you had the money to buy them; Lawler hadn't. But if he could lift a wallet off a financier in the Bank of England, surely he could lift a pistol off a drunken thug in the Rookery.

Lawler sidled into one of the thieves' kitchens in the Castle. Attention was focused on two dogs biting each other to death, and coins were clinking on the stone floor as bets were laid. A fire burned in the centre of the kitchen and herrings were frying in a huge pan of black fat.

Lawler selected his victim carefully. The main consideration was that he had to be drunk, and what few wits he had left should be concentrated on the fighting dogs. Lawler spotted a tall, bushy-haired drunk leaning against a pillar, a cup of gin in one hand and a double-barrelled pistol stuck in his belt. His empty hand was on his hip drawing back his moulting green jacket away from the pistol.

Lawler took up a position beside the drunk who turned, regarded him through glazed eyes and then turned his attention back to the fight.

Lawler took his last coin, a penny, from his pocket and asked: 'Who's your money on?'

The drunk turned again. 'The Staffordshire,' he said slowly. 'Put your blunt on it, culley, before it eats the other game little bastard for dinner.'

Lawler leaned forward, stumbled against the drunk, tossed the penny at the man taking the bets, and left the kitchen with the pistol under his coat.

'Got a piece of rope or string?' Blackstone asked.

Oh yes, Lawler thought, and the Crown Jewels in my waistcoat pocket. He searched his pockets and found a piece of string about four feet long.

'Tie the barker on it and lower it through the grating,' Blackstone ordered.

Yes master, Lawler said to himself. He tied the string round the trigger guard and lowered it through the grating.

'Now drop it,' Blackstone said.

Blackstone caught the gun as it fell. 'Wait outside,' he told Lawler. 'If I'm not out in five minutes get round to Bow Street.'

Lawler moved away from the grating, watching phantom figures drift by in the fog. He was cold and mortified and frightened. Perhaps a bed in Mrs Rawlinson's establishment wouldn't be such a bad idea after all; he felt the great mounds of her body enveloping him, warming him...

His reverie was shattered by the explosion as Blackstone blew the lock off the cellar door with one barrel of the pistol.

Gun in hand, Blackstone made his way stealthily along a passage that smelled of stale beer and mildew. If anyone had heard the explosion they hadn't rushed into action; but then explosions weren't exceptional in Rats' Castle and its environs.

He reached a heavy wooden door decorated with rusty studs, a Spanish type of door. In the lock was a big rusty key. Gently Blackstone turned it and pushed the door, which opened with a sigh. Beyond, another passage. Blackstone moved along it and realised that he was climbing. He was still shivering with the cold and yet there was heat inside him. His chest ached and there was sweat on his forehead: Blackstone had a fever.

Another door, another key. But this time, as he opened it, he heard singing and shouting and music and he smelled herrings cooking and the bite of hard liquor lacing the musty odour of stale beer.

There was a man on the other side of the door, leaning against the wall talking to a girl in a low-cut blouse. It was a very low-cut blouse and the girl was red-haired and pretty, and Blackstone could understand the man's dereliction of duty. The man, big and burly with hairy forearms, saw Blackstone too late. First the shock on his face, then his hand reaching for the pistol in his belt.

Blackstone jerked his flint-lock. 'Don't,' he said.

'How the hell—'

'It doesn't matter how,' Blackstone said. 'I'm out and I want to know why I was *in*.'

Afterwards he blamed the fever, but suddenly the girl was between them and the man was away, through another door and, Blackstone realised, lost. And if you were lost in Rats' Castle and didn't want to be found, then you were well and truly lost.

Blackstone swore and pushed away the girl, who looked at him curiously and said: 'So you're the great Edmund Blackstone. Shouldn't you—'

'Yes,' Blackstone said, 'I should be at the Bank of England.'

'Why don't you stay here for a while?' she said. 'You look cold and ill. I could warm you up ...'

Blackstone managed a smile. 'Another time,' he told her.

He made his way through the kitchen, still holding the gun, aware that he no longer commanded the old respect. Why should he? Dirty, cold, feverish, with time fast running out in the Bank affair. There was some laughter, a few jeers; Blackstone pushed through a throng round the door, walked down another passage and finally emerged in the street where Lawler was waiting.

'Get a cab,' he told Lawler. He leaned against the wall feeling the fever spread through his body. He shivered and stuck the old pistol into his belt.

In the cab he asked Lawler how he had managed to find him. Lawler told him about Windmill Street and Ruthven and his own contact in the Black Bull and waited for gratitude.

But Blackstone was asleep.

CHAPTER TEN

The clue presented itself to Blackstone during a night of feverish dreams. When he awoke he knew he had glimpsed it but he couldn't identify it; so he lay quiet trying to distinguish between fantasy and reality. His body was bathed in sweat and the sounds of life from outside his rooms – a bird singing, a dog barking – seemed to reach him from a long way off. The walls of his bedroom looked very high, the ceiling very small.

It was some time before he realised he wasn't alone in the room. He turned and saw Mercy Bristow sitting on a chair beside the bed gazing at him. He smiled, put his hand to his jaw, felt the thick stubble. Then he realised that, despite the sweat and stubble, he was clean and the sheets were dry. And that he was naked under the bedclothes.

'You?'

She nodded. 'You were in a terrible state. You've still got a fever.'

He turned and stared at the receding ceiling. A clue. A clue to what? Had he glimpsed a way to save Johnny Bristow? Had he glimpsed a way to foil the Diddiki? Had he glimpsed any damn thing?

He began to shiver again.

The girl tucked the bedclothes around him but he continued to shiver. 'I'll get you some hot broth,' she said; but when she brought it he couldn't drink it and the shivering continued.

'There's only one way to stop that,' she said. He heard the rustle of clothes being discarded. Then she was in the bed beside him and he felt her small breasts pressed against him, her arms round him, her hair against his cheek. 'For God's sake,' he said. Then, as the shivering became less agitated, he slept again; and the dreams were more composed and somewhere among them was a clue which he still couldn't catch as it fluttered like a moth inside his skull.

'What day is it?' he asked.

She was still there beside him, arms around his body.

'Friday,' she said.

'Hell!' He sat up but he was still weak and gently she pushed him down again. 'That leaves two days…'

'Don't worry,' she said.

He lay still, not wanting to make any move that could be interpreted as 'intimate'. She was seventeen and she was working for him and her brother was due to die at 8 a.m. on Monday.

'How long have I been here?'

'A long time.' She hesitated. 'You've had some callers.'

'Who?' Blackstone raised himself on one elbow so that he was looking down at her.

'Lawler. He said something about some Italians.'

'What did he say?'

One breast with a small pink nipple was bared and Blackstone covered it with the sheet.

'Nothing very much,' she said, frowning. 'He'd found where they lived but they weren't there. Something like that.'

'Who else called?'

'A bad-tempered old man,' she said.

Blackstone sighed. 'With a face like a mountain goat?'
She giggled.

'That'd be Birnie,' Blackstone said. 'What did he want?'
As if he didn't know.

'He wanted to know what was the matter with you, where
you'd been, what I was doing here…He wanted to know
everything, Mr Blackstone.'

Blackstone laughed aloud. 'Blackie, for God's sake. How
can you call me Mr Blackstone when you're lying in bed
with me with no clothes on?'

'Blackie,' she said softly, tasting the word.

'And what did you tell him?'

'I didn't tell him anything. He wanted to see you and
I said he couldn't because you were ill. He tried to come
in but…'

'But what, Mercy?'

'I closed the door in his face.'

Blackstone was philosophical about it, wondering who
his next employer would be.

'Any others?'

'A big man with a pale face. And a smaller man, younger
and very enthusiastic. I think they were both Bow Street
Runners like you…Blackie.' She smiled at him anxiously.

'And you closed the door in their faces?'

'I wouldn't let them in.'

'I hope you checked your pockets after they'd gone.' She
didn't understand and he went on: 'Now I've got to get up.'

'You mustn't yet.' Arms pulling him down.

'I've got to,' he said.

But she held him down. He could feel sleep seduc-
ing him once more, filling the vacuums in his body with
soft wool, calling him back through time. The ache in his
body was blurring; a lullaby was taking up the rhythm

of his heartbeat. He fought it for a moment, then succumbed making a last vow to try and return to those slumbrous, far-off places where there … was … a clue … to something …

The girl watched him for a few minutes. She didn't move, hardly breathed for fear of disturbing him. Blackie … She finally moved and pulled the bedclothes up round his stubbly chin. This was the man who would save her brother and yet here she was making sure he stayed in bed, with the gallows only a week-end away. She knew as she lay there gazing at him that this was where she always wanted to be, by his side, and she knew at the same time that dollymops born in the stews were never meant to expect such favours from life. They were dollymops and that was that. Swollen knees, the master's unwanted attentions, the rough side of the mistress's tongue, £7 a year and one day off a month, perhaps marriage to a second footman or a first gardener, and then children and another sort of servitude: that's what dollymops were supposed to expect and it was impudence to expect more.

But it wasn't a crime to hope, so once again she slipped her arms round his chest and lay there listening to his breathing and his heartbeat. And hoping.

He was back in Newgate.

He was a boy again and he was visiting his accomplice who had been less lucky than he. The boy who was less lucky had three days to live, three days in which to meditate on the error of his ways before the hangman, William Brunskill, commonly known as Jack Ketch, hanged him with the theatrical sort of flourish for which he was famed. After the drop, when the bodies were still twitching, it was his custom to bow to his audience, hand to his breast.

The boy who was to die was standing in the Press Yard. It was freezing in the yard and the boy was drunk and terrified.

Through the bars Edmund Blackstone, aged fourteen, caught the infection of fear. I should be standing there with him, waiting for the drop. I was as guilty as he. Beside Blackstone stood Mr Sweetman, a handkerchief drenched in lavender-water to his nostrils to keep out the jail stink.

'So there's nothing to be done?' the boy mumbled.

'We mustn't give up hope,' Mr Sweetman said.

But all three of them knew there was no hope. Everything had been done; there was to be no reprieve. The French wars had begun and there was a temporary shortage of adult fodder for the scaffold because the press gangs had taken so many criminals. In fact times were so hard for Brunskill that he had asked the Court of Aldermen for an increase in his allowance.

Blackstone, who had already tried without success to give himself up, said: 'Isn't there any chance of escaping?'

'It's been done,' his friend said, swigging from a pewter tankard. 'Jack Sheppard did it. He filed through the spikes on the hatch where the condemned prisoners used to talk to their visitors. He was talking to his visitors while he was filing away. He left it almost sawed through, then he had two more judies visit him and he broke off the spikes and they pulled him through while the turnkeys were boozing at the end of the passage. Then, blow me, if he wasn't captured and got clean away again.'

Blackstone listened, but he didn't pay too much attention. Who didn't know the story of Jack Sheppard, thief and jailbreaker extraordinary? Born in 1702, he had rapidly become the hero of the underworld and much of the world above as well. When he was returned to jail he was visited by hundreds of sightseers who brought him food and money. He was handcuffed and fettered but he found a nail with which he managed to open the padlock chaining him to the floor. Still festooned in his fetters, he managed to chip away the stones holding an iron bar in the chimney; with the bar he then forced door after door. The escape preparations took five hours; the climax was to have been a leap on to a roof-top next to the prison. But it was now dark, so Sheppard went all the way back to his cell, fetched a blanket, hammered a spike from the wall of the chapel into the wall of the prison – and slid down the blanket. He rested in a garret next to the prison for two hours before escaping, fetters clanking in the night.

But he was caught again and hanged in 1724 aged twenty-two.

(In his sleep Edmund Blackstone twitched and moaned and the girl in his bed held him tight.)

'There's only one way these days,' the boy in the Press Yard said, trying to douse the fear with ale. 'And that's on the scaffold – after the drop.'

'What do you mean?' Mr Sweetman asked.

In a disjointed fashion the boy explained bronchotomy. Blackstone listened in terrible awe.

Bronchotomy needed phenomenal luck – and an amenable hangman. It had worked once with an Irish thief named Patrick Redmond who was led to the scaffold in 1767. Six hours after he had been hanged he made a public appearance at a theatre and thanked an actor friend named Glover for saving him. One theory was that a surgeon had made an incision in his windpipe enabling air to reach his lungs and the hangman had taken a bribe to cut him down before the prescribed hour had passed.

It saddened Mr Sweetman to think that the boy was building hope on this kind of tale. 'What are you suggesting?' he asked. 'That we should bribe the, ah, Mr Brunskill?'

'I don't know, sir. It was just that Blackie asked if there was any chance of escaping.'

'I just thought...' Blackstone began, but he couldn't finish the sentence because there was nothing really to say.

The condemned boy said: 'I thought that Brunskill might take a finny to hold me up. Or maybe you could get me some sort of pipe...'

(Blackstone moaned again in his sleep because they had tried everything, even approached Brunskill, but there was nothing they could do. Not when it was just a bit of a boy who was going to be turned off. He frowned and the girl smoothed his forehead.)

Another visit took place only one day before the boy was due to be hanged. He was talking about a ghost that was said to haunt Newgate. He said he had seen it wandering outside the salt-boxes. The spirit of all those who had died inside and outside the prison – that's what they said because such was the catalogue of death that you couldn't single out one victim to fill the ghost's shroud.

And there was a sound of water, the condemned boy said, when he saw the ghost. Running water – but perhaps it was the liquor he had drunk.

(Ghosts and running water. In his sleep Blackstone twitched, tried to sit up. 'There, there,' said the girl.)

Mercifully the dreams skipped the execution, and it was fifteen years later and Blackstone was a Runner and this time it was a woman they were going to string up. They no longer burned women at the stake, which reflected the humanitarian spirit of reform sweeping Britain.

The woman came from Liverpool and moved to London, and, such was her personality, she recruited a gang of women pickpockets from under the noses of the professional fine-wirers in Rats' Castle. While her team spread across fashionable London, she herself concentrated on churches, sliding jewelled rings from gentlemen's fingers as they helped her to her pew.

She then decided upon a simulated pregnancy and went down in the history of crime as the originator of the device. Into the depths of her pillow-stuffed belly went the pickings and no one dared search her, particularly as she posed as a rich and titled pregnant lady. Sometimes she collapsed in theatrical labour, relieving of their watches and purses those who came to her aid; sometimes she knocked on the doors of mansions, fainted in the hallway, and collected her loot while the agitated lady of the house went for the brandy. Being extremely pretty she was also able to blackmail many suitors – having aborted the pillows at her waist – by waiting until they were stripped and excited in her bed; then, at a prearranged signal, an angry 'husband' would enter the room; scandal was averted by a payment from lover to 'husband'.

She was finally caught and transported; but London called and she returned, knowing that the penalty would be death. She was caught and taken to Newgate, where she awaited the gallows with the sort of composure expected of highwaymen.

A vast crowd gathered outside Newgate to watch the female fine-wirer turned off. But, when the officials went to her cell, stomachs rumbling in anticipation of the post-execution breakfast, the reason for her composure became apparent: she had vanished. And the turnkey guarding her was sitting against the wall in a state of equal composure, his skull shattered.

There were no signs of escape, no signs of forceful entry. She had disappeared, vanished, evaporated, as if some celestial fine-wirer had lifted her from her cell.

Blackstone awoke with a start. It was still light; the girl had gone. He listened and heard movements in the kitchen. He wondered what he would do about Mercy Bristow. But at the moment he had more important things to wonder about.

The clue was assembling from his excursions into the past. A ghost, a prison escape that had been greeted as a miracle. But Bow Street Runners are not impressed with theories of divine intervention. A fragment of the clue was missing; Blackstone hungered for it.

The heat had left his body; his chest still ached but his brain was clear. Gingerly, he swung his legs out of the bed and walked unsteadily to the mirror where he regarded his hard, scarred body speculatively; his prickly face was pale but his eyes looked bright enough. He put on a dressing-gown and went to the kitchen for shaving water.

Mercy had anticipated his awakening from the fluttering of his eyelids. Coffee was made, water boiling on the hob.

'Hallo ...'

'Blackie,' he said.

'Blackie,' she said.

He poured himself some coffee. The kitchen clock ticking away above the coal fire told him it was two o'clock in the afternoon. Time wasn't running out: it was galloping away. He drank the coffee, felt it land in his stomach. His hands were trembling, and for a moment he felt as though he was going to faint; he fought it and won.

He stood up and Mercy asked: 'What are you going to do?'

'I'm going out.'

'You shouldn't—'

'I have to.'

'Shall I make you something to eat?'

Blackstone thought about it. The last thing he wanted was something to eat, but it looked cold outside – cold enough for snow – and he decided that he should have some fuel in his belly because God knows what lay ahead of him. 'All right,' he said, 'Something light.'

He took the boiling water into his bedroom and began to sheer away the bristles. Why, he wondered, had his captors been so decent, comparatively speaking that is? In the Rookery you never took prisoners: you blew out their brains or clubbed them to death if you didn't want to waste a bullet. Perhaps Lord Hardinge drew the line at murder.

He washed himself down with the remainder of the hot water, then dressed. He opened the chest containing his guns. It was difficult to choose the right weapon because he had no idea what he might have to use it for. To shoot a ghost? He decided once more on the Mantons – you couldn't go far wrong with the work of Joseph Manton, unless your opponent fired first – two pocket pistols and a horse pistol. Into the leg of his black leather boots he slid another long-bladed French stiletto.

She had fried ham and eggs and made more coffee. He forced down the food, slugged the coffee with brandy.

'Where are you going?' she asked, watching him eat with maternal pleasure.

Blackstone, who wasn't sure, said: 'I expect I'll go to Newgate.'

'Johnny will be pleased to see you.'

'He's a nice lad,' Blackstone said, wondering what he could do about her blind faith in his ability to save the boy.

'You will get him off, won't you, Blackie?' Not so blind now?

'You mustn't pin your hopes too high.'

'I know that,' she said. 'You've been ill…'

'It's not that. You know, the law can be very hard.'

'Can anyone be so hard that they can allow a boy' – a sob – 'to be hung?'

Blackstone thought of Lord Hardinge. 'They don't see it like that,' he said.

'But you're the law, Blackie.'

'I know,' he said.

'Do *you* think children should be executed?'

Blackstone shook his head. But the implication was there: he was a part of a vast, ruthless stratum of class distinction and privilege, either inherited or bought like an army commission, that dispatched members of lower strata to the hulks, the treadmill, the convict ships, the gallows. Why did he carry out the wishes of a society whose unpardonable crime was not just lack of compassion but total lack of interest in the 'dangerous' classes? Blackstone didn't know, never had known; except that sometimes the gilt-crowned baton implemented his own ideas of justice.

'No,' Blackstone said, 'I don't think children should be executed.'

'Is there any hope at all?'

'There's always hope,' Blackstone told her.

'But not much?'

He looked into those big eyes, owlish through lack of sleep. 'Not much more,' he said.

She nodded. The dangerous classes always accepted injustice, just as the privileged stoically accepted inclement weather during the hunting season.

He stood up, finished his coffee, hesitated. Then he kissed her gently and was gone into the cold and cruel afternoon outside.

CHAPTER ELEVEN

Several people wondered about Blackstone's absence from duty with varying degrees of interest and emotion. Page was in a ferment of emotion. The humiliation over Lawler and the financier Jenkins in the Rotunda rankled: so did many other incidents in which their careers had touched each other's. He was exultant that he had been assigned to the Bank of England investigation, hurt that he had not been put in charge of it, suspicious about Blackstone's movements, sick with fear that he himself might fail.

With Bentley he went to the Bank and interviewed the directors and staff, who were by this time weary of being interrogated by representatives of Bow Street exuding little confidence in their own ability to trap the Diddiki. In any case it seemed to have become a personal vendetta between Bow Street and the gypsies, with the Bank merely providing the site for the denouement. If the Diddiki only wanted to prove what daring fellows they were, and had no intention of stealing any bullion, then let them get on with it; meanwhile there were graver problems to consider, such as the run on gold as companies went bust like puffballs underfoot.

The directors were condescending in their attitude to Page and Bentley; the staff openly sneered. Page contributed to the general lack of decorum by snapping at 'young'

Bentley whenever he got the chance. One way and another the status of the Bow Street Runners was at its lowest ebb.

Among the others brooding about Blackstone was the girl at the Brown Bear – but she had heard there was another girl installed in Blackstone's rooms and had no intention of calling there. Another was Sir Richard Birnie.

Birnie brooded as he dressed his scraggy frame in front of a blazing fire. He brooded all the way down to breakfast – porridge, toast and tea – brooded as he opened *The Times*, and exploded with wrath and frustration when he reached the letters.

'A plague on them!' He pushed his bowl of porridge away and began to read, while a frightened maid removed the bowl, poured him some more tea and scurried away to the kitchen.

The Diddiki repeated their threat and went on to inquire where Edmund Blackstone had been for the past forty-eight hours. Had he admitted defeat and gone to some bolt-hole? Had the Bow Street Runners admitted defeat? No doubt Peel would be interested to hear about their frantic and futile endeavours on his return to England.

Birnie stared out of the window at the bleak day outside. The bare branches of a tree rasped together and the wind ruffled the feathers of a sparrow perched on it. The bleak day seemed to epitomise Birnie's future. Another five years of this life, perhaps; another five years of disgrace as the Runners were disbanded and Peel introduced some uniformed substitute. The climax of his own ruthless ambition a charade, a farce.

Past, present and future fused icily.

Once a mere saddlemaker, Birnie had attracted the attention of the then Prince of Wales; then he had married a rich woman and begun his climb to power. Finally only the incumbent Bow Street magistrate, Sir Robert Baker, stood in his way. Happily for Birnie the funeral arrangements for Queen Caroline were bungled – two demonstrators were killed – and Baker was sacked.

Now it was his turn.

He put on his long black coat, tall hat and muffler and went into the street, heading for Bow Street. Ice on the rutted road crackled under his feet, and the eyes of the beggars thrusting their bowls in front of him were running with the cold.

Blackstone was up to something – of that Birnie was positive. Something not connected with the investigation in hand. Birnie remembered the cheek of the girl who had refused him admittance to Blackstone's home; he growled at a beggar with a wooden leg.

Was it possible that Blackstone was responsible for the leakage of information about the Bank affair? Birnie walked past the Theatre Royal and turned into Bow Street scowling like winter. Surely not. But with a background like Blackstone's you could never tell.

Shoulders bunched, Birnie strode past clerks and officials without answering their greetings. God help anyone in the dock this morning, they said as his office door slammed.

The fire was lit; smuts were settling on his desk. From the walls Birnie's predecessors stared at him with mocking eyes – Henry Fielding; his brother John, the blind beak; Thomas de Veil, father of twenty-five children.

Who would know what Blackstone was up to? His only confidant was George Ruthven. Typical, Birnie thought – the roughest and toughest of the Runners. A thug, in fact – but, Birnie admitted, a useful one. Birnie summoned him to his office from the Brown Bear.

'Well, Ruthven, what's he up to?'

'I've no idea, sir.'

Birnie recognised the lie and worried at it. 'You realise your future is at stake as much as anyone's?'

Ruthven said he did.

'Then why did Blackstone go missing in the middle of this assignment. This vital assignment?'

'I don't know, sir. Perhaps the Diddiki got him.'

'The Diddiki!' Birnie muttered something that sounded to Ruthven like a Gaelic curse. Then he lit his long pipe, pointed the stem at Ruthven and said: 'Go and get him, Ruthven.'

'I've tried,' Ruthven said, 'but Blackstone's servant turned me away.'

'Blackstone's wench, you mean.'

Ruthven shrugged.

Birnie said: 'If a Bow Street Runner of your size can't get past a serving wench then perhaps it is time the Runners were disbanded.'

'I'll see what I can do, sir.'

Moodily, Birnie watched Ruthven leave the building – and walk straight into the Brown Bear. Birnie marvelled at Ruthven's sense of urgency.

By lunchtime there was still no sign of Blackstone. Birnie went to a chop-house in the Strand, where he endured some baiting at the hands of the businessmen who dined there. He drank half a bottle of hock that tasted like vinegar and went back to Bow Street.

Blackstone was waiting for him outside his office.

The recriminations were long and bitter.

Blackstone told Birnie that he had been waylaid and imprisoned, and Birnie commented that Blackstone's vigilance left a lot to be desired. Birnie asked Blackstone if he had any idea who his captors were, and Blackstone said he had no idea.

So it went on, and in the middle of it all a letter from Lord Hardinge arrived by special messenger.

'Odd,' said Birnie, ripping open the envelope with a paper-knife.

Blackstone hoped the paper-knife would be out of reach when Birnie finished reading the letter.

Birnie read the letter, then re-read it, then put it down on the desk in front of him and said again: 'Odd. Very odd.'

'Why's that, sir?' Blackstone asked.

'An invitation to dinner,' Birnie said. 'I hardly know the man.' He picked up the knife and tested its blade with a bony finger. 'An invitation to dinner and a veiled inquiry about you, Blackstone.'

'Really, sir?'

'He seems to be questioning your capabilities.' Birnie sighed. 'I suppose it must be in connection with this wretched affair of the gypsies…'

Or a move preparatory to prosecuting me, Blackstone thought. But at least it proved one thing; Lord Hardinge was too scared of what might be revealed in Windmill Street to launch an impetuous prosecution. He was sounding out the ground, and Blackstone decided he would have to pay him another visit. No one, not even a judge, could be allowed to get away with a kidnap.

Birnie was still muttering about how odd it was that Lord Hardinge of all people should suddenly invite him to dinner. Blackstone thought it was odd that *anyone* should invite Birnie to dinner.

'Anyway,' Birnie was saying, 'so you really haven't anything to report at all?'

'Nothing, sir.'

'That girl told me you had a fever and couldn't be disturbed.'

Blackstone apologised on behalf of the girl. He wished Birnie hadn't seen her. Birnie was a shrewd old bastard.

'Who is she?' Birnie asked.

'Just a girl who works for me.'

'Bit young for you, isn't she?'

'She's seventeen, sir. There are a few dollymops of fourteen and less working in London—'

'When she answered the door,' Birnie interrupted, 'she was wearing one of your coats and nothing else underneath.'

Shrewd, lecherous old bastard!

Blackstone said in a voice that totally lacked authority: 'Perhaps she was having a bath.'

Birnie clearly didn't believe that dollymops had baths. 'Perhaps,' he said, 'she was sharing your bed of fever.'

'With respect, sir,' Blackstone said, 'this is a private matter—'

'Nothing's private when the Bow Street Runners' name is at stake.'

'I *did* have a fever, sir. I still do …'

Birnie asked: 'Who is that girl?'

'I told you—'

'What's her name?'

'I forget—'

'Her name, Blackstone.'

'Bristow, sir.'

Birnie stared at him. 'Bristow, eh?' He paused, tapping the paper-knife on the desk. 'Now where have I heard that name recently?'

Later that day Blackstone went to the English Bastille, as Newgate was known. It was the most feared prison in Britain, and had been since 1188.

The boy was in the yard, sitting by himself at the foot of one of the towering walls. He was ashen-faced, and Blackstone thought he looked as if he'd seen a ghost.

When the boy came to the grating he told Blackstone that he had.

CHAPTER TWELVE

L awler objected strongly. 'I'm not going to lodge with that old bitch,' he told Blackstone. 'Absolutely definitely not, Mr Blackstone. Do what you like to me. Sell me to the press-gang, chain me to the treadmill, keelhaul me – but I'm not going back to that old cow. On my life I'm not.'

'Then I'll have to tell those punters you welshed on where you are,' Blackstone told him.

So Lawler packed his meagre belongings and they set out by cab for Kilburn.

It was the only potential lead to the Diddiki and Blackstone decided that he had to make at least a token effort to nail them. In the morning he would pay a visit to Lord Hardinge at his country residence – see how he warmed to the notion of his wife and children hearing about the waif in Windmill Street.

It was cold and dark outside the cab – taverns and parlours beckoning, horse-shoes striking sparks on cobblestones, the calls of the girl street-vendors sharp and sad, the sky jewelled with stars. The fog had lifted but it had left behind its reek; the night Blackstone thought, smelled of gunpowder.

But where the hell was the snow?

All the way Lawler grumbled. 'She'll bed me, Mr Blackstone, and then I'm done for. Once they've bedded you they've got you, make no mistake. The law's on their side, see?'

'Well, don't let her bed you,' Blackstone said. 'Keep a tight hold on your trousers, man.'

'She'll get me kanurd,' Lawler mumbled. 'Like she did last time, and then she'll bed me and I'll be stuck in sodding Kilburn for the rest of my born.'

'A pleasant place,' Blackstone said. The fever was fading but it hadn't made its final exit; his eyes felt hot and his head ached.

'I was followed last time I came here,' Lawler said. 'You promised me protection, Mr Blackstone, and yet the bastards came after me. What sort of protection is that? You know, I carry out my part of the bargain and you—'

'They were working for me,' Blackstone said.

'Go on.'

'They were your protection,' Blackstone said. 'Except that you shook them off.'

Lawler thought: He's almost as good a liar as me. You had to admire him – even though you hated him for the ungrateful bastard he was.

Blackstone said: 'Tell the driver to stop about a hundred yards away from the house.'

'Why?' Lawler asked.

'Because they might be there.'

'I don't want any trouble,' Lawler said.

'Who does?' Blackstone said. And when the driver had reined in the horse and they had paid him to wait, Blackstone told Lawler to walk ahead and knock on the door. Blackstone waited behind a tall privet hedge while Lawler knocked; light suddenly beamed down the front path as the door opened, and Blackstone heard the voices of Lawler and a woman.

'Frank!'

'Good evening, Mrs Rawlinson.'

'Welcome back. Have – have you come to stay?'

'I thought I might stay for a few days. But if you're full up—'

'Always room for a decent little man like you.'

'I've brought a friend with me.'

A pause. 'A lady friend?'

Lawler, hastily: 'No, a man.'

Mrs Rawlinson, eagerly: 'Really? Where is he?'

Blackstone stepped out from behind the hedge and walked up the garden path towards the two silhouettes, one very slight, the other elephantine by comparison.

She was wearing a pink satin dressing-gown and her hair was in curlers. She was eating some sort of sweet and under one arm she held a lap-dog. She greeted Blackstone with hideous coyness, and for a moment he felt sorry for Lawler. Perhaps she had poisoned her husband.

They went into the sitting-room where Mrs Rawlinson poured them each a glass of Madeira and offered them chocolates surmounted by crystallised fruit.

'Well,' she said, allowing the dressing-gown to fall open and reveal a plump leg mottled by the heat of the fire, 'who would have thought my Frank would have a friend like you?'

Blackstone grinned at Lawler. 'Frank?'

'I christened him,' Mrs Rawlinson explained. 'He ... he just looked like a Frank to me. My husband was a Jack – he was a seafaring man, you know.'

Blackstone glanced at the ships in the bottles and nodded.

Mrs Rawlinson said: 'And let me guess your name Mr ...'

'Whitestone,' Blackstone said.

She popped a chocolate into her mouth and looked at him speculatively. 'Whitestone … Now what would go with a distinguished name like that? And what would suit a distinguished gentleman like yourself?'

Lawler suggested Judas.

'You could be a Richard or a Charles or a James … but no—' She pointed a finger heavy with rings. 'I've got it – Edmund.'

Blackstone stared at her in astonishment. 'How on earth did you guess that?'

'I have these powers,' Mrs Rawlinson explained. 'Spiritual powers. It's this house, you see. It gives me the feeling that I can read people's minds – and speak to the dead. Although I haven't been able to reach my Jack,' she said reflectively.

No fool, Jack, Blackstone thought.

Mrs Rawlinson went on: 'It's got a definite *feeling* about it, this house. Can you feel it, Mr Whitestone? You know, a feeling that we're in touch with the past. As a matter of fact,' she said, ignoring a yelp of terror from Lawler, 'it is haunted. I've seen our ghost once or twice. He's quite friendly. You know, he doesn't carry his head under his arm or anything like that.'

London, Blackstone reflected, was full of ghosts this winter. And again he had the feeling that he was on the brink of a revelation. He forced himself to concentrate.

A knock at the door.

Mrs Rawlinson rose and peered through a chink in the curtains. Then she turned to Lawler and said: 'Why, Frank, it's one of those Italian gentlemen you were asking about.'

It was very simply executed.

Blackstone stood inside the bedroom so that he was concealed when the door opened. When the man came in, Blackstone shoved the Manton in his back and told him to raise his hands. Then he searched the man, finding a screw-barrelled Barton pocket pistol in his coat; he threw this into the corner of the room, stepped back and told the man to turn round.

On the landing Lawler and Mrs Rawlinson watched spellbound. Blackstone closed the door and told the man to sit down on the edge of the bed. Blackstone pulled up a chair and sat facing him, pistol aimed at his chest.

So far the man hadn't spoken. Now he did – an hysterical tirade of protest in broken English.

Blackstone asked: 'When did you arrive in this country?'

The man began to calm down. 'About three weeks ago,' he said, his Italian accent making the words bounce.

'From where?'

'From Rome. But I don't see—'

'Why did you come here?'

'Business. I am an Italian businessman and I have my rights, and I want to know who you are, *signore.*'

'Police,' said Blackstone who had experienced difficulty in explaining the role of the Runners to foreigners.

'Why do you want to question me?'

'Because,' Blackstone said. He waved the gun at the Italian. 'Your name?'

'Vittorio. Vittorio Vincelli.'

'And you're a businessman?'

'*Si* – I already told you—'

'A big businessman?'

The Italian began to use his hands. They said he was a pretty big businessman.

'Then why do you lodge in a place like this?'

Why not? the hands asked.

Blackstone asked: 'Where are your two business associates?'

'In the city – doing business.'

'Delivering letters to the newspapers? Making keys to get into the vaults of the Bank of England?'

The Italian looked puzzled. 'Please, *signore*, I don't understand ...'

'Why did you sign yourselves the Diddiki?'

'You make fun of me?'

'I might shoot you if you don't answer my questions truthfully.'

The hands said: You're mad.

'What were you doing in the Bank of England the other day?'

'I told you, *signore*, business.'

'Monkey business,' Blackstone said, glad that he had checked with Jenkins the financier.

'Monkey business?'

'Yes, monkey business, Signor Vincelli. You sold some bonds to a Mr Robert Jenkins knowing them to be worthless. Only a raving idiot would buy stock in a South American mine at the moment. Mr Jenkins is no fool and you should have known better.'

'But—'

'The money he paid you with is also worthless,' Blackstone said.

'Then he is a fraud.' The hands were excited.

'No, *signore*, you are the fraud – a hanging offence in this country.'

Signor Vincelli began to look extremely alarmed.

Blackstone said: 'But, if you were able to help us with this business about the threat to break into the Bank of England, we might just deport you ...'

'But I don't know what you're talking about.'

'Then you'd better find out. Meanwhile I'm taking you to Bow Street. Get your things together, Signor Vincelli, there's a nice comfortable cell waiting for you.'

Lawler said: 'So I needn't stay here, Mr Blackstone?'

'What makes you think that, Lawler?'

'I mean now you've got this cove there isn't any point, is there?' Lawler appealed.

'There are two other coves.'

Mrs Rawlinson stepped forward from the shadows. 'You're Edmund Blackstone, aren't you?'

Blackstone nodded.

'And I *was* right about the first name.' She paused. 'It's this house you know…'

'Tell me,' Blackstone said, prodding the Italian's back with his pistol, 'does anything else occur when you see this – this ghost?'

She shook her head. 'Nothing really except…'

'Yes, Mrs Rawlinson?'

'Except that I seem to hear the sound of running water.'

CHAPTER THIRTEEN

Captain Kidd was seen walking that night. And many other ghosts. It was a fine night for ghosts and it promised to be an excellent winter season for them. In a room above the parlour of the Brown Bear, Blackstone sat up late reading about them.

Captain Kidd was seen where he was always seen, at Execution Dock, the gallows beside the Thames at Wapping where those convicted of crimes on the High Seas were turned off. They are taken from Newgate, sitting beside their executioner in a cart. In front rides the Marshal of the Admiralty, behind him two City marshals on horseback. The bodies are left hanging until the tide has washed over them three times.

Captain Kidd had been given a brief to sail a gunship against pirates plundering shipping. But he was accused of having turned pirate himself and on 23 May 1701 was duly hanged at Execution Dock, despite claims that the authorities had encouraged his piracy.

Since then Captain Kidd had repeatedly returned to the site, according to local residents, in particular those rolling out of local hostelries. He was said to rise from the water, a slender, silvery figure, and move gracefully upstream until he submerged again to protest his innocence to the fish.

On this particular night he was seen by a drunken navvy helping to dig Brunel's tunnel under the Thames. According to the navvy, Captain Kidd was angry at the excavations taking place at his grave. Plied with more liquor, the navvy said that Kidd, with whom he seemed to have struck up a friendship, had cursed Brunel and his tunnel, which he said would know many disasters before it was finished.

Blackstone, seeking to establish a common denominator to the hauntings, read on. Among the ghosts he analysed was a headless woman who was always seen on the lawns of St James's Park. She was said to be the wife of a sergeant in the Coldstream Guards who, in 1816, knifed her and cut off her head before dumping her body in the foul waters of the lake. She was seen by the lake wearing a dress dripping with water.

Another was a bearded gentleman in a frock coat who appeared beside a plane tree, known as Dead Man's Tree, not far from Piccadilly. Here many duels had been fought, and many suicides had hanged themselves from its branches. The bearded man was believed to have shot himself there after hearing that his wife and four children had died in a fire. At the dead of night, so it was said, you could still hear his sighs.

Eventually Blackstone decided that he had read enough: he had isolated the common factor that he had suspected – *water!* For Captain Kidd, the Thames. For the headless woman, the lake in St James's Park. For the bearded man in the frock coat, the river Tyburn.

And for Mrs Rawlinson's ghost?

Blackstone consulted a book about London's rivers – and discovered the Westbourne, which rose near White Stone pond on Hampstead Heath and made its way towards London via Kilburn.

So Mrs Rawlinson's ghost also emerged from a watery grave.

Blackstone flipped through one of the books and, towards the end, found support for his theory.

It is not beyond the bounds of possibility that there exists a connection between London's rivers, many of them underground and long since forgotten, and the manifestations of the supernatural which occur at regular intervals. Ghosts have, it is true, been sighted at locations where, as far as is known, there is no known river flowing; but, in this context, it should not be forgotten that water flows in many forbidden places, i.e. where a sewer has been constructed against the wishes of the law.

The candle was burning low. God knows what secret waterway lay beneath the Brown Bear; and, in any case, the Fleet wasn't far away. Blackstone took a pinch of snuff and read on, occasionally glancing into the darkness beyond the candle's glow. He didn't believe in ghosts; but then again he didn't disbelieve in them.

We cannot but guess at the juxtaposition of these watercourses, and supernatural phenomena, but those with a cynical turn of mind might postulate the theory that the sound of hidden water, no doubt eerie in the early hours of the morning, might, to an extent, account for the existence of these manifestations. It is but a short step – the mingling of the senses, perhaps – from the aural to the optical, especially to those of a sensitive disposition.

Blackstone heard a noise in the corner. He carried the candle across the room – and found a moth fluttering there. He returned to the table by the window and read on.

*We are not necessarily of that cynical frame of mind, and
readily acknowledge that ghosts may well swell London's
nocturnal population, but it would be remiss of us not to
elaborate on the coincidence of the presence of water and, in
particular, underground water. Is it not possible that gases
arise from these subterranean rivers and sewers, become
ignited and, aided and abetted by the sound of running
water, give the appearance of ghostly apparitions? Is this
not, perhaps, the explanation for the phenomena known as
Jack o' Lanterns which, from time to time, have been sighted
flitting around the tors and crags of Dartmoor? Could those
weird sprites who have struck terror into the hearts of the
most hardened travellers be the result of gases escaping from
the bogs and mires of that wild and inhospitable region?*

Thoughtfully, Blackstone snuffed out the candle and
made his way to the headquarters of the Runners across
the street. The offices were in darkness and he had to light
a lantern. In the record office he found the case histories
of criminals who had been dispatched to Newgate, many of
them to the scaffold.

It was midnight. The parchment sheets rustled under his
hands. So much evil and death contained inside the bind-
ings. Once he though he heard a tapping. John Fielding, the
blind beak, tapping his way through the corridors? Perhaps,
Blackstone thought, I'm still feverish.

After some while he found what he was looking for: the
case of the Liverpool woman who had disappeared from a
condemned cell.

Occupation of husband: tosherman – someone who
made his living by combing the underground rivers and sewers of London for treasure. Blackstone closed the heavy vol-
ume and tied its covers with a leather strap. So the husband

of the woman who had vanished had been an expert on underground London!

Blackstone still needed some more information. If you wanted historical or statistical information at an hour when libraries were closed, you reluctantly approached 'young' Bentley.

Blackstone let himself out of the building. Across the road business was still flourishing in the parlour of the Brown Bear. Blackstone glanced up and down the moonlit street. And, with some relief saw a familiar figure entering the tavern. No one could accuse George Ruthven of having a ghostly appearance.

First his own explanations to the other Runners, giving away as little as possible. Yes, the Italian locked in a cell across the road might be an important lead; yes, time was running short.

The girl hardly spoke to him. Page left shortly after his arrival, pointing out that it hadn't snowed yet and he would be around on Monday to collect his sovereign. Finally there were just himself, Ruthven, and Bentley, who always left last in case he missed anything.

Blackstone worked the conversation round to famous escapes in general. Then famous escapes from Newgate. Bentley plunged in eagerly.

He started with Jack Sheppard. Ruthven yawned and said he was going home, but Blackstone restrained him.

Bentley recalled the Gordon Riots in 1780 when a mob had sacked Newgate, reducing it to a smouldering ruin, and all the inmates had escaped. The odd thing, Bentley said, was that so many were recaptured simply because they stayed around the place as though it was their own home that had been razed.

'Didn't anyone ever escape through a sewer?' Blackstone asked.

Ah, did they not! In 1731, Bentley said, six prisoners managed to dig their way into a sewer. Four got away but two died somewhere in the stinking passage. And in 1737 a man named Daniel Malden managed to reach the sewer through a vault. He escaped to the Continent but was stupid enough to return to England and was hanged at Tyburn.

Then why, Blackstone wondered, hadn't anyone surmised that the Liverpool woman who had so mysteriously vanished had escaped through a sewer. Bentley supplied the answer. After the last escape they had strengthened the floor above the sewer and blocked all its entries. Which didn't exclude the possibility, Blackstone thought, that her husband had known of a river, or the tributary of a river, or an old sewer constructed illegally. And that the woman hadn't broken *out:* her husband had broken *in,* from beneath the prison.

Johnny Bristow had seen a ghost. Johnny Bristow had heard water. There was still a chance.

Ruthven and Blackstone walked together to the stables.

Ruthven said: 'Sorry I didn't get to Rats' Castle, Blackie.'

'Don't worry about it,' Blackstone said. 'Lawler got there.'

'Another little rat,' Ruthven said. 'Is there any hope, Blackie?'

'Of what?'

'Of saving Bristow.'

Blackstone nodded. 'But I shall need your help.' He paused. 'And I think I should warn you that Birnie may be on to something ...'

'Christ,' Ruthen said.

'Are you game?'

'I might as well finish what I've started.' 'There might be a little glory in it, too, George.'

Ruthven creased another fold into his furrowed brow. 'Blind me, Blackie, how do you make that out?'

'Because,' Blackstone said, 'I think we might be able to beat the Diddiki at their own game.'

Chapter Fourteen

It was dawn and the tide was rising swiftly, and the boy crouched inside the drain couldn't remain there much longer. But he couldn't leave yet because in his hand he grasped a rough ball of metal with a golden heart, and at the other end of the drain there were thieving hands waiting.

He gazed through the grating at the rising, mud-coloured water outside. There was no escape through those bars, and soon the water would be pouring through them. Higher, higher till it was at his neck.

The boy shivered with the cold – he was half naked – and with fear. But the fear wasn't strong enough to overcome the desire to keep the ball of metal, a desire born of poverty and starvation. With its glittering yolk this ball was worth at least £10, enough to keep him in food and ale for a year or more.

The boy's name was Tom and he was an apprentice tosherman. His world was the sewers, rivers, culverts, passages and tunnels of London. The ceilings of his work-places dripped with slime; the air he breathed stank; his spoils were the coins and other valuables that found their way into underground London. Once in a lifetime you struck gold, and you didn't part with it easily.

He was a thin boy with sharp features that gave him a rodent-like appearance; but if anyone had bothered to fatten him up he would have been pleasing enough to look at – brown hair, brown eyes, undistinguished nose, impudence in the lines of his mouth.

Water gurgled at his feet. Driftwood floated past from the direction of the sea he had never seen. Now, now. Wait, wait. The golden egg in his hand. The rats fleeing. Canny, sensible rats.

But it wasn't the first time that he had left it till the last moment. Never before with gold in his hand, but with enough to warrant split-second timing to avoid handing over the takings to the older toshermen who couldn't squeeze down the sewers emptying into the Thames.

Water poured over his bare feet and swept down the drain, bringing with it the smell of boats and paint. The sewer was about four feet in diameter, made from bricks and iron hoops. The water reached his ankles.

The boy rolled the ball in his hand. It had been underground a long time. Moulded and smoothed by the movement of water for decades, wedged in a hole left by a dislodged brick until the boy spotted it in a green nest of moss.

The water rose up his legs.

And suddenly he was more scared than ever before. He scrambled away from the grating, the water pursuing him. Had he left it too late? He moaned to himself, praying to God and promising to go to church. His head grazed the top of the drain, the water reached his waist. He thought of the great kitchen where he slept and ate and drank and fought; he thought how rich the life behind him had been, how bountiful the life ahead would have been with gold to spend…

He hit his head on an outcrop of stone and fell dazed into the water, feeling it pour through his nostrils and down his throat.

Fifty yards away, in a cavern where the sewers divided and the water went its different ways, the group of waiting men shook their heads and hurried away to their various exits, emerging in streets, gardens, yards, and even a cemetery or two. Another tosherboy drowned, the second that month.

One man stayed behind.

He was forty, old for the trade, and he was a big man with a back bowed like a miner's. He was known as Gold because of the number of sovereigns he had found; he was feared and respected and was the king of the toshermen.

Kneeling down, Gold peered down the drain. The water rushing at him was halfway up the wall, rising swiftly. He could see nothing at first, then a hump, then a face wild with its first introduction to death.

'Hold on,' Gold shouted, meaninglessly. 'Try and crawl forward.'

The boy's face disappeared, then rose again.

'I'm coming for you,' Gold shouted.

No chance of reaching him. But near the cavern the drain did widen. Gold knew his drains and he looked around for one thing that might save the boy. Sweet mother of God! – there it was, a long pole with an attachment at the end, like a wide garden hoe, which sewermen used for pushing the sludge back into the Thames.

Gold grasped the pole and pushed it towards the boy. But it didn't reach. The water had almost covered the boy and soon it would cover Gold.

'Grab hold of it,' he shouted, mouth filling with water, as he threw himself into the drain, pushing the pole in front of him. He pulled. Nothing. He pulled again – there was some resistance, too late now to check. Gold pulled the pole, backing out of the drain, pushed and shoved by the tidal water racing upstream.

Then they were out in the cavern like exploding corks, the boy half-conscious hanging on to the pole. The water was around Gold's waist, and no one except Gold would have been able to reach an exit in time; perhaps not even Gold.

Carrying the boy under one arm, Gold made for a man-hole cover concealed by beards of hanging moss. Few knew of its existence, the fewer the better to Gold's way of think-ing. The water was pushing around his chest, trying to take them with it. With one arm he managed to keep the boy's face above water, with the other he shoved the pole at the manhole cover.

The cover moved slightly. One more heave and it opened…gradually…then toppled backwards. Daylight streamed into the tunnel. Gold pushed the boy head first through the opening, then hauled himself out.

They were lying in a ditch, and nearby the sun shone on the free waters of the Thames sweeping through London. They lay for a few minutes. Finally Gold spoke.

'What had you found yourself down there, culley?'

The boy gazed at his empty hands and began to cry.

Gold lived in St Giles' Rookery, three lanes from Lawler, but he had been born on the banks of the Thames and he could only relax when there was the smell of river mud in his nostrils, the sight and sound of moving water in his eyes and ears.

He came from a family of toshermen who scavenged the subterranean world of the Isle of Dogs – a pocket of land surrounded on three sides by a bulge in the Thames. The Isle had its ghost like most parts of London; in fact the Isle went one better: it had a ghost accompanied by phantom dogs. Centuries ago the Isle had been covered by a forest known as Hainault. In this forest – according to legend eagerly substantiated by late-night tipplers – a newly-wed nobleman accompanied by dogs went boar hunting; but during the hunt his bride drowned in a swamp; and, ever since, the nobleman and his dogs had been seen in the sky searching for the bride.

The story had terrified Gold and the other young mud-larks who tramped the ankle-deep mud of the Thames at low tide in search of treasure; but, being their leader, fear-less and strong, Gold was forced to mock the phantoms even if he believed they existed, and he had himself seen a ghost across the river at Greenwich at the palace where Anne Boleyn was arrested before she had her head chopped off at the Tower.

Ghosts and water. It wasn't till years later that the con-nection occurred to Gold, and it was to provide him with the means to become the uncontested king of the underground.

But *not* the underworld – because Gold was an honest man. And so rare a commodity was honesty that he was regarded almost as a mystic among his colleagues. Not that mysticism was omnipotent in Gold's London; but when you had the muscles to support it then few bothered to chal-lenge your authority.

From the Isle of Dogs the young Gold wandered up-river, to the underground passages and taverns – many haunted – of Rotherhithe, on the opposite bank, where warehouses were being built like castle walls beside the moat of the Thames. From there he roamed to Southwark, the site of Shakespeare's Globe Theatre.

It was here that Gold first struck gold – a Spanish coin lying deep in the silt near Clink Street. He found it with his bare foot, raised it as gently as a chicken's egg, wiped away the slime, and gazed at the majestic lustre that seduces men to glory or the grave. Gold was seduced, enslaved, at the age of fourteen.

He had no parents and so he held on to the coin while embryonic business instincts got to work. First of all, like any young man seeking a fortune, he had to move to the centre of London, the centre of the world. The tide was sweeping in fast and he couldn't search the mud any longer; in any case he didn't want to attract attention by concentrating on one area. Invest, young man. Wasn't there some story in the Bible that said it was wrong to merely save money?

So Gold re-crossed the river, made his way to the slum at Westminster known as Devil's Acre, and sold the coin for £1 to a legless money-lender who carried on his business in a basement filled with caged birds. With five shillings of the money he rented a room. He lay down on the bed, covered himself with a tattered blanket, and wondered how to hook more goldfish from the Thames mud without being seen. It had to be at night, he decided, when most toshermen were in bed, and mud, water, roof-tops and even gold were silver in the moonlight.

For six weeks he combed the mud near Clink Street, named after an ancient prison for heretics, and during that time raised two more Spanish coins which he sold for £2 each. But that was the end of the treasure hunt. The time had come to diversify his business.

He moved to the deep sewers and rivers beneath the mansions where the swells lived. At first he was resented; but those who resented him met his fists and relented; finally they began to follow him because he had this magnetism – an alchemy, according to some – for gold. Sovereigns and, occasionally, those balls with the hearts of gold rose to his fingers from the mud and slime, beckoned from dripping alcoves, implored his bare feet to tread on them.

By the time he was eighteen Gold was established in his twilight kingdom. He worked with a select band of six men and boys who operated as a pack, beating off pursuit as they moved through the tunnels. But those outside the pack were treated kindly; if they could prove hard times – or harder times than usual – they were given a few coins to buy food or drink or medicine.

Soon the pack knew every manhole, every exit into a premises, in central London. Or almost every one, because Gold kept a few to himself.

By the age of twenty he was married, with a small house nudging the mansions along the Strand. From its windows, more like portholes, he could see the Thames and so, with his pretty wife and a child on the way, he was as content as any man can be who had heard the call of gold in his youth.

By the age of twenty-three he had three children; still happy, but restless. In his dreams he saw Spanish galleons plundered, their gold pouring into the sea; he saw nuggets gleaming in the dark depths of the mines of Africa and South America. Gold, gold...ah...the man known as Gold drooled in his sleep.

One day he told his wife that he planned to sail to South America and make their fortune. He would be back within two years, he told her, and he would buy a fine house in Greenwich and, cured of his fever, he would settle down. Finally she agreed, and she wept as he waved farewell and headed for the more easterly reaches of the Thames where a ship bound for South America was moored.

In his money-belt he carried a small fortune in gold pieces, in his trouser belt he carried a twin-barrelled pistol to protect those pieces. Spring was in the air, sunlight glinted on the river.

But those with the Midas touch are often cursed as well; sometimes the scales balance, sometimes they tip. For Gold that spring day they tipped away from Midas, and Gold's journey to South America ended at pistol point in a tavern in Wapping a few miles from his home.

The tavern he entered for a last grog on English soil was used by shofulmen, but Gold, set fair for a fortune across the Atlantic, was not to know. It occurred to him that some of the customers were a bit flash, but there was nothing to associate them with the faking of coins; nothing to indicate that some of them were carriers who brought the forged loot from the coining shops of London to certain taverns where they passed it to the smashers who, in their turn, circulated it around the country.

Had any of the shofulmen tried to pass a sovereign to Gold, then he *would* have guessed their profession. Not for him the shell of a sovereign filled with lead; he wouldn't even have had to bite it to know it was a fake – the weight would have registered the moment the coin changed hands. Not that the customers in this particular tavern specialised in lead-filled gold-boys. Silver was their merchandise – good flats pressed from a mixture of silver and copper and burnished with nitric acid; other imitations struck from pewter, hence the shortage of pewter tankards in many inns.

Another factor unknown to the king of the underground was that during the night a coiners' den had been raided off the Ratcliffe Highway. In an attic high above the bawdy houses frequented by sailors, the constables had caught five men red-handed with their crucible and hammers. As the constables burst in, the bit-fakers tried to destroy their coins in the crucible because without these the law had no case. There was a fight and one constable was badly burned, but enough coins were saved to ensure a conviction. As a conviction meant the gallows the men were prepared to nose. Next day raids on taverns all over London were carried out. Wherever the cream of the profession was expected to consort, the Bow Street Runners were called in.

As Gold sat at a table staring serenely at the sails of the ships anchored in the Thames, coiners and smashers were fighting and cursing and demanding to know who had betrayed them at taverns in St Giles, Islington, Bethnal Green, Whitechapel and Westminster. Gold's time was nigh.

The raid on the tavern in Wapping was organised by a new Bow Street Runner named Blackstone. The tavern was surrounded by constables, and Blackstone, young and scowling, thrust his way into the parlour and ordered everyone to stop doing whatever they were doing. He seemed to think that everyone would obey the authority of his baton; that everything would go according to plan, and the wanted men would accompany him meekly to Bow Street. Such is the stuff of policemen's dreams.

Within seconds the parlour was a heaving mass of bodies. Fists, cudgels, bottles, life-protectors – all these flew. An amazed Gold watched from his window-seat; then, as someone fired a pistol and the ball punched out a pane of glass behind his head, he decided it was time to go. He watched Blackstone laying about him with gusto, then made for the door. But the constables had now confined the brawl to a tight circle with Blackstone at its centre. Gold was inside its circumference, and ten minutes later he was in a cart bound for the cells.

Two days later he tried to explain the gold coins in his belt to Edmund Blackstone. Blackstone, facing him across a table in a cell, admitted that, as far as could be ascertained, none of the coins was forged. But where did they come from? From the mud of the Thames? From the sewers and underground rivers of the city? Blackstone laughed. Now, where the hell *did* they come from?

Gold repeated his story, realising with despair that he was being interrogated by a novice anxious to make his name. And what better way than to organise a round-up of shofulmen – and catch a cracksman with a belt-full of gold in the process?

'Why were you carrying the coins?'

Gold struck the table with his fist. 'I told you – to pay my passage and keep me in funds when I got to South America.'

'And what was the name of the ship?'

'The Golden Horn.'

'But there was no such ship berthed in the Thames.'

Gold leaned across the table. 'I told you. She was due to sail on the noon tide. By the time you got there she had gone.'

Blackstone took some snuff. To Gold's mind he was too much of a dandy by half – a prizefighter trying to look like Beau Brummel. God help me, Gold thought.

'Your wife backs up your story.'

'Of course she does.'

'But she would, wouldn't she?'

'Would she? I don't know. I'm not a criminal. I don't know about these things.'

Blackstone looked unimpressed. 'Can anyone else support your story?'

'My children?'

Blackstone sighed. 'Anyone else?'

Gold thought about it. He had never sought honesty in the pack who hunted with him. If he named any of them they might soon be sharing his cell. 'No one else,' he told Blackstone, who frowned and said: 'I want to make every possible check. If you're innocent then you've got nothing to fear.'

'Do you really believe that?' Gold asked.

'Of course,' Blackstone said, adding: 'At least when I'm in charge of a case.'

'Then you've got a lot to learn,' Gold said. And made the mistake of asking: 'In any case, what's a cove like you doing in the Runners?'

'What sort of a cove would that be?' Blackstone asked, a rasp to his voice.

'You weren't born on the side of the law, culley. You're from the Rookery, aren't you?'

'So?'

'So you should keep to your own kind,' Gold said.

'Not everyone in the Rookery's a villain, Gold.'

'Not quite everyone,' Gold said.

'You're not helping yourself, Gold.'

'I don't have to. Like you said, culley, if I'm innocent then I don't have anything to worry about, do I?'

'Nothing except your mouth,' Blackstone said.

'Should I be frightened of you?'

'You should respect the law.'

'Pull the other leg; it's got bells on,' Gold said.

Blackstone stood up – big and strong and keen and none too sure of himself, but dangerous for all that. 'I'll try and trace some of the coins.' he said.

Two days later Blackstone returned and explained the snag in the theory that an innocent party had nothing to worry about. 'Five of those coins of yours were stolen,' he told Gold.

'I didn't steal them,' Gold said, despair like bile in his stomach.

'They were in your possession.'

'That doesn't make me a thief.'

'It makes you a receiver of stolen property.'

'I didn't *receive* the bloody things. I found them.'

'The trouble,' Blackstone said carefully, 'is that the matter has been taken out of my hands.'

'Taken out of your hands?' Gold looked incredulous. 'What the hell are you talking about, man? It's your case.'

'Not any more.' Blackstone explained that the coins were part of a robbery from a silk merchant's house five years ago, and that the robbery had been investigated by another Runner, a Runner held in much esteem, a Runner many years senior to Blackstone. The silk merchant was a miser and he had marked every sovereign in his possession with tiny nicks. Gold's five sovereigns were all nicked. Blackstone looked unhappy about it, but not as unhappy as Gold.

'What are you trying to tell me?' Gold asked.

'Just that I'm not in charge of the case any more. But, if you're innocent, you've got nothing to worry about.'

Gold snarled at him: 'For God's sake stop saying that. Who is this other Runner?'

'A man called Griffiths,' Blackstone said.

'Is he straight?' Gold asked, thinking what a futile question it was.

'What do you expect me to say?'

Gold buried his head in his hands. 'Why? Why me? I've been honest all my life, and now this. Why?' he implored Blackstone.

'I'll do whatever I can,' Blackstone said.

'Do you believe I'm innocent?'

'I believe you're an honest man.'

'Sweet mother of God, that's the same thing!'

'I'll see what I can do,' Blackstone said.

Gold stood up and went to the barred window. He gripped the bars and said: 'Scragging job, ain't it, pinching gold coins?'

'It depends on the value of the coins,' Blackstone told him.

'Aye. And it depends who they was pinched from. If they was pinched from some poor bloody lurker in the Rookery I'd get my knuckles rapped. If they was pinched from Lady Muck from the Boneyard it'd be a topping job. That's right, isn't it?'

'The court often undervalues stolen property to save a thief from the gallows.'

Gold turned and faced Blackstone. 'How can they undervalue five gold coins?'

Blackstone didn't reply. Then he got up to go. 'I'll see what I can do.'

'So you keep saying.'

'On my oath.'

'All right, culley,' Gold said, 'I believe you.'

One month later Gold was sentenced to five years' imprisonment for being in possession of five gold coins, knowing them to have been stolen.

One of the chief prosecution witnesses was the new Bow Street Runner, Edmund Blackstone. He gave evidence that Gold had admitted to him in an interview that he knew the coins had been stolen.

Gold went to jail and began to plan his revenge. Blackstone visited him but Gold refused to see him. Blackstone didn't blame him: Gold didn't know the truth.

To save Gold from the gallows Blackstone had risked his career. Pitted against him was William Griffiths, a vindictive and crooked Runner, peering into retirement. His failure to catch the thieves who had burgled the home of the silk merchant still rankled; if he could nail Gold for the job then he would finish his career in a burst of glory. Griffiths was after blood.

Blackstone proved the existence of an open sewer near the silk merchant's home. Wasn't it possible that the thieves, who had been surprised and chased, had dropped some of their swag in the sewer? Possible but unlikely, said Griffiths, announcing that he could produce the merchant's butler who had given a description of one of the thieves, a description that fitted Gold.

Blackstone took legal advice and consulted the Chief Magistrate, who told him that his business was the prosecution rather than the defence of villains. If Blackstone persisted in interfering with Griffiths's case then he stood an excellent chance of being sacked.

But Blackstone did persist and discovered that the butler had been dismissed from his previous employment for dishonesty. Finally a compromise was reached: Gold would be prosecuted – but on the lesser charge of being in possession.

Blackstone knew that injustice was being condoned. He also knew that if he didn't agree and give evidence against Gold, the tosherman would be hanged. He gave his evidence, averting his eyes from the man in the dock.

During his imprisonment Gold tried to control his bitterness. He spent his time making plans to reclaim the throne of his underground kingdom and to extend the boundaries of that kingdom when he was released. And all the time he believed that he would stumble across a way to revenge himself on Blackstone.

His wife brought him maps and surveys of London, but his research was hampered by his inability to read. So he taught himself to read. Then she brought him historical books about London, and after a year or so Gold was able to lie on the wooden boards of his bed and transport himself to a perch in the clouds from which he gazed down on London, down and through its surface so that he saw another city, a city of tunnels and rivers, of foundations of bygone palaces and mansions, of the rotting bones of ancient men and extinct animals of grotesque proportions, of hidden vaults and cellars nestling deep in blue clay.

Soon the city beneath the city became more real to Gold than the slums and fine avenues that partnered each other on the surface.

There was the River Fleet, rising in the pastures of Hampstead Heath, diving and surfacing as cockily as a cormorant on its way to the Thames at Blackfriars, passing through a hollow near its outlet and adopting the name Holbourne, or Holborn. Once it was 600 feet wide as it neared the Thames under Fleet Bridge, and ships would moor in its waters to discharge their cargoes; now its lower reaches were treacle-thick with sludge. Then there was the Tyburn, also rising in Hampstead but taking a more aristocratic course through Marylebone, Oxford Street, Piccadilly before emptying itself into Father Thames at Westminster. There was the Westbourne which helped to fill the stinking Serpentine, Counter's Creek, the Effra – beneath London was another Venice.

It was during all this research that Gold became aware of the connection between ghosts and water. He remembered the nobleman and dogs of his childhood, and the apparition in Greenwich, both adjacent to water. He delved into his books and found that nearly all the ghosts seemed to appear above a submerged waterway. Find a ghost and you find an entrance into underground London. The possibilities were enthralling: with this sort of knowledge in his possession King Gold would reign again.

But it was one underground river in particular that intrigued Gold. The Walbrook. If he wasn't much mistaken it flowed beneath the Bank of England.

CHAPTER FIFTEEN

Saturday.

Less than two days left.

Behind him years of planning. Gold was forty now, old for his age, stooped from life in underground London, but as strong as a prizefighter. His fair, cropped hair was shot with grey, his knuckles were scarred from contact with rough walls, his face bore the lines which spell prison to those who know.

Two factors had sustained Gold since his release from jail. One was his integrity. Somehow he had preserved it; this was a miracle in the company he kept, and sometimes a saintly light seemed to shine from his eyes, a light which blinded the unwary to their shrewdness.

The other factor was the plan. He had nursed it, nourished it, examined it and tested it, for more than ten years while he reestablished himself in his kingdom. The object of the plan was simple: the total humiliation of Edmund Blackstone. Not death, torture, blackmail, double-crossing, nothing that betrayed Gold's code of honour. Just sweet, simple humiliation. Often Gold imagined he could hear the mocking laughter of London's under-world, of London Society, echoing through the caverns of his kingdom; and in the dripping darkness he grinned fiercely.

In the basement of the house in St Giles which he had bought after the death of his wife and two of his children, Gold read the *Morning Post* and the last declaration of the Diddiki. Why Diddiki? The name had come unsolicited to Gold and he supposed it was because, in a way, he and his men were gypsies of the darkness.

He turned to the boy whom he had rescued that morning: 'Can you read?'

Tom shook his head.

Gold smiled; it had been a stupid question. 'Have you heard about the Diddiki?'

Tom said: 'You mean the gyppos who're going to break into the Bank of England?'

The very same, Gold told him.

'Everyone's heard of them. They've got the Runners on the run, ain't they?' The boy grinned showing strong white teeth, one of them chipped. 'Do you think they'll manage it?'

'I hope so,' said Gold, looking speculatively at the boy. 'Do you?'

'Course I do. I'd like to see Blackstone's face on Monday morning. Be as red as a foot patrolman's waistcoat, I shouldn't wonder.'

'Any idea who the Diddiki are?'

'Gyppos, I suppose. But I don't see how they're going to do it, do you, Mr Gold?'

'No idea,' lied Gold, who that morning had made a last check of the foundations of the Bank. Blackstone had checked them too; Gold knew that. But the Bow Street Runner had only checked them from above; the floors of the bullion vaults appeared immovable and Gold didn't blame Blackstone for not suspecting that one flagstone had been doctored from beneath. According to Gold's

RICHARD FALKIRK

information – the best – Blackstone had also studied plans of the drains, which he had obtained from the Commissioner of Sewers. Doubtless the drains would be well guarded on Sunday night, but the tunnel along the course of the Walbrook wouldn't be guarded, because only Gold, one other man and a boy knew about it. And so they should, because they had dug it, working like moles for two long dark years.

'I thought they might try and get up through the sewers,' the boy said.

'Too obvious,' Gold told him.

'Then I don't see—'

'Nor do the Bow Street Runners. Nor does Mister bloody Blackstone,' Gold said, venom in his voice.

'Then how?'

'Ours not to reason why,' Gold said.

The boy's stomach rumbled and Gold asked him if he was hungry. Men wouldn't be hungry after they'd nearly drowned, but London's urchins would still be hungry after a banquet at the Mansion House. Gold's question was answered by another sound from the boy's stomach, a noise like a violin string being plucked.

Gold put bread and cheese and pickles on the table; and a side of beef and some apples and a jug of ale. The boy didn't begin to eat: rather he launched an attack on the food, fighting the bread and cheese with a knife and cramming the spoils of war into his mouth with his hand.

Soon Gold began to feel hungry too. He poured himself some ale and ate some cheese, fine crumbly stuff from Cheshire. Royalty always ate well and King Gold was no exception. As he ate he tried to read the character of the boy, always a difficult task with London's waifs whose better qualities were often smothered at birth. One last-minute complication had arisen in the plan. A boy named Dick Hatchard, who was to be sent up into a cavity beside the doctored flagstone, had fallen sick; he was still willing to go underground but he was coughing badly and Gold thought the waters of the Walbrook might kill him. So Gold surveyed with interest the ravenous boy sitting opposite him.

After the first impetus of the attack on the food had died down Gold began to test him. Why had he tried to keep the crown jewel – the nugget with the gold centre – to himself? Didn't he know the rules? All spoils to be shared?

'I didn't know you was out there,' Tom said.

'What's that got to do with it?'

'The others would have pinched it.' The boy munched a pickled onion and belched. 'They don't share everything – you know that, Mr Gold. They shares about half of what they finds. They reckon you don't notice too much these days. As if your mind's somewhere else.' The boy stared warily at Gold; you didn't criticise a monarch, but Gold *had* asked the question.

Gold, whose mind *had* been elsewhere recently, said: 'Are you trying to tell me you'd have brought that crown jewel to me?'

The boy guzzled some ale and bit into an apple. 'You want the truth?'

'Of course.'

'Then I doubt it, Mr Gold. You know, like I say, nobody reckons you know what's being netted these days. So I would have probably said to myself, "Tom, why hand over to Mr Gold what he won't miss anyway?" I know I should have handed it over like a good 'un. But I could have made myself a pound or two out of that nugget and bought some clothes and everything. You know how it is, Mr Gold, we ain't all as honest as the day is short.'

'Long,' Gold said.

'Huh?'

'Honest as the day is long.' Gold drank from his tankard of ale. 'But that was a pretty honest answer, Tom.'

The boy didn't reply.

'You could have said you would have handed it over. It would have been the obvious thing to say, wouldn't it. I mean, seeing as there isn't any crown jewel to hand over.' Gold finished his ale and lit a clay pipe. 'Why did you say you wouldn't have handed it over?'

"Cos I wouldn't have,' the boy said, pushing his chair away from the table and glancing towards the door because he didn't like the drift of the conversation.

'You're being very honest about your dishonesty,' Gold said, smiling. He stood up, crossed the room and locked the door. 'Don't worry about that crown jewel any more. The tide's not gone down yet but the chances are that, when it does, the gold will go with it.'

'Then again it might not,' the boy said, wondering if he was in for a thrashing. 'It might lodge in the grating.'

'And you'd wait there again until you nearly drowned?'

'I expect so,' said the boy.

'Honesty of a sort, courage …' Gold sat down again and drummed his fingers on the table. 'How old are you?'

'Thirteen,' the boy said. 'At least I think so.'

The same age as Dick Hatchard. Gold didn't like taking chances, not after all those years of planning. But he couldn't send a sick child to possible death. There didn't seem to be much choice.

'Would you like to work for me?'

'I already do,' said the boy in a surprised voice. 'We all do, don't we?'

'Not all the time, it seems. No,' – Gold put his elbows on the table and leaned forward – 'I was thinking of some rather special work.'

'What sort of special work?' the boy asked suspiciously. 'I'm not a snakesman, Mr Gold.'

'Nor am I a kidsman,' Gold snapped.

The boy said he was sorry.

Gold said: 'A special job underground at night-time.'

'I suppose it would be all right,' the boy said. 'When, Mr Gold?'

'At a dark and midnight hour,' Gold said.

After they had eaten, Gold returned to the *Morning Post*. His letter had received more space than ever before. He re-read it with pleasure, smiling when he remembered how Blackstone had called on the best screevers in town to try and trace the author. Who would have believed that a tosher-man, an ex-jailbird, would have such a literary flourish?

Gold read the letter to the boy, who was sitting in front of the fire enveloped in some of Gold's old clothes.

The Diddiki repeated all their old challenges, then threw down the gauntlet. There was no intention to steal, said the letter; in fact the directors of the Bank of England should be grateful to the writers of the letter for discovering flaws in security...

The boy interrupted. 'That's what I can't understand. That's what no one can understand – why they're doing it. I mean, what's the point if they ain't going to pinch any gold bars? It seems daft to me.'

'Listen,' Gold said, and read on: *'However it would hardly befit the directors of this great establishment to ignore the diligence expended by us in uncovering the weaknesses in the Bank's defences. If we can present ourselves in the bullion vaults, then surely it is not outside the bounds of probability that others with tendencies more criminal than our own can arrive at the same conclusions as ourselves, present themselves in the vaults without a reception committee present and vanish the way they came with the bullion on their persons. Within a comparatively short space of time these rascals could bankrupt the Bank and perhaps the country.'*

'Blind me!' exclaimed the boy.

Gold held up his hand. *'We believe therefore'* – Gold read on – *'that it would be a noble gesture on the part of the directors to reward us, their humble servants, for our efforts on their behalf and, indeed, on behalf of our country. We have searched our souls and come to the conclusion that £1,000 would be a small price to pay for our endeavours.'*

'Cripes,' the boy said.

Gold said: 'Just listen to this. When the Fancy reads this next bit the Bank will have to cough up.'

'If the Diddiki get to the vaults.'

'They'll get there,' Gold said.

'What do they say, then?'

Gold read on: *'We are also led to believe that the said directors are of a sporting disposition and we believe, this being so, they will appreciate the sporting nature of our challenge. If we present ourselves in the bullion vaults at the dark and midnight hour we have previously mentioned, then we feel convinced that these sporting instincts will triumph and that we shall be suitably rewarded.'*

'Gawd,' said the boy, 'if the directors don't cough up the Fancy'll wreck the place.'

'Just like the mob did in 1780,' Gold said.

'Why did they do that?' the boy asked.

'No popery,' Gold answered mysteriously. He re-lit his pipe and read the last paragraph of the letter with a smile on his face, murmuring: 'Perfect, just perfect.'

'What's perfect, Mr Gold?'

'This last bit.' Gold read out the last sentences. *'It has come to our notice that Mr Edmund Blackstone, the eminent Bow Street Runner, has been making some blundering attempts to thwart us in our mission. To Mr Blackstone we would say, beware, you are not dealing with the sort of petty criminal whose apprehension you have made your speciality. This time you are not dealing with vagrants, beggars, pickpockets, coiners or receivers of stolen property. This time you are dealing with men who are more than a match for you.'*

'Lor,' exclaimed the boy. 'They're really chancing their luck, these gyppos, ain't they?'

Gold continued reading: *'We know your every move Mr Blackstone. We know that you have apprehended some unfortunate Italian gentleman who, we can assure you, is totally innocent of any participation in our schemes. We know that you have searched the vaults, interviewed the staff, even interviewed the professional letter-writers of London in an effort to identify us. Amateurish stuff, Mr Blackstone. We expected better of you! Already the streets of London are filled with sniggers as you pass by. Wait until Monday, Mr Blackstone, by which time they will resound with gales of laughter such as no red-nosed clown ever extracted from an audience.'*

'I wouldn't laugh at him.' Tom said.

'Why the hell not?'

'Because he'd clout me. He's got a lot of respect has Blackstone,' the boy added guardedly.

'You mean people respect his baton.'

'No, they respect Blackstone himself,' the boy said, knowing that he was angering Gold.

'Why should anyone respect a bent lawman?'

'There's those that reckon he ain't so bent. Those that reckon he'd let a stock buzzer go free and pinch the kidsman who was forcing him to go thieving.'

'Blackstone's bent,' Gold said, his voice as cold and as sharp as an icicle. 'As crooked as a corkscrew. A turncoat who came from the other side of the law. There's nothing as low as a bent lawman, Tom, and don't you forget it.'

The boy said diplomatically: 'So it's the Diddiki versus Blackstone now, eh, Mr Gold?'

'Something like that,' said Gold, staring at the stem of his pipe which he had just broken in his fist.

'My money's on the gyppos.'

'Mine too, lad.'

The boy swallowed, cleared his throat, poked the fire with the iron poker and watched the sparks chasing each other up the chimney. After a while he said: 'You're one of the Diddiki, ain't you, Mr Gold?'

Gold nodded.

'And you want me to help?'

'That's what I said.'

'You mean you trust me?'

'You've got to trust someone.'

'I don't understand,' the boy said.

'Nothing to understand. Are you game or aren't you?'

'Course I'm game,' the boy said. 'Who wouldn't be?' He shook his head in wonderment. 'Me one of the Diddiki, God blind me!'

'Maybe he will,' Gold said. 'Maybe I will if you don't do what you're told.'

'Are you the arch cove?'

'I'm in charge. There's only me, another fellow, a lad, and now you. We've been working at it for years, so, you see, you've come in rather late, but you'll be reaping the benefits just the same. You might have lost the crown jewel, Tom, but you've fallen lucky.'

'But why me?'

Gold explained the plan and said: 'There's a hollow beside the flagstone. Only a lad can climb in and do what has to be done to release the flagstone. Once that's done then we can all climb through. The lad who goes up there has got to be a skinny little devil,' Gold said. 'There's not much meat on you, is there? And, what's more, you're used to working underground. Wouldn't do to have a surface worker down there at a dark and midnight hour, would it?' He paused. 'So you be here tomorrow morning. Better still, don't leave. Have you got any folk to worry about you?'

The boy shook his head. 'What about you, Mr Gold? Have you got any of your own?'

'Got a son nearly twenty,' Gold said. 'The other two snuffed it.'

'Will there be anything in it for me?'

'Of course – there's £1,500 to be split between us.'

'I thought you said £1,000.'

'I did,' Gold said. 'But I haven't read the last sentence of the letter to you, have I? I've made a side bet with Blackstone. If he doesn't stop us getting into the vaults then he owes us £500.'

The boy laughed and hugged himself. 'They do say he likes a bet. But he won't like this one so much, will he, Mr Gold?'

But Gold didn't answer. He had just noticed the letter in the paper signed Edmund Blackstone. It commanded as much space as Gold's, perhaps more. It was at the top of the page whereas Gold's was halfway down, and he had only missed it because he had been searching for the Diddiki's imprint.

Blackstone's letter read:

It has been brought to my attention that the so-called Diddiki – a common term used to describe half-breed gypsies – have personally involved me in their flamboyant challenge to the directors of the Bank of England. I should like to take this opportunity to inform readers that I, the undersigned, who have been put in charge of the inquiries into the activities of the Diddiki – perhaps mouchers would be a more appropriate vulgarism – am fully aware of their every movement and it would be premature indeed to assume that the activities of these men are in any way mysterious to the authorities at Bow Street.

Gold frowned. He remembered the young but shrewd features of the young Runner who had once interviewed him and then doublecrossed him, and he felt vaguely uneasy.

Having said this, let me throw down a challenge. It has come to my knowledge through my inquiries that these half-breeds propose to wager me £5oo that I am powerless to stop them entering the Bank of England vaults at this dramatic 'dark and midnight hour'. I will improve upon that. The Diddiki are, apparently, of a sporting turn of mind and presumably will not flinch if the stakes are increased. I therefore make the following challenge: If I prove that I am fully aware of how they propose to gain entry to the vaults of the Bank of England, then they shall pay me £1,000.

Gold swore. How could Blackstone possibly know that he had intended to make the £500 wager? Could it be true, as they had feared at one time, that he was on to something?

The boy asked: 'Anything the matter, Mr Gold?'

'I don't know,' Gold said.

'What was you reading?'

'A letter from Blackstone.'

'What did it say, Mr Gold?'

Gold told him.

'He's bluffing, Mr Gold.'

'Maybe. But I want you to do something for me.'

'What's that, Mr Gold?'

'Tomorrow we go underground. Today I want you to stay on top.'

The boy nodded, puzzled. 'Doing what, Mr Gold?'

'I want you to follow Blackstone,' Gold said.

Gold had a good reason for buying the small house in the Rookery. With his income, he could have bought a decent place in Islington or Highgate Village. But no – he chose a two-storeyed tenement in St Giles. Certainly it was trim, with its whitewashed walls, woodwork freshly painted blue, its window-box planted with bulbs for the spring; so neat and clean, in fact, that it looked like a milk tooth in a row of rotting stumps. But why St Giles? The answer lay not in the location, not in the portion of the house above ground; as might have been expected with Gold the answer lay in the basement.

It was from the basement that Gold went to work. And, after the boy had left, Gold opened the door to his kingdom. He pulled back the table, lifted the scrubbed floorboards with their polished knots of wood, and, with a grunt, lifted a trapdoor. The smell rose, filling the room, musty, rotten and chill; but not unpleasant to Gold because he had breathed this air all his life. The smell of rotting seaweed isn't pleasant but it has a certain salty healthiness about it; this was how the underground breath of London smelled to Gold. And indeed it was preferable to many of the odours on Gold's front doorstep.

Gold lowered himself into the aperture, feet finding the iron rungs of the ladder he had clamped to the side of the manhole over which the house was built. Then he descended into the dripping gloom to try and find out if there was any substance in Blackstone's letter in the *Morning Post*.

CHAPTER SIXTEEN

Blackstone awoke as the tide was sweeping up the Thames and almost taking the boy Tom's life with it.

It was another bright day, with frost left by the mist and fog lying thickly on the fields and making patterns on the windowpanes. Blackstone lay for a few minutes gazing through the patterns – angels' wings and stars and diamonds and white peacocks' tails – thinking that it was going to be the most brilliant and beautiful day of the year and that he was going to spend it underground. He also thought that it could be the most decisive day in his career. He recalled that time was running out for his wager about the snow and, judging by the blue light shining through the frost-patterns, he thought he stood an excellent chance of losing it – not to mention his job and £1,000 to the Diddiki.

He decided that there wasn't time to visit Lord Hardinge, swung himself out of bed and went into the kitchen, where the scene was now familiar. And that was another problem: what the hell was he going to do about the girl, irrespective of whether he managed to snatch her brother from the noose? He was, Blackstone realised, beginning to enjoy the routine – the smell of coffee had become the alarm that awoke him in the mornings and he didn't fancy any substitute. There on his plate were five rashers of bacon, three sausages, two eggs, two slices of liver and a kidney. There was Mercy Bristow standing in front of the black cooking range, her face flushed from its fire, smiling at him and asking: 'How do you feel this morning?'

Blackstone felt fine and told her: 'Better, Mercy, thanks to you.'

'You should look after yourself more.'

Blackstone drank some coffee and tackled the food.

'A man on horseback brought this.' She handed him the *Morning Post.*

'Ah.' Blackstone took it from her and opened it. There they were, the two letters, the duel of words. Blackstone smiled and nodded as he read: he thought his letter was rather well done. Especially the bit about the Diddiki's £500 wager. It hadn't been too difficult – all Blackstone had done was ask the editor about the contents of the letter before it was published. Blackstone didn't imagine it would fool the authors for very long; but at least it would keep the populace guessing and perhaps muffle some of their scorn until his ultimate triumph, or debacle.

'Will you be seeing Johnny today?' Mercy asked, pushing hot muffins towards him.

Blackstone wiped his plate and told her he would. 'But I have told you not to hold any false hopes. All I can promise is that I'll do my best.'

'I know you'll do that, Blackie.'

Blackstone took his coffee to the kitchen window and rubbed away the steam. The day sparkled and beckoned. It was a day to take your horse and ride till you and the horse ached with the joy of it.

But not today.

'Shall I lay your clothes out?' Mercy asked.

'Not my clothes,' Blackstone told her. 'Today you lay out my rags. The shabbiest and dirtiest you can find, and if they aren't shabby and dirty enough make 'em so.'

Then Blackstone tried to explain to her that their relationship, innocent though it was, had no permanency. They had met because of her brother's plight, and he had taken her into his home because she was cold and wet and worried. It was good having her around and she was a wonderful cook and nurse but there was just nothing ahead of them. How old was she? Seventeen? Blackstone laughed at her youth – then reflected that girls were already women at fourteen in the stews of London. Suddenly she was in his arms, which was wrong, and he kissed her gently, without passion, and went on explaining, but she didn't seem to take much notice. So he stroked her hair, tilted her head with one finger beneath her chin and looked into her eyes, gentle with trust, and thought to himself, God what shall I do? First save the boy! But what if he hanged? What would he see then in those eyes? 'Don't worry,' he said. 'It'll be all right.' He meant this to apply to the boy but knew she interpreted it as applying equally to their future. So he retired to the bedroom and put on his rags and emerged hoping that he looked sufficiently ridiculous to put a stop to this acceptance of permanency; but, no, she stood there gravely examining him as a wife studies her husband before he leaves home for an important meeting. Then she opened the door, kissed him and watched him as he walked down the garden path and round the corner towards the mews where Poacher was stabled.

He was out of her sight when Sir Richard Birnie leaned out of the waiting carriage and said: 'Time we had a chat, Blackstone.' 'So,' Birnie said, 'the girl is the sister of a condemned boy?'

'That's right, sir,' Blackstone said.

They were sitting in the carriage outside the mews; it was 9 a.m. and Birnie's churchwarden pipe was glowing furiously.

'You realise I got out of bed at dawn in order to catch you?'

'You must have got up early.' Blackstone agreed.

'Because I suspected that you had no intention of coming to Bow Street this morning.'

'I did have other plans, sir,' Blackstone said.

'I knew the name Bristow rang a bell. There was a petition to reprieve the boy, was there not?'

'It failed,' Blackstone said.

'They usually do. The law is the law. If it's flouted, then those responsible must pay the penalty.'

'Even if they're only thirteen?'

'The law as it stands makes no concession to thirteen-year-olds.'

'Then the law disgusts me,' Blackstone said, staring at the threadbare knee of his trousers and adjusting the cloak he had last worn ten years ago.

'It is your job to implement the law irrespective of your views. Let those more fitted to the task occupy themselves with law reform. Peel isn't doing such a bad job,' said Birnie, making a capital crime out of reform. 'Leave it to the likes of him.' He screwed up his old face into an expression of ferocity. 'Am I to understand, Blackstone, that you have some scheme to save this wretched boy from the gallows?'

'I don't believe he should be hanged, sir.'

'Other boys have been hanged before him.'

'That doesn't make it any more right, sir.'

'You were never much concerned about the other victims, Blackstone. Odd that you should suddenly be so concerned when Bristow's sister comes and stays with you.'

Blackstone said: 'The girl is merely staying with me. She's very upset...'

Birnie said: 'I dined with Lord Hardinge last night. For some reason a lot of the conversation concerned you. I can't think why, can you, Blackstone?'

Blackstone shook his head vigorously.

'He asked some odd questions. Questions relating to the extent of your authority. Almost as if he feared you, Blackstone. Although, of course, that is quite ridiculous,' Birnie added, his tone betraying that he was not at all sure that it was ridiculous. He leaned out of the carriage and knocked out his pipe, then asked: 'Why should Lord Hardinge be so concerned about you, Blackstone? Is it connected in any way with the fact that he was the judge who sentenced Johnny Bristow to death?'

'Perhaps his conscience is bothering him,' Blackstone suggested.

'Nonsense. Why should it be? Lord Hardinge merely implements the law as it stands.' Birnie paused. 'Have you been to see Lord Hardinge, Blackstone?'

Blackstone said: 'Yes.'

'You didn't ... You didn't threaten Lord Hardinge?'

'What with?' Blackstone asked quickly.

'It doesn't matter.' Birnie looked worried. 'Some, ah, some gentlemen in high places have curious habits. The strain, the daily rubbing shoulders with corruption ...'

You know, Blackstone thought. You old bastard – you know. 'What sort of curious habits?' he asked.

'It doesn't matter. We're all human, all fallible.'

'Unless we're thirteen years old,' Blackstone said.

'I suppose ... I suppose all this had nothing to do with you being locked up in a dungeon in the Rookery?'

'Why should it?' Blackstone asked.

'I don't know ...' For a few moments, his face drawn and creased with the cold, Birnie became a very old man, hesitant and unsure of himself, the pressures and threats of the situation too much for him. He reminded Blackstone of an elderly gentleman walking along a pavement, trying to avoid the frozen puddles, searching for the grass verge with his stick. It didn't last long. Birnie soon found the grass verge, anchored himself with his stick, and snapped: 'And what the devil is the meaning of this letter in the *Post* this morning?' He produced a copy of the newspaper and prodded Blackstone in the ribs with it. 'What's all this about a £1,000 wager, eh? Do you really have any idea how these gypsies are going to do it? And, if you have, why in God's name haven't you thought fit to tell me?'

'I think I may be on to something,' Blackstone said carefully.

'Think? Think, man?' Birnie's breath steamed on the cold air. 'Do you mean to say you've involved the name of Bow Street in a wager just because you *think* you may be on to something?'

'It is a personal wager,' Blackstone said.

'I think,' Birnie said with deliberation, 'that the time has come for you to share some of your personal involvements.' He slapped the copy of the *Morning Post* across his knee. 'I don't know why you pulled in that Italian, but he'll have to be released now. Meanwhile I want to know just what the position is with Lord Hardinge and I want to know what the position is with the Diddiki. In particular I want to know exactly why you're wasting your time trying to save a thirteen-year-old criminal from the gallows when your assignment is to prevent a gang of scoundrels making a mockery of the law and in particular a mockery of the Bow Street Runners.'

'Well,' Blackstone said, feeling the maps and plans of underground London in his pocket, 'it's like this—'

'And I also want to know,' Birnie said, 'what the hell you're doing dressed like a rag-and-bone man.'

'It's like this—'

'And if you don't have a reasonable explanation for your conduct, you can stay in rags for the rest of your life because, as far as I'm concerned, you'll no longer work for Bow Street.'

Blackstone had known they would reach this confrontation sooner or later; but it seemed unfair that it should happen on a jewelled morning like this. A shepherd was taking a flock of sheep to the fields and they shouldered their way past the carriage as though it didn't exist, a black and white dog nipping at their heels. In the distance Blackstone could see the buildings of London which in future years would reach out and draw Paddington into the city. But, at this moment, city and country were one beneath the thick hoar-frost. A bird perched on the icy air singing, berries shone brightly in the hedgerows – a glorious, chiming day. A great day on which to be sacked.

'Well?' Birnie asked.

'Supposing,' Blackstone began, 'I was to tell you that the fate of Johnny Bristow and the threats of the Diddiki are not unconnected.'

'I wouldn't believe it,' Birnie said.

Blackstone said: 'It would take a long time to explain, but I promise you, sir, there is a connection. At the moment it's a question of time. What I'm asking is that you trust me and give me two days. If I haven't beaten the Diddiki at their own game by Monday then I deserve to be sacked.'

'You deserve to be sacked now,' Birnie said.

'I'm the only man who can prevent these gypsies from making the Bow Street Runners the laughing-stock of London.'

Birnie digested this. 'Not if you shared your knowledge.'

Blackstone said: 'I would if there were time. But I've got to act now.'

'It's about time the Runners stopped having secret contacts, informers...'

Blackstone sensed a weakening in Birnie's attitude. He said: 'Just two days, sir.'

'If you fail it doesn't matter any way, does it, Blackstone? The Bow Street Runners will be finished and Peel will be organising a celebration banquet. If you fail, you might as well put all the Runners in the stocks and throw rotten cabbages at them.'

'Two days,' Blackstone said. 'If I fail I'll put myself on a ship to Botany Bay.'

Birnie shook his head. 'No,' he said, 'I'll do that.'

The Poacher galloped with zest, infected with the bright promise of the day, hooves thudding on the frozen mud, mane flying. Man and horse became one, a single rippling sinew.

Blackstone had arranged to meet George Ruthven in the Cheshire Cheese to make their final plans. If Blackstone's theories were correct then the Diddiki had more than the humiliation of the Runners at stake: they were conducting a personal vendetta. Which meant that it was between him and one other man. But who? In all probability it was a criminal whom Blackstone had arrested and dispatched to the hulks, to prison, to Van Diemen's Land, anywhere but the gallows. As the Poacher galloped in the direction of Tyburn, Blackstone tried to think who could harbour enough grudge to plot such an elaborate revenge.

There were hundreds who would harbour the grudge. Henry Challoner, for instance; but Challoner would seek more than ridicule: he would seek blood. The strange aspect of the mystery was its core of honesty. We'll prove we can steal your bullion but we won't actually take it. What sort of a villain was that? Unless he wasn't a villain, unless he had been arrested and convicted unjustly...

By now Blackstone was convinced that the attempt to enter the Bank would be made from underground. There was no other way, unless it was the directors themselves who planned to present themselves at a dark and midnight hour. Blackstone had checked the drains, the flooring, and found nothing suspicious. But until last night he hadn't considered the rivers and streams; nor had he considered the significance of ghosts.

So it was fair to assume that the man pitted against him was someone with a knowledge of underground London who believed that he had been the victim of a miscarriage of justice. The Poacher was galloping into Oxford Street when Blackstone remembered.

Gold!

But that hadn't been the tosherman's real name. Blackstone hugged Poacher with his thighs. Gold, Gold...What was the name in the records? It wouldn't be difficult to find; it was a question of time, and time was running out.

Blackstone tethered the Poacher outside the Cheshire Cheese and stroked the horse's steaming flanks. He needed Gold's real name, he needed his address, he needed a guiding light through the tunnels of London, he needed the luck of the devil. Perhaps the devil would hear him from the sewers.

At first the landlord refused Blackstone the tramp entry. Ruthven thumped him jovially on the chest and the landlord changed his mind.

They went to a private room upstairs where Blackstone spread his maps and charts on a table. He had marked a route in ink which terminated at the Bank of England.

After they had ordered brandy Blackstone asked: 'Did you do what I asked?'

Ruthven, who had just left one of the Bank's directors, nodded. 'He thought I was as mad as our late King, God bless him.'

'But what did he say?' Blackstone asked impatiently.

'Are you sure you're quite right in the head, Blackie?'

'For God's sake spit it out,' Blackstone said.

'All right.' Ruthven drank some brandy. 'I asked him if anyone had seen a ghost in the Bank recently and he looked at me as if I were soft in the head and finally said yes one of the guards in the vaults reckoned he had seen one only the other night. Then he asked me if the Bow Street Runners were reduced to chasing ghosts and, well, there wasn't much I could say, was there? Are we chasing ghosts, Blackie?'

Blackstone was pacing round the room smacking the palm of one hand with his fist. 'I knew I was right,' he said. 'I knew it, George.'

Ruthven stamped on the floor and bawled for more drink. 'Now calm down, Blackie, and let old George into the secret. Gypsies, ghosts – what the hell is all this about?'

Blackstone said: 'Johnny Bristow saw a ghost in Newgate the other day.'

'So?'

'And a ghost was seen in the Bank at just about the same time.'

'So?'

A girl brought more liquor. Blackstone waited till she had gone before continuing. 'To the best of my knowledge there haven't been any ghosts seen at either place for years. Now it's a fact, George, that almost every time a ghost is sighted there's water not very far away. If it isn't on the surface it's underground. It's a fact,' Blackstone said, noting the expression on Ruthven's face, the expression of a doctor treating a disordered patient.

'Since when were ghosts facts?'

Blackstone ignored him. 'So it looks as if there's been some underground activity at Newgate *and* at the Bank.'

Ruthven said: 'Still got a fever, Blackie?'

Blackstone unrolled a map of London – overground. 'Now Newgate's not too far from the Bank, eh, George?' Blackstone prodded the map with his finger. 'Newgate Street, Cheapside and there you are.'

'In the vaults?'

'Why not,' Blackstone said. 'You see, I thought at first that Hardinge had put the mob on to me to scare me off, to keep me quiet until after Johnny Bristow's hanged, or perhaps to polish me off at a later date. Now I'm not so sure. In the first place he wouldn't be so crude; in the second place he would probably guess that I had confided in someone like you and then the fat would be in the fire. No, Hardinge is just going to brazen it out. You know, George, what does it matter in this society of ours if a peer of the realm indulges his whims, corrupts little girls? Nobody would give a hang.'

'To quote a phrase,' Ruthven said.

'He dined with Birnie last night and didn't say a word about it as far as I can gather.'

Ruthven had begun to look interested. 'So who did attack you?'

'I'm not sure,' Blackstone told him. 'But I've got a theory.'

'Ah.' Ruthven sighed; you couldn't twist the arm of a theory, and Ruthven had little time for them. 'Nothing stronger?'

'The Diddiki seem to know my every movement, right?'

'Right,' said Ruthven.

'Then, if they thought I was on to something, they'd want me out of the way. Is that a fair conclusion?'

'Fair enough – if you were on to something.'

'If they went to the bother of kidnapping me then they must have thought I *was* on to something.'

'If it was the Diddiki who kidnapped you.'

'George,' Blackstone said, 'for God's sake stop saying *if*.'

'*If* I don't, what will you do?'

'Cut your tongue out,' Blackstone said.

'Pray continue, master.'

'So, I'm assuming that I was kidnapped by the Diddiki – or someone working for them – because I was on to something. But what, George?'

Ruthven gestured helplessly: it was Blackstone's theory, his copyright.

'Supposing I had visited a key-point in their plans to break into the Bank. They would be pretty worried, eh, George? Especially if they didn't realise I was only there by chance.'

Ruthven rolled brandy round his mouth. It tasted strong and clean and he decided to order some more. He stamped on the floor.

'Now what places have I visited since all this began?'

'The Bank,' Ruthven said promptly.

'The Bank, naturally. But where else?' Blackstone waited for understanding to dawn on Ruthven's features. Nothing happened. Blackstone went on: 'I've been to Bow Street obviously. And I've been up west looking for the skeleton in

Hardinge's cupboard. I've been round the Rookery and I've been home to Paddington. None of these movements would have agitated our gypsy friends – they're all too far away.'

'Too far away from where?'

'From the bloody Bank,' Blackstone said as the girl put a bottle of cognac on the table. 'Where else?'

'It's your round,' Ruthven said, pointing at the bottle.

Blackstone gave the girl a shilling. She marked the level of the brandy and left the bottle behind.

Blackstone said: 'Don't you see, I've only been to one place that could have got them worried, and that's Newgate prison.'

'And ghosts have been seen at both Newgate and the Bank.'

Blackstone raised his glass. 'George,' he said, 'you're a genius.'

Ruthven smiled modestly. 'So you think there's an underground tunnel from the prison to the bank.'

'If you'd gone to college,' Blackstone said, 'you'd have conquered the world.'

Ruthven leaned back and put his large feet on the table.

Blackstone elaborated. 'When I visited Johnny Bristow they must have thought it was a ruse. I mean, who would think that a Bow Street Runner would bother about a thirteen-year-old boy?' Blackstone smote the table with his fist. 'I think that one of the Diddiki is inside Newgate Prison.'

'So why don't we pinch him?' Ruthven asked.

'For several reasons,' Blackstone said patiently. 'Firstly I want to save that boy from the gallows. I can't get him a reprieve so I intend to rescue him. What better way than underground?'

'Birnie will like that,' Ruthven said.

'Confound Birnie,' Blackstone replied.

'Secondly, I don't think it's as simple as a direct tunnel from Newgate to the Bank. There wouldn't be any reason for such a tunnel. I think they must have worked out a route underground from prison to bank. But, if we pinch the accomplice inside the prison, if we knew who he was –'

'Steady with those *ifs*,' Ruthven said.

'– then we wouldn't be able to find the way.'

'I could, ah, persuade him to help us,' Ruthven suggested.

'So we've got to box a little clever,' Blackstone said, ignoring him. 'Now, let's take the ghost at the Bank and the reason for him being there. The reason, I think, is a river called the Walbrook. I found it marked on one of these maps last night.'

Blackstone spread another map on the table – this time a map of subterranean London – and told Ruthven about the Walbrook.

Its source, Blackstone said, was a swamp near Old Street and Shoreditch. It appeared to have several tributaries and it meandered through the City in its search for the Thames. It finally emptied itself into the parent river opposite Southwark. In fact, said Blackstone, it was quite probably navigable in pre-Roman times.

'Really,' Ruthven said, yawning.

Blackstone returned to the map of overground London and Stabbed with his finger at the area between Cheapside and Cornhill. 'But that's the part of the river that concerns us. That's where the Walbrook flows under the Bank of England.'

'Well I'll be damned,' Ruthven exclaimed. 'Doesn't anyone else know about it?'

'They did,' Blackstone told him. 'Back in 1732 and 1803 they found water trickling through the Bank's foundations when building was in progress. But everyone seems to have forgotten about it. I traced it in these old maps.'

'What put you up to it?' Ruthven asked.

'The ghosts,' Blackstone said. 'Don't you believe in ghosts, George?'

'I believe in spirits,' Ruthven said, pouring himself more brandy. 'Now this Walbrook. I suppose it flows under Newgate as well, eh, Blackie?'

Blackstone shook his head. 'That's the snag, George, it doesn't. All I know is that the Walbrook flows under the Bank, and I'll wager someone's widened its banks and made a decent tunnel out of it. Something flows under Newgate. Another river, maybe, or an illegal sewer. And it's up to us to link the two, just as the Diddiki have.'

'And that's all we've got to go on?'

Blackstone rolled up the maps. 'I've worked out a sort of a route,' he told Ruthven.

'A sort of a theory?'

'You could call it that,' Blackstone said, grinning. 'But, like I said, we've got to box clever.'

'Well,' Ruthven said, 'I have done a bit of milling in my time.'

They went downstairs, settled the bill and walked out into the winter sunshine. Ten feet beneath them a man named Gold made his way towards Newgate prison.

CHAPTER SEVENTEEN

Tramping through a high-walled sewer running into the Fleet, Gold felt uneasy. As an adversary Blackstone was coming up to expectations. Now he was on the loose, a rogue Runner, and probably more dangerous than if he was hunting with the pack.

For a moment Blackstone's knowledge of the £500 side-bet had worried Gold. Then he had realised that Blackstone had merely asked the editor what was in the letter before it was published. You had to admire the low cunning of the bastard, Gold thought, wondering once again how Blackstone had got hold of a pistol when he was locked in a dungeon under Rats' Castle.

As he neared the Fleet, Gold took from his pocket a large handkerchief soaked in lavender-water and tied it round his face. Even after years underground Gold couldn't stand the stench of the Fleet. It would have been easier to have journeyed this part of the route overground, but Gold didn't want to be seen and today he wanted to check all his escape routes.

The sewer grew narrower and Gold had to crouch. Water and waste flowed over his hobnailed boots. Now he had to cross under the Fleet, one of the routes discovered by toshermen less scrupulous than Gold, who envisaged flight from the law. Any pursuing constable would presume that they would have to surface to cross the foul reaches of the Fleet. Not so – years before, when the Fleet was deep and clear and ships discharged at Seacoal Lane, an experimental tunnel had been bored underneath, preparatory perhaps to building a tunnel under the Thames.

Near the mouth of the sewer Gold removed some bricks from the wall and scrambled through the hole into the old tunnel. Then he replaced the bricks and continued on his way beneath the Fleet.

'Now what?' Ruthven asked, as they stood outside the bank.

Blackstone took out one of his maps. As far as he could make out the Walbrook flowed directly beneath them. But how to gain access to it? How would a tosherman manage it? Blackstone scanned the map for the nearest drain; it appeared to run directly under Threadneedle Street. So now he needed to find one of the manholes through which the sewermen lowered themselves to empty the bowels of London.

They found it in a baker's yard a hundred yards away. At first the baker, a cadaverous man with flour on his hands, was reluctant to allow them into the yard. He talked about trespass and the rights of the individual and questioned the authority of the two strangers, implying that a baton with a crown on it didn't entitle the owner to intrude on to innocent people's property. However, Ruthven's clenched fist two inches from his nose made him more conciliatory, if not less surly.

Blackstone pulled up the iron cover of the manhole and they both stood back grimacing as the foul air emerged, followed by two fat rats.

'I'll go first,' Blackstone said.

'Wait a minute,' Ruthven said.

He went back to the bakery and reappeared five minutes later wearing some old clothes.

Blackstone lowered himself tentatively until his feet found the rungs of an iron ladder. Ten rungs and he was at the bottom of the drain, the light from his oil-lamp throwing shadows on the streaming walls. He gazed up at the circle of blue sky and felt like a drowning man; then the sky was blotted out by the descending bulk of Ruthven.

Bending low, they began to make their way slowly in the direction of the Bank of England.

Half a mile away Gold was also working his way cautiously along a tunnel. And he was moving towards Blackstone and Ruthven.

This was one of the worst stretches Gold had to navigate. The air was foul, walls were cracked. You could *feel* the weight of sludge above you, see it seeping through the cracks. And the rats seemed to be bigger and bolder, resenting intruders into what they had made their own. As Gold hurried along the flame in his oil lamp burned low.

Then he was across. Light and air filtered through a broken manhole, the flame regained its power.

To the left lay the drains that led to Newgate prison. In the prison, with enough blunt to bribe the turnkeys to give him freedom of movement, was a man known as the Mouse because of his agility underground.

At first, when the Mouse had been thrown into Newgate for debt, Gold had cursed and decided to pay the money owing. But then, poring over the charts of his territories one night, Gold had realised that a sewer underneath Newgate led to other drains which led to the Walbrook at the point where it passed under the Bank of England. What better refuge if, for any inconceivable reason, the plan to enter the

Bank vaults misfired? Who would dream of searching for the Diddiki in Newgate prison?

Gold remembered the case of the Liverpool woman who had disappeared from a condemned cell. It was obvious to him that, with help from underground, she had escaped through the sewer. If it had been subsequently blocked then it could soon be unblocked. So, with one of the team languishing in stir, Gold and a man named Harry Booth, who had subsequently sailed to America, and the boy who had since fallen sick had turned their attentions to the slimy corridors beneath the prison.

Now the tunnel was clear and the stone in the wall of the prison that was to be removed was clearly visible. In fact the route passing beneath the prison was clear all the way from Gold's basement to the bullion vaults.

Gold branched left and hastened towards the Bank, pausing beneath the jail to check the stonework at the point where the Mouse would make his descent. Could Blackstone have guessed that Newgate played any part in the scheme? Gold doubted it because he hadn't returned to the prison, hadn't made any move; his visit must have been a coincidence and they had overestimated his intelligence by kidnapping him.

Gold hurried on, skirting the foundations of St Paul's, arriving at the Bank just as Blackstone and Ruthven arrived at a point 7 feet 3 inches ahead of him.

Twenty minutes after he had lowered himself through the manhole Blackstone noticed that the darkness ahead of them seemed even darker, impenetrable. He whispered to Ruthven to stop and pointed ahead. 'Looks like we may have found something,' he said.

'A wall perhaps,' Ruthven said.

'A sewer wouldn't just end like that,' Blackstone whispered. 'There wouldn't be any point to the sewer if it did. You know, all this stuff' – Blackstone gestured in the flickering light at the liquid flowing over their feet – 'wouldn't be able to get away.'

'But it's getting away now,' Ruthven said.

'Then they must have made an outlet for it.'

'I wish,' Ruthven said, 'that you'd consulted someone else at Bow Street and never involved me in your theories.'

'You stay here.' Blackstone crept forward until the light from his lantern reached a wall blocking the drain. Blackstone felt the brickwork with his free hand. It was covered with slime, and yet…

Gold had reached the wall and was now separated from Blackstone by one foot of bricks. He froze, listening. Was there someone on the other side of the wall? He drew a pistol from his belt and waited.

When Blackstone returned Ruthven whispered: 'I think someone's following us. I can't be sure. Just a sort of slithering noise.'

'Rats,' Blackstone said.

'A bloody big 'un by the sound of it.'

They listened for a while. Nothing except the dripping and gurgle of water, the scurry of tiny feet. But, just the same, the feeling that they were being watched.

'Time to go,' Blackstone said softly.

They turned with difficulty and, as they moved, they both heard it. A slithering, splashing noise in the direction of the manhole. Ghosts, Blackstone reflected, neither slithered nor splashed. 'Get a move on,' he told Ruthven.

They reached the manhole and stared with relief at the circle of blue light above. Ahead lay more sewer. If anyone had followed them then he was along there somewhere. But, if he knew his underground London, there wasn't any point in giving chase. Not that Ruthven had any intention of giving chase.

Above ground once more, they leaned against the fence encircling the yard and sucked down lungfuls of fresh air while Ruthven waited fatalistically for the next theory.

'Right,' Blackstone said, obliging him, 'that leads into the Walbrook and they've blocked it with a wall just in case anyone came nosing around. No doubt about it. The wall was built fairly recently. There's slime on it but no moss, and you can feel the roughness of the bricks. What's more there's a bit of rubble at the bottom of it.'

'Let's smash it down,' Ruthven suggested.

Blackstone shook his head. 'We want to catch 'em, not scare 'em off.' He took some snuff to clear his nostrils of the sewer fumes.

'Box clever, I suppose,' Ruthven said.

'Aye, George, box clever. That's just what you'll have to do tomorrow.'

'And you?'

'I'll be in jail,' Blackstone said. 'Because, when you've dressed and made yourself look like a Bow Street Runner again, you're going to throw me into Newgate prison.'

Gold waited beside the wall for ten minutes. Then he relaxed. He thought he had seen a light through a chink in the bricks; but there were often strange lights down here. It was, after all, the presence of ghosts that had helped him to trace the highways and byways of his domain. He turned and headed back the way he had come.

An hour later he was back in the basement of his home taking off his hobnail boots, trousers with their leather knee-pads, leather jerkin and three wool vests beneath.

He was brewing a pot of tea when the boy Tom arrived to tell him that he had followed Blackstone to Threadneedle Street and had trailed him and another big fellow along the drain leading to the wall.

Chapter Eighteen

Lawler shifted miserably in the embrace of Mrs Rawlinson. She was asleep but her arms enfolded him tightly, and whenever he moved they gripped tighter. Once she half awoke and caressed him, murmuring 'You dear little man', and then fell asleep again, snoring gently. It was only four in the afternoon but Mrs Rawlinson had insisted on going to bed for 'a little bit of fun'. Now the fun was over and Lawler considered himself to be in danger of suffocation from the two great pillows of her bosom.

Really, it was too much. As far as he could see, Blackstone hadn't given him any protection whatsoever – he didn't believe for one second that the men who had followed him had been Bow Street Runners – and, in any case, being bedded by a grizzly bear was too high a price to pay. If there had been any possibility of the other two Italians returning he might have put up with it; but now there was no chance because there was a reference to the Italian at Bow Street in the *Morning Post* and no one, not even a foreigner, would be stupid enough to risk arrest by reclaiming their possessions.

Inch by inch Lawler worked his way down the bed under the pile of blankets and the eiderdown. For a second her grip loosened; Lawler slid his head between her breasts and was free.

He sat on the edge of the bed shivering and searching for his socks. His clothes were distributed all over the room, flung around as he dodged Mrs Rawlinson's skittish advances, determined to strip off as quickly as possible and get it over with. He found his socks, then his shirt, then his waistcoat. The floorboards creaked and Mrs Rawlinson's eyes fluttered, but when he was finally dressed she was still asleep, hugging the pillow that Lawler had substituted for himself.

Down the stairs, a creak at every footstep. He paused at the door to the parlour, noticing the half-finished bottle of port on the table. His downfall! He slipped inside and drank a couple more glasses to keep out the cold. Then he took his coat and scarf from the hat-stand and made for the front door, knocking a ship becalmed in a bottle to the floor on his way.

Upstairs he heard Mrs Rawlinson call: 'Frank, Frank, where are you?' He fled.

It was almost dark when Ruthven presented his villainous-looking charge, dressed in rags and smelling like a dung-heap, to the two turnkeys at the main gate to Newgate prison.

'He's all yours till Monday,' Ruthven said, pushing Blackstone up the steps.

'Who says so?' The senior turnkey backed away from Blackstone. 'We've got enough filth here without having the likes of him dumped on us. Got any blunt to buy his victuals, has he?'

'Does he look as if he has?' Ruthven asked.

'What's he here for?'

'Suspicion of murder,' Ruthven said.

'A topping job, eh?'

Ruthven shrugged. 'Who knows. He hasn't been in court yet.'

'Then why can't you keep him in your own bloody cells at Bow Street?'

'Because they're full,' Ruthven told him.

'And so are ours. Full of filth and vermin.' The turnkey turned to Blackstone. 'He looks a right villainous bastard this one. Hey, you got any blunt?'

Blackstone shook his head.

'Any snout?'

Blackstone shook his head again.

'Have you got any bloody thing?'

Before Blackstone could reply the other turnkey asked Ruthven if he had any papers authorising them to admit a prisoner.

'No papers,' Ruthven said. 'Only this.' He showed the turnkeys his baton.

'I suppose it's all right,' the first turnkey said.

'What's his name?' the second asked, turning and kicking Blackstone. 'You, what's your name?'

'Edmunds,' Blackstone said.

'First name?'

'Jack.'

The first turnkey wrote laboriously on a sheet of paper. Then he said to Blackstone: 'Sign this, and get on with it.'

'I can't write,' Blackstone said.

'Blind me,' the second turnkey said, 'the class of criminal we have to lock up gets lower every day. Here, make your mark here.'

The first turnkey said: 'Come on then, culley, but don't get too near me. I don't want to catch the plague.'

The second turnkey said: 'And don't make no trouble. There's a few scraggings on Monday and some of the lags gets a bit restless. We have to cut down on their liquor a bit before a scragging. Unless, of course, they're in a position to make contributions to jail funds.' The turnkey winked elaborately at Ruthven.

Ruthven winked back and said: 'All right then, I'll be off.'

He walked down the steps, turning at the foot of them to watch the great doors closing on Blackstone.

Blackstone knew the priorities of jail: first make your peace with your wardsman, then your fellow lags, then the turnkeys. These were the three keys to survival. If you hadn't any currency – money, tobacco, food – then God help you unless you had the strength of a sedan-chair carrier with which to assert your rights.

The wardsmen had the sharpest teeth of the vermin inhabiting England's jails. They were prisoners who had ingratiated themselves with the authorities and received, in return, the trappings of power. They drew double food rations, they were given beds, they prescribed punishments, they sold tea, sugar, snuff and tobacco, they issued knives, forks, wooden plates, mugs and blankets – for a fee. Most of them were totally corrupt.

After you had greased the wardsman's palm you had to distribute some of your wealth to the other lags in your ward. If you refused you ran the risk of a mock trial. Judge, jury and counsel were appointed; you were allowed to defend yourself, but if you resorted to eloquence a fist in the mouth silenced you. The punishment was usually an improvised pillory.

The least dangerous arms of authority were the turnkeys, who took their orders from the Keeper of the jail. Their goal was a quiet life and, if the bribes were adequate, they were happy to turn a Nelson's eye to trouble.

The new prison, designed by George Dance after the Gordon Riots, comprised three quadrangles encircled by wards. The northern quadrangle was reserved for debtors, the other two were for male and female felons and were separated by a fifteen-foot wall. There was a chapel, an infirmary, and several taps for the sale of ale.

But Blackstone didn't want to be thrown into the new prison: he wanted to be held in the old quarters which had survived the fire, the quarters where the condemned spent their last days on earth.

The privilege cost him two shillings, paid to another turnkey taking him to the men's quadrangle. The turnkey was surprised that the man in rags possessed a penny, let alone a couple of shillings. (In fact Blackstone had much more than a few shillings hidden beneath his rags.) The turnkey hesitated. Why in the name of God did Edmunds want to spend the week-end with the damned?

Blackstone told him that he had promised Johnny Bristow's sister that he would try to spend his last week-end with him.

'I don't see why not,' the turnkey said, chinking the two coins together in his hand. 'Can't help feeling sorry for him, can you?' He glanced at Blackstone. 'How did you end up like this? You look strong enough, tough enough, to earn a decent living.'

'I was double-crossed by the Bow Street Runners,' Blackstone told him.

The turnkey was sympathetic. 'I'd like to see some of the Bow Street Runners strung up,' he said. 'They're worse than any villains you'll find inside the walls of Newgate.'

'That they are,' Blackstone agreed.

They walked past the male felons' ward where the prisoners with private means – the euphemism for hidden swag – were singing robustly, swigging ale, playing with dice, besporting themselves with whores smuggled in by the turnkeys, and fighting.

As they walked down an echoing passage with the darkening sky high above them, Blackstone asked his tame turnkey if there were any toshermen inside.

'You're a rum 'un,' the turnkey said. 'What do you want to know that for?'

'I've been living with them,' Blackstone said. 'They're a decent bunch.'

'They're all right,' the turnkey conceded. 'We don't get many of them in here. In any case it can't be much worse here than the places where they earns their keep.' He frowned, thinking about a tosherman's lot in life.

'Well?'

'Can't say that I can think of any,' the turnkey said. Then he snapped his fingers. 'Wait a minute, I heard one of the other twirls talking about a body in the debtors' quarters. Apparently he's got plenty of blunt. This mate of mine couldn't understand it. You know, what's he doing in with the debtors if he's got plenty of money?

'And he's a tosherman?'

'That's right,' the turnkey said. 'Fellow known as the Mouse.'

Even the condemned prisoners in the Press Yard had a wardsman. He was a fat man named Haggerty who would probably be reprieved; he had claimed Benefit of Clergy – the law which saved men of the cloth from the gallows – but there was some confusion about his case because the law was in the process of being repealed.

Haggerty had been accused of theft, and while awaiting trial had managed to learn the first verse of the Fifty-first

Psalm, known as the Neck Verse. To claim Benefit of Clergy you had to recite this, and Haggerty managed it in court before sentence was passed.

Falling on his knees in the dock he babbled:

'Have mercy upon me, O God, according to thy loving kindness;
    According to the multitude of thy tender mercies, blot out my transgressions.'

But judge and jury had been reluctant to blot out Haggerty's transgressions because evil was printed so indelibly on his fat face that his guilt was indisputable. So Haggerty had been sentenced to death, but there was little doubt that his sentence would be commuted to transportation; meanwhile he ruled the Press Yard on the understanding that he put in a word for the condemned lags when his reprieve came through.

Haggerty viewed Blackstone with distrust. 'What do you want to see Bristow for?' he asked.

'It's none of your business,' said Blackstone, slipping Haggerty a sovereign.

Haggerty, who had been flogged for stealing less, gazed at the coin in wonderment. 'What do I have to do for this?'

'Nothing,' Blackstone told him. 'Just leave me alone.'

Which left the other lags to deal with. About thirty of them sitting around a fire drinking, the flames from the blazing logs finding the fear and hopelessness in their faces. Johnny Bristow was sitting on the perimeter of the circle, a pot of ale in his hand, staring into the flames.

Cautiously Blackstone sat down beside him, putting his finger to his lips when Johnny recognised him. 'Blind me,' the boy whispered, 'who have you done for?'

Blackstone told him to be quiet and listen.

'But I've only got one day left,' Johnny said, a catch in his voice. 'I thought you'd abandoned me, Mr Blackstone. You know, I heard you was more interested in catching these gyppos.'

'I'm interested in you *and* the gyppos,' Blackstone said. 'Now don't drink too much of that stuff.' Blackstone tapped the pot in the boy's hand. 'And don't despair.'

'I'll try not to,' the boy said. 'They take us to chapel tomorrow and we sit beside a coffin and listen to some prater telling us why we're being scragged. Nice of him ain't it.' The boy's lips began to tremble.

Blackstone squeezed his arm. 'Just don't let on that you know me.'

Blackstone distributed some tobacco and money to the other prisoners and told those that asked that he had been sentenced to death for shooting a bailiff in an alley off Holborn; but no one was particularly interested; there were to be eight hangings within the next forty-eight hours and the crime of a beggar with the stink of the sewers on his rags didn't interest them.

Half an hour later George Ruthven turned up at the grating at the end of the yard. Ruthven sent the turnkey on an errand and passed Blackstone a set of the best, Birmingham-made house-breaking tools. Chisel, jemmy, set of bettys, twirls, pliers with tapered jaws for gripping the end of a key inside a lock, and a drill for cutting out the locks of safes made with exceptionally hard Sheffield steel.

'I hope you know what you're doing,' Ruthven said.

'Don't I always?'

'No,' Ruthven said.

'Did you check Gold's real name?'

'All in good time,' Ruthven said.

'We haven't got any good time. In fact,' Blackstone said, 'we haven't any time at all.'

'I'll go through the records tonight,' Ruthven told him.

'Find out where he lives and pay him a visit. He used to live in the Strand in the good old days – before I sent him to stir for a crime he didn't commit. But I did my best for him,' Blackstone said, 'although the poor bastard never realised it. Still doesn't, it seems, and can't wait to get his revenge. A pity we're going to deprive him of that…'

'*If* we're going to deprive him of it.' Ruthven frowned, then said: 'Gold! Why didn't I think of it before. King Gold – the leader of the toshermen. He's got a place in St Giles.'

'Then get round there,' Blackstone said. 'See what King Gold's been up to of late.'

'Aye,' Ruthven said, 'and I'll keep a barker handy. He's a tough 'un, is Gold. Tough as a badger's arse.'

'On your way,' Blackstone said.

A few minutes later a bell rang for prayers. Some of the men knelt and prayed fervently, some remained standing, staring at the cold stars; two highwaymen walked arrogantly around the yard maintaining their bravado because that's the way men of their profession were expected to behave. Prayers were followed by supper – a pint of gruel and half a pound of bread – then the bell for roll call. The men lined up; they were all present and correct and no one seemed aware that there was one extra.

Then off to the condemned cells. Blackstone joined Johnny Bristow in his cell and dispatched the turnkey to buy two pints of gin for the three of them. The turnkey, who often made errands like this, locked the doors behind him. While he was away Blackstone took the bettys and twirls from under his rags. The bettys, or picklocks, were instruments with a handle like the handle of a key and a powerful hook at the other end; the twirls, or skeleton keys, came in various shapes, sizes and patterns, each one having a key-head at both ends. If, by any chance, the turnkey had left his key in the outside of the door then Blackstone would try an outsider, as the pliers with the tapered jaws were known; if not he would have to try the twirls. The turnkey hadn't left the key in the lock so Blackstone went to work with the skeleton keys.

The boy watched breathlessly as Blackstone worked. 'It's no good, Mr Blackstone,' he said. 'Even if you get out of the cell you can't get out of the Bastille.'

'Jack Sheppard did,' Blackstone said. Despite the cold, sweat trickled down his forehead and into his eyes. 'Where exactly did you see that ghost?'

'Down the passage,' the boy said. 'About ten yards away. As a matter of fact I've seen it twice now, at the same spot both times.'

One of the skeleton keys turned with a ponderous click. The door opened a couple of inches and Blackstone peered out. No one in sight. He beckoned to Johnny Bristow. 'Where exactly?'

'Where what?'

'Where was the ghost?'

Johnny pointed down the stone-walled passage. 'There, about the fourth flagstone along. But why...'

Blackstone closed the door and returned the housebreaking equipment to his rags.

'But I thought...'

Blackstone winked at him. 'There's a few things to be arranged yet. But don't you worry, little 'un. You won't be keeping that appointment with Jack Ketch.'

The turnkey returned and applied himself to the serious business of drinking himself into a drunken stupor.

That evening George Ruthven called on Gold. He had intended to check the tosherman's real name at Bow Street; but Birnie was on the prowl and Birnie was the last person Ruthven wanted to see. Ruthven was quite confident that one day Blackstone would get them both dismissed, but he might as well postpone the inevitable for as long as possible.

Gold was on the point of leaving when Ruthven arrived at the house near Rats' Castle. He was dressed in his working clothes and yet it didn't seem to Ruthven that he had been intending to leave by the door leading into the street. Odd.

Ruthven, one hand on the pistol in his coat pocket, was courteous to Gold. Courteous, that is, by Ruthven's standards: he didn't kick the door in and he didn't shove Gold against the wall before introducing himself. Where, Ruthven asked, was Gold going?

Gold tapped the leather elbows of his filthy jacket and told Ruthven that he had been on the point of going up West to dine at his club and maybe take in a theatre at the same time.

'Don't be funny,' Ruthven said mildly, peering into parlour, kitchen and bedroom, remarkably trim for the area, the parlour smelling of lavender and polish like a room reserved for family reunions and wakes. 'Where do you live?'

Gold asked what he meant? Where did Ruthven think he lived? In the latrine?'

'Where do you eat, sleep, drink? Got a basement?' he asked conversationally, and when Gold said he had, Ruthven asked: 'Do you mind if I have a look?'

'Any authority?'

Ruthven produced his baton and began to wonder why Gold was so reticent about his basement. Outside they could hear the voice of a woman selling vinegar and the obscenities of two men limbering up for a brawl. He told Gold to lead the way to the basement.

Warmth. A smell of food. The breath of a bottle. Gold led the way down the stone steps with a candle lantern. The basement was also trim, but it was lived in. Ruthven glanced round, noticing that the dishes and cutlery on the sink had catered for two. Blackstone would have been proud of him. Had Gold had a guest, he asked.

'None of your business,' Gold said.

Ruthven sniffed the bottle on the table. Brandy. Understandable if you spent half your life in the dripping dungeons of London.

'Do you mind...?'

'Help yourself,' Gold said. 'Your sort always do.'

Ruthven helped himself, drinking straight from the bottle and staring speculatively at Gold. He considered telling Gold that he knew about the affair of the stolen coins all those years ago. But that would only alert Gold to the fact that he was suspected of complicity in the campaign to discredit Blackstone.

'How's business?' Ruthven asked.

'What's it to you?'

'Look,' Ruthven said patiently, wiping the neck of the bottle with his hand, 'there's no need to adopt this attitude. Makes a man suspicious. A routine inquiry about a brooch lost down a drain in the Haymarket and all of a sudden Mr Gold is acting like he's got a corpse in his pantry. You see, you're the obvious person to come to if anything's lost down a drain, aren't you, Mr Gold, you being a tosherman and all. It stands to reason I should come and see you, doesn't it, especially when you're the king of the underground, as it were, and must know if any valuable brooch has been found in the vicinity of the Haymarket.'

Gold said: 'I don't know anything about any brooch.'

'Mind if I have a look in the pantry – just in case there is a body in there?'

'Please yourself,' Gold said.

Ruthven pleased himself, then returned to the table. And sat on a chair directly above the trapdoor leading to the sewer.

CHAPTER NINETEEN

S unday.

A day of rest and worship. A leisurely day in which the hours pass like becalmed galleons. A long dose of a day. Unless, of course, it's your last day alive, in which case the hours pass like minutes and the certainty that you are going to be the victim of mankind's ultimate barbarism freezes like an icicle inside you.

It was 8 a.m. and, if the phenomenon known as justice completed its course, Johnny Bristow had twenty-four hours to live.

It was a bright, chiming day with a touch of frost in the air to polish the cheeks of the ladies on their way to church; the sort of day to coax the gentlemen into the taverns for a tankard or two of mulled ale before carving the joint; a day to repair to the fireside and reflect on the invulnerable ceremony of Sunday in the haven of civilised living that was England.

Unless, of course, you had the misfortune to awake in an overcrowded garret with frozen feet, an empty belly and an empty purse.

Lord Hardinge went to church as usual in the village near Windsor. He read the lesson and knelt in prayer beside his wife and children, wondering as he prayed what had stopped Blackstone from carrying out his threats. His thoughts strayed to the little girls of Windmill Street and, glancing at the sun streaming through the stained-glass windows, he decided to forgive the Bow Street Runner. He gave generously to the collection and later distributed a few coins to the villagers lining the path from the church to his carriage. They doffed their caps in gratitude and Lord Hardinge glowed with the decency of life. If you transgressed, if you abused this wonderful birthright, if you took the calculated risk of crime, then you deserved retribution. Someone had to dispense justice, and God, fate, circumstance, breeding and education had decreed that Lord Hardinge should be in the seat of judgement. The stability of the English way of life had to be preserved, and Lord Hardinge was not the man to duck that responsibility. Later, as he tucked into a plate of underdone beef washed down with a passable claret, he recalled that the court wasn't sitting tomorrow and he had to preside at a meeting of the hunt committee.

Sir Richard Birnie passed the day in a less charitable frame of mind. London was laughing at Bow Street, and Birnie wanted to weep with frustration. Blackstone had vanished again, Ruthven with him. Crowds were gathering outside the Bank of England to witness the shame of Bow Street before moving on to Newgate for the executions. Birnie had posted constables around the Bank, inside the Bank, and in the vaults under the Bank. He met the bewildered directors and, with an expression of deep gloom on his face, informed them that the last laugh would be with Bow Street. They stared at him as though he was an old fighting-cock about to show the white feather.

Mercy Bristow spent the day tidying up. What else was there to do? In the evening she would visit Newgate but until then there was nothing for it but to tidy up and pray that her brother would be saved and that the future would take a turn for the better. In fact, the immediacy and gravity of her problems apart, she passed the day much like other dollymops all over the country, tidying up and hoping that circumstances would improve. In Mercy's case the circumstances revolved around Blackstone. Surely he sensed her devotion, surely he needed her? But did a man like Blackstone need anyone? Whenever this doubt arose she tucked it away, popped it into drawers and closets with his errant snuff-boxes or cravats. Thus she preserved her hope throughout the day, and it remained strong because it was all she had.

Lawler spent much of the day tramping country roads in Hertfordshire. Better lie low for a while and keep out of Blackstone's way – much more to the point Mrs Rawlinson's. To keep himself going he imagined Blackstone in the stocks and himself in the jeering crowd armed with mouldering cabbages, rotten eggs and stinking chicken giblets. He saw an egg splattering on those arrogant features, he saw the yolk spilling down the fine clothes. Ha ha, ho ho. Lawler laughed aloud.

Gold's day didn't really have a beginning. It was the continuation of a long and desperate night spent with George Ruthven in the basement of his home. By dawn Ruthven showed no sign of leaving and crisis-point in the plan had arrived. Gold abhorred violence and, despite the great injustice of his life, had always veered away from crime. But what now? If Ruthven stayed any longer then everything was lost and Blackstone would have won. So now he had to deal with the crude ox of a man sitting directly over his private gateway to the underground London.

Ruthven's chin was dark with bristles and his eyes were slitted with fatigue. But he was still drinking and showing no inclination to move, so Gold asked again: 'Just what the hell are you waiting for?'

'Biding my time,' Ruthven said.

'For what?'

'For you to make a move.'

'What sort of a move?'

'Any sort of a move,' Ruthven said, pouring himself some more brandy.

'Do you think I stole the brooch?' Gold leaned across the table and glared into Ruthven's red eyes and shouted: 'If you want to arrest me, for God's sake arrest me.'

'You don't like my company?'

'I don't like your company,' Gold said. 'I don't like your company and I don't like you.'

'Then you're at liberty to leave,' Ruthven said. 'But I'll come with you, of course.' He yawned. 'A breath of fresh air would do us both good.'

Gold sat down. Any master-plan had to be flexible; there had to be allowances for the unexpected. It wasn't essential to use the trapdoor to get to the sewers; there were dozens of other entrances. But not with Ruthven shambling along beside him. *If Ruthven knows I'm the Diddiki why doesn't he pinch me?* Gold glanced at the clock on the wall. It was 9 a.m. He had to act now and there had to be violence; not brutality, just a simple act that was almost farcical. He went to the chest of drawers where drinking mugs hung from hooks, pulled one incongrously large hook and, as Ruthven disappeared with a yell through the trapdoor, said: 'That's the tradesman's entrance.'

Blackstone spent the first daylight hours of Sunday in the yard, on the fringe of the crowd around the fire. The atmosphere in the jail was tense for two reasons: not only was it

Execution Eve, but that afternoon Elizabeth Fry was paying one of her visits to Newgate.

In April 1817 Mrs Fry had formed the Association for the Improvement of Female Prisoners in Newgate. Throughout the next decade she pushed through reforms for the women, and had recently won the case for the appointment of wardresses. Now she was working for the separation of women prisoners at night, regular work, more religious education. Thus Mrs Fry was as unwelcome as the plague inside the walls of the English Bastille.

Blackstone finished his gruel. It was disgusting but he had to have sustenance for the rigours ahead. He believed he had now found the secret exit from the jail. On the wall beside where Johnny Bristow had twice seen a ghost was a large iron ring to which recalcitrant prisoners had once been chained. The ring was attached at ground level to a block of granite, and this had to be the exit because there was no way in which anyone could prise a flagstone from the floor; as it was, it would require an immensely powerful man to move the block with the ring on it. If Blackstone's theories were correct this was the way the Liverpool woman had escaped years ago. Behind that block of stone lay the drain which had subsequently been blocked up – and unblocked again by human moles. Blackstone could either wait till nightfall, break out of the condemned cell with Johnny Bristow and pull out the stone block himself, or he could wait until the member of the Diddiki inside the jail made his move. Neither alternative was foolproof and Blackstone decided to insure against failure: he would seek out the lurking Diddiki and make sure that they all left together.

By 10 a.m. he had made contact with the first turnkey he had bribed. He bribed him again and was admitted to the debtor's yard, where he went looking for the man known as the Mouse – so named, Blackstone assumed, for his agility. The assumption was correct, except that subterranean agility implied someone of small, twitching build. The Mouse was 6 feet 2 inches tall, with the chest of a Cornish wrestler; his biceps had burst the arms of his velveteen jacket, and his trousers were as tight as gloves around his thighs. He was completely bald and possessed only one ear. He was not, Blackstone decided, the sort of man to be beguiled by threats.

'A word in your good ear, culley,' Blackstone whispered.

The Mouse looked at him suspiciously. 'Who the hell are you?' he demanded. He was standing in a corner of the yard, arms crossed, watching a game of dice.

Blackstone's hand slid to the Manton concealed beneath his rags. He told the Mouse that his name was Edmunds and he had a message from outside.

'Message? What sort of a message?'

'Come over here and I'll tell you.'

They went to the far corner of the yard, where a turnkey hovered uncertainly. The Mouse told him to shove off and the turnkey shoved off obediently.

'Well?'

'Gold sent me,' Blackstone said.

'Gold? Who's Gold?'

'Gold the tosherman.' Blackstone watched the skin tighten over knuckles like billiard balls; beside the Mouse, George Ruthven would look like a jockey. Still, nothing ventured nothing gained. Blackstone said: 'Gold the Diddiki,' and stood his distance.

The Mouse polished his knuckles with the palm of his other hand and said: 'I don't know no Gold. No Diddiki neither.' His voice was curiously soft and high-pitched, like the voice of a eunuch.

Could Blackstone be wrong? The king of the tosher-men outside, a tosherman with agility and three men's muscles inside. No, the coincidence was too great. Warily, Blackstone explained to the Mouse how entry to the Bank was to be gained. He described the tunnel along the course of the Walbrook, the newly-built wall underground; he also chanced his luck and described the tunnels leading from the prison to the Bank.

The knuckles of the Mouse shone. 'If what you says is right, matey, then I should do for you here and now.' He sucked his knuckles and began to polish them again. 'Because if what you says is true I'm a candidate for a lag-ging at the very least if you peaches on me.' His voice rose an octave.

'Look,' Blackstone said, 'would I be telling you if I was going to peach on you? Would I be talking to you at all if Gold hadn't sent me with a message? If I hadn't been enrolled into the Diddiki?'

'You a tosherman? Never,' the Mouse said emphatically.

'I didn't say I was, did I? Come to that you haven't got the stamp of one. No stoop, no smell.' One blow from that fist, Blackstone thought, and my head would come off like a doll's.

The Mouse asked: 'Why did this man Gold send you here?'

'To help you.'

'I don't need ho help. And there's never been no talk of me needing help. Why couldn't he come here himself?' the Mouse asked, dropping all the pretence.

'Because the Runners are on to him,' Blackstone said, employing one of the many faces of truth.

'I don't believe you.'

'A Runner called Ruthven.'

'I've heard of him,' the Mouse conceded. 'What about that bastard Blackstone?'

Blackstone shrugged. 'Perhaps he's given up the ghost.'

'So, what's Gold doing about Ruthven?'

'Leading him through the sewers to drown in the Fleet, I shouldn't wonder. Anyway, I don't think we've got to worry about Gold too much. He can take care of himself. But he was worried in case anything went wrong if he wasn't on time, so he sent me here to help you.'

'I could have managed by myself. Myself and the boy, that is.' The Mouse took a step towards Blackstone. 'What happened to the boy, then?'

'He's all right,' Blackstone said, wondering: What boy? 'But Gold wanted to be sure. You know how he is.'

'I wouldn't want anything to happen to the boy.'

'Nothing will,' Blackstone said, and hearing the compassion in the voice of the big, bald man, told him about Johnny Bristow and the plan to spirit him away from Newgate.

'Poor little bastard,' the Mouse said when Blackstone had finished. 'Poor little sod,' he said, prompting Blackstone to ask if he'd help them.

'Why not? Anything to save a little 'un from Jack Ketch.'

'What time do we move?' Blackstone asked.

'Didn't he tell you?'

'He said you'd tell me.'

'Where was you then when Ruthven turned up?'

'In his house.'

'Got out through the basement, I suppose.'

Blackstone nodded. 'He just had time to tell me what was what before Ruthven broke down the door.'

'How did you get in here then?'

'That's not difficult,' Blackstone said. 'The difficulty's getting out – unless you know how.' He winked broadly.

'I asked how you got in.'

'Easy,' Blackstone told him. 'Easiest thing in the world to get into stir when you think about it. I said I was visiting Johnny Bristow. A little blunt in the right direction and you're in as easy as pie. No trouble in getting into stir, no trouble at all. Then, when they're chucking out the visitors, you just stay. Ask any blower wanting to stay inside to dab it up with her old man. She'll tell you – a little more blunt and in you go. And here I am,' Blackstone said.

'And here you are,' the Mouse said, flexing one arm so that a seam in his jacket split a little further. 'So it's up to you and me and the little 'un if Goldie's lumbered with this Ruthven.'

'What time?' Blackstone asked again.

'As soon as it gets dark.'

'How are you going to get out of here?'

The Mouse looked surprised. 'The turnkeys will do anything for me,' he said, thrusting a fist under Blackstone's nose. 'Why, I reckon they'd give me Jack Ketch's job if I asked nicely.' He laughed, the laughter like wind chimes stirred by a breeze, incongruous and faintly sinister. 'So you be on your toes at dusk, culley.' He paused. 'How are you going to get past the turnkeys? No disrespect – you look like you can take care of yourself. Look as if you've done a bit of milling in your time. But—'

Blackstone told him how he intended to get out of the condemned cell.

'Look after the little 'un then,' the Mouse said. 'Poor little sod.'

Outside, the crowds were gathering because it was expected that the Diddiki would make a public appearance after they had entered the vaults. Threadneedle Street, Bartholomew

Lane, Lothbury and Princes Street were thick with people; Tivoli Corner was the assembly point for every pieman and vendor of baked potatoes, fried fish, fruit, toffee-apples and chestnuts in London. As the sun rose in the winter sky mulled ale and grog flowed freely from the taverns, and the more freely it flowed, the more urgently the pickpockets, whores, beggars, duffers, magsmen and thimble-riggers went to work. Already the purveyors of confessions from the condemned cells at Newgate were selling their wares, and several of the doomed would have been surprised at the extent of their contrition. After the Diddiki had made their appearance the crowd would swarm down Cheapside to grab the prime positions for the 8 a.m. executions at Newgate.

Bookmakers were still offering odds on the Diddiki, but the odds were so short and the general conviction that the gypsies would succeed was so strong that there were few takers; only a few punters who knew Blackstone well, punters like the one-eyed pieman, parted with their money and kept close to the bookmaker.

There hadn't really been a week-end like it since the great ice-fair of 1814 on the Thames, which ended only when the ice melted and the booths were swept downstream.

Among the crowd were those members of the Fancy who were connoisseurs of hanging. They had come from all over England because, as a wag put it, it promised to be 'a topping morning'. Eight felons to be scragged, two of them highwaymen, who always gave good value with their speeches, curses and the arrogant removal of their shoes. A dead highwayman's shoes had been known to fetch as much as three pounds, and a piece of the rope that hanged him three shillings.

With luck there might even be a repetition of the scenes when Charles White, an arsonist, was hanged. As the lever was pulled he managed to leap forward and balance himself on the edge of the open trap. He fought the executioner and his assistants until they hurled him into the hold with the hangman swinging on his legs like a pendulum. The connoisseurs recalled a murderer who had managed to haul himself up the rope four times before falling exhausted to his death. Who could know what sport lay the morning ahead, after the bonus attraction at the Bank.

The boy Tom had been waiting outside Gold's house warming his hands on a baked potato. And now, as they hurried towards Fleet Street, Gold told him about Ruthven's visit.

'Is everything going to be all right, Mr Gold?' the boy asked.

'If we hurry,' Gold replied, steering him through the crowds heading for the Bank. 'We're a bit behind time but I made allowances for that. I made allowances for everything,' he added, squeezing the boy's thin arm.

'Is … is that Runner dead?'

Gold shook his head. 'Take more than a fall down a ladder to kill a great oaf like Ruthven. I went down and had a look at him. He was out cold but he'll come to all right. No fear of that.'

The boy sank his teeth into the floury heart of the potato. 'But what happens when he does come to?'

'Nothing much. If he can move the trapdoor then he's a stronger man than the Mouse.'

'The Mouse?'

Gold explained as they crossed Fleet Street. 'Even if he escaped, the Runners are back where they started. They've been down a drain near the Bank and come up against a brick wall, so to speak. They don't know about the Walbrook; they don't know about Newgate.' Gold chuckled.

'By one o'clock in the morning Edmund Blackstone will be a candidate for a travelling circus and, if I'm any judge of the feeling of this country, you and I will be richer by more blunt than you've ever set eyes on, young 'un.'

The boy grinned and chewed and swallowed and ran beside the long-striding Gold as they entered Bouverie Street. They stopped outside number 29.

Gold told Tom that there used to be a monastery on the site known as Whitefriars Priory. Everyone thought it had been destroyed in 1545. 'But,' said Gold, winking, 'I knew better.' He pointed downwards. 'There's a room down there forty foot high and cellars going right under Britton's Court and a fair old tunnel leading to the Thames. But we don't go that way. We head back and branch off to the Fleet and then' – he punched the boy in the ribs – 'we head towards the Old Lady of Threadneedle Street.'

He led Tom round a ruined wall to a patch of waste ground covered with coarse grass, dead nettles and ivy. He knelt and tore at the weeds and ivy which covered so many of the doorways to his kingdom. Then he removed some bricks and heaved out a chunk of sandstone imported centuries ago by the masons who had built the monastery. Gold and the boy stared down into the dark mouth of a tunnel.

'Here we go,' Gold said.

'Here we go,' the boy echoed.

They began to descend a flight of steps. The time was 12.30 p.m.

Ruthven came to twenty minutes after he had crashed down the ladder under Gold's basement. Water was dripping on his forehead, a rat was sitting on his chest. He groaned and tried to think where the hell he could be. At first he thought he had drunk too much in the Brown Bear and they had thrown him in the cellar to cool off. Then he remembered. Despite his bluff appearance Ruthven had a secret store of sensitivity and he was fully aware that he wasn't the brightest of Birnie's men. Only he could have sat directly on top of a trapdoor in a tosherman's house, he admitted to himself, groaning with the pain and the indignity of it. With the second groan the rat scuttled away; Ruthven sat up and felt his body for damage. There was blood in his mouth, a lump on the back of his head, a throbbing ache at the base of his spine; his shins were skinned and he thought he might have sprained his ankle. He tried to stand up, cracked his head on the roof of the tunnel and sat down again. What the hell was the time? Day or night? Sunday or Monday? Cautiously he struggled into a kneeling position and explored the floor of the tunnel. Slime, water, stones as cold as ice. He moved on his hands and knees, found the bottom step of the ladder. He began to climb it. High above was a chink of light which, Ruthven reasoned, must come from Gold's basement. Sunlight or lantern-light? Had the Diddiki succeeded? Had Johnny Bristow been hanged?

He reached the trapdoor, placed the flats of his hands against it and pushed. Daggers of pain inside his skull. Pain in his legs. Pain everywhere. The trapdoor didn't give an inch. What he needed was a battering ram. What he needed was some sort of light. What he needed was a bloody miracle.

Then, as his head cleared a little, he remembered his gun. He searched his pockets: it was gone. He went down the ladder again, cursing as he reached the bottom and once again cracked his skull on the roof of the tunnel. He found the gun on the ground and, with the butt nestling comfortably in the palm of his hand, he fingered the mechanism. Broken! With his forefinger he felt the jagged outlines where the hammer had snapped. Now what? His free hand encountered a rock of some sort, but it wasn't big enough to batter his way through the trapdoor. He could, he supposed, try and attract attention; it was worth a try even if the only person who heard him would be Gold. Perhaps a cleaning woman, a friend... Ruthven went up the steps again and hammered at the trapdoor for a couple of minutes. Nothing – just the drip, drip, drip around him as though the crust of the earth was being squeezed dry of its moisture.

Down again to the tunnel, one ankle weak and tender under his weight. Left or right? Ruthven shrugged, convinced that whatever decision he took would be wrong. He went left into impenetrable darkness which seemed to thicken with every foot of progress he made on his hands and knees. Five minutes, ten minutes... God knows how long. The shafts of pain had become blunted into a steady ache; the cold and wet encased him in icy armour; he yearned for daylight as a man dying of thirst yearns for water. Soon he began to wonder if this was how it had been written he would die – in a grave running with filth beneath the city of his birth. Perhaps even under Bow Street – or, worse still, the cheerful parlour of the Brown Bear.

He stopped and rested, listening to the sound of water and the furtive movement of rats. If only there was a single ray of light, a ray of hope. He blinked and peered ahead but it was as dark as ever, darker than night. He straightened up and found that he could just manage to stand with his head bowed. Was there a reason for making the tunnel higher? Perhaps he was nearing one of the intersections of the sewers, perhaps he was nearing the Thames – and one of the sewer-grills that would trap him until the tide covered his body.

Ruthven stumbled on.

Then stopped.

Ahead the vaguest glow of light. And the sound of water. Not dripping water: this was greedy gushing water seeking the sea. He hadn't been wrong: the Thames lay ahead. And imprisoning bars?

Ruthven lurched forward, praying as the light took on shape and the smell of the river reached him. The clean smell of running water, not the stagnation of the sewers. He imagined he heard seagulls and the sound of waves slapping the hulls of ships. Please God, don't let there be bars!

But God didn't please him. There were bars, in geometrical squares, and beyond were the free river and the sky burnished bright as metal and the seagulls floating in the air currents.

Ruthven gripped the bars of the grill and stared out. He was overcome not only by despair but by reproach to the God he hadn't consulted for thirty years or more. Soon the tide would spend itself, begin its return journey and plunge into the sewer. All Ruthven could do was to return the way he had come.

His hands gripped the bars tightly. But wasn't there something odd about them? They were so smooth, so bright – as well-tooled as the barrel of a gun. Not the pitted and rusty surface that one would expect. Ruthven frowned. Hadn't he read something recently about experimental grills being fitted to make the cleaning of the sewers easier? Something about operating like a drawbridge...

Ruthven let go of the grill and looked around. There, at the bottom of the grill, hidden by a buttress, was a big iron handle. Ruthven gripped it and turned it; it moved easily, as though it had been recently greased; chains clanked and the grill opened outwards.

Ruthven kicked off his shoes and dived. But the water was shallow and he surfaced almost at once. He began to wade with the current towards a quay a hundred yards down river. And so great was his joy that he forgot to apologise to the God he had doubted.

When he reached the quay it was 3 p.m.

Throughout the day the prescribed preliminaries to death were duly observed.

After Blackstone had gone to the debtors' quarters Johnny Bristow was taken with the seven other felons to the chapel. They were seated in the condemned pew, an oval-shaped box capable of seating thirty, in the centre of the chapel. In the middle of the box stood a table bearing a symbolic coffin. Until 1824 visitors who paid a shilling had been allowed into the gallery to observe the doomed men; but, such was the momentum of reform, this practice had been discontinued and only other prisoners were admitted.

This morning the clergyman, known as the Ordinary, was determined to extract the last ounce of contrition from his lambs being prepared for the slaughter. He was a tall, gaunt man who would have liked a comfortable country living, but it was God's will that he preach to scum and so he carried out his duties conscientiously, pausing occasionally during his sermon to press a scented handkerchief to his nostrils to counter the stench of the jail which permeated the House of God.

His first words from the pulpit were: 'You wretched sinners who have defiled God's wonderful gift of life, ponder on the fact that this is the last sermon ye shall ever hear.' He then castigated each in turn for their crimes, allocating Johnny Bristow minimal reproach because of his age.

After the service the Ordinary went to a tavern for his lunch and drank a bottle of Burgundy to prepare himself for the doleful duties ahead, which would culminate in the morning as his voice rang through the stone-walled passages: 'I am the resurrection and the life...' As he poured the last glassful of wine he determined to apply once more for a parish in the Cotswolds.

In the Press Yard the eight condemned souls, always accompanied by a turnkey, kept themselves apart from those still hoping for a reprieve. They were allowed to drink as much as they liked and to receive visitors. On this, their last day on earth, they all wore their best clothes, such as they were, and the two highwaymen appeared in morning suits specially tailored for the occasion.

In the afternoon, as Mrs Fry toured the women's quarters, one of the condemned tried unsuccessfully to cheat the gallows by cutting his wrist with a knife smuggled into him by his fiancée. Gloom settled heavily on the jail, and the turnkeys doubled their vigilance because they recognised this as the prelude to trouble.

As dusk began to settle Johnny Bristow asked to be taken back to his cell, one of the fifteen dungeons in which it was always dusk.

There, as time slipped past and Blackstone failed to appear, Johnny Bristow was assailed by a fear more piercing than anything he had experienced since his conviction.

The reason for Blackstone's absence was the tightening of security on Execution Eve. Not even a sovereign would persuade the tame turnkey to admit him to Johnny Bristow's salt-box; not even the flexing biceps and massive bunched fists of the Mouse could persuade the other turnkeys, reinforced for this macabre day of rest, to allow either of them out of the debtors' yard.

Blackstone said: 'So much for Gold's perfect timing.'

'And so much for yours, culley,' the Mouse said, pulling at his good ear.

'Do you have any ideas?'

The Mouse said he hadn't. He had based his plans on brute force and the brute had failed.

Blackstone fingered the house-breaking implements under his rags. 'I can get us out of here,' he told the Mouse, 'if you can fix the turnkeys.'

'There's too many of 'em,' the Mouse said.

'Then you'll have to create a diversion. It shouldn't be too difficult – there's always trouble the day before a hanging.'

'Not in the debtors' yard,' the Mouse said. 'They ain't criminals. They'd just as rather watch a scragging as riot about it.'

'Not if they're drunk,' Blackstone said thoughtfully. 'They'll riot about anything if they're lushy enough, especially if they heard trouble over the felons' side.' He took some coins from his rags. 'Here, the turnkeys may be acting up a bit today but they won't refuse a few free pints of Geneva. Who would?' Blackstone asked the Mouse.

Five minutes later gin and ale were being guzzled in the debtors' yard as Elizabeth Fry completed her tour of the women's quarters, and on the other side of the jail trouble began to break out among the felons.

By 5 p.m. most of the debtors and the turnkeys guarding them were drunk. 'Time to go to work,' Blackstone said to the Mouse.

At 5 p.m. Gold and the boy Tom arrived at the point below the vaults of the Bank of England where they had arranged to meet the Mouse. They sat down beside the waters of the Walbrook and waited.

211

Chapter Twenty

A bove the tunnels, the sewers, the caverns and vaults of underground London fires burned in the vicinity of the Bank of England, their sparks flying high into the black night. Now it was time for the whores to go to work and, on the fringes of the great concourse awaiting the 'dark and midnight hour', they besported themselves with gentlemen in the alleyways and courtyards of Cornhill, Moorgate and Cheapside. The frosty air smelled of frying sausages and onions and echoed to the shouts of the Fancy who had improvised a cock-fighting pit to while away the time. The one-eyed pieman sold more pies than he had all year, backing Blackstone with the money and getting fantastic odds from the bookmakers, who knew and loved a mug when they saw one.

Inside the fortress walls of the Bank, Sir Richard Birnie met the directors in the board-room. There were six hours left until midnight and the mood of the meeting was defeatist. The atmosphere was not enhanced, to Birnie's mind, by the arrival from abroad of Robert Peel, former Undersecretary of War and Colonies, Chief Secretary of Ireland, and now Home Secretary and sworn enemy of the Bow Street Runners. He sat at the head of the long table, his features aloof as always, awaiting the midnight debacle which would hasten the dissolution of the Runners and the formation of his brain-child, the Metropolitan Police Force.

Gloating, Birnie thought. Praying for law and order – *his* law and order – to be flouted. Zealot, hypocrite!

Peel, the most enlightened and humane politician in England, stared down the table at Birnie and said: 'Do you have any idea of the whereabouts of this man Edmund Blackstone, Sir Richard?'

Birnie stuffed tobacco into the cramped bowl of his pipe and lit it with a taper. 'He has been given a free hand,' he told Peel. 'I can only presume he is at the heels of these … these Diddiki.'

Peel said: 'These men appear to have intimate knowledge of the inner working of Bow Street, Sir Richard. Have you any idea how they have been able to publish letters in the newspapers reporting your progress – or lack of it?'

'We're looking into it,' Birnie said hopelessly. 'At the moment the threat of unlawful entry into the Bank has been uppermost in our minds.'

Birnie occupied himself with his pipe again to escape the cynical stares of the rich and powerful men gathered around him.

'Surely the two aspects of the investigation complement each other,' Peel said and went on: 'The Bow Street Runners have long been, ah, famed for their knowledge of and, indeed, participation in criminal activities in the ultimate interests of justice. Surely this much-vaunted network of informers should have produced some lead to the identity of these, ah, gypsies?'

'Perhaps they have,' Birnie said, wondering if they would give him a big enough pension to buy a cottage in Scotland and end his days where he was born.

'Then they don't seem to have confided in their superior officer.'

'I'm concerned with results,' Birnie said.

'Irrespective of the means employed to obtain them?'

'I'll answer your questions at midnight,' Birnie snapped, reflecting that his impertinence could hardly worsen the enormity of his failure.

Peel smiled and shrugged.

One of the directors picked up an envelope lying on the table. It was stuffed with bank-notes printed on the new paper provided by Henry Portal at Bere Mill in Hampshire. One thousand pounds worth of Mr Portal's paper.

The director, who had glossy cheeks, glossy white hair and glossy manners, said: 'We've decided to reward the Diddiki with this if they make good their threats.'

Birnie looked aghast. 'Reward them for breaking into the Bank of England?'

The director smoothed his glossy hair. 'They're national heroes. If we don't reward them the mob will sack the Bank. Beside,' the director said, 'it only seems fair. They *are* pretty audacious gentlemen, are they not?'

Birnie turned to Peel. 'Does this have your support, sir?'

Peel drummed his fingers on the table. 'In theory no, but realistically speaking yes. You could say' – Peel stared past Birnie at a portrait of John Soane, the architect – 'that we're rewarding them for their honesty. After all, they are performing a public service in a way. Showing us the chinks in the Bank's armour, the chinks that your men have failed to find. Or appear to have failed to find,' Peel added.

'Perhaps, sir, we should have knighted the Cato Street Conspirators instead of executing them.'

Peel smiled. 'There are many that would agree with you there.'

'But this will only encourage the criminal element. Who knows, soon they'll be threatening to present themselves at a dark and midnight hour to the King.'

'I'll wager they won't be the only ones in his bed-chamber,' another director said.

Birnie said: 'It's preposterous—' and bit on the stem of his pipe as Peel interrupted.

'They won't be the first in London to be rewarded for nefarious practice, will they, Sir Richard?'

'Are you implying –?'

'I'm implying nothing,' Peel said. 'It's a well-known fact, is it not, that a thief-taker is paid a reward for his capture?'

'My men are not thief-takers.'

'Gentlemen,' said the glossy-voiced director, 'should we not pay more attention to the matter in hand?' He glanced at the gold watch in the pocket of his waistcoat fitting snugly across his plump belly. 'It's 7.30 – five and a half hours left.' To Birnie he said: 'Is there anything else you wish to check, Sir Richard?'

'Nothing,' Birnie said. 'Every available Runner is stationed in and around the Bank, not to mention three dozen constables brought in from all over London.'

'Then perhaps we should adjourn for a bite to eat,' said the glossy-voiced director.

'Perhaps we should prepare a celebration banquet for the Diddiki,' Birnie said bitterly.

The trouble started in one of the felons' wards where a cash-carrier, a pimp, had been accused in front of a prisoners' court of being a nose – an informer. Not only that but he had refused to buy grog and share the food that a visitor had brought him. But these weren't the principal charges, because they didn't involve much sport – and sport, with its many definitions, was the essence of life inside and outside Newgate's walls.

The pertinent charges drawn up by a crooked lawyer were: coughing at night to the distress of other malfactors; slandering one Edward Appleyard, a notorious footpad; failing to keep himself in a state of cleanliness and thus endangering the health of other prisoners; trying to undermine the authority of the wardsman by questioning his competence; and accepting his ration of gruel before he was duly authorised so to do.

The judge was the wardsman, wearing a filthy towel as a wig, and the jury was a collection of the most villainous-looking lags in the ward. Conviction and punishment – an improvised pillory – was inevitable unless the accused was in a position to buy himself out of the dock.

But the real cause of the violence that followed was not the mock trial: it was the unease that sweeps any prison on the day before an execution; a revulsion, not necessarily recognised as such, at the savage within us. And it was highly infectious.

At the end of the mock trial one of the prisoners on the jury, who believed the accused had peached on him to a turnkey, said: 'They're stringing up better than him tomorrow. Why don't we top this bastard?'

The ward became quiet, as quiet as a grave. Everyone looked at the judge, a thief who had twice escaped the noose on technicalities – imperfections in the charges – that humane judges had spotted. But he was full of cheap brandy, incensed with the injustice of life. 'Aye, lads,' he shouted, 'why not? What's worse than a nose, I ask you? What's worse?'

The crook lawyer intervened: 'That's not what he was charged with.'

'Who cares what he was charged with? Anyone got a rope?'

Someone had. But not everyone wanted to lynch the shivering cash-carrier who was pleading for his life. And it was then that the riot started, watched through bars by the turnkeys, who preferred to let the lags batter each other senseless rather than intervene.

The noise reached the debtors' yard where turnkeys and prisoners were boozing together.

'Now,' Blackstone whispered to the Mouse.

The Mouse raised his hands and shouted: 'Hear what I hear, lads?' They stopped drinking and listened and the Mouse went on: 'It's a break, that's what it is. They've overpowered the twirls on the other side. Do you want to spend the rest of your lives rotting here because you owe some dirty moneylender a couple of pounds?'

'I don't for one,' Blackstone shouted.

'Nor me,' someone else cried.

The Mouse stepped on to a low wall. 'I say let's get out now. Let's show them what we think of scragging the poor innocent sods in the salt-boxes.'

The Mouse picked up one of the turnkeys and threw him into a group of prisoners passing a jug of gin from hand to hand. The jug broke and the gin flowed across the flagstones.

'Come on lads,' Blackstone shouted. 'Let's get out of here.'

Within seconds the debtors' yard was filled with fighting, screaming prisoners and turnkeys. Blackstone knelt and applied himself to the lock of the main door. There was a key on the other side of the lock and he tried to turn it with the outsider, but it wouldn't move and he punched it out with the skeleton key. He turned the skeleton key. No movement.

A turnkey with a bleeding nose and an eye swollen like an egg lurched up. 'Hey,' he said, 'what—'

The Mouse hit him once on the jaw and the turnkey slid to the ground.

'For God's sake hurry up,' the Mouse said.

'I can't go any faster, culley.'

'Then try the other end of the bastard.'

'Just what I was going to do,' Blackstone said, withdrawing the skeleton key and plunging the other end into the keyhole. He turned the key and grinned as it moved and the door opened.

Then they were outside in the high-vaulted passage.

'Come on,' the Mouse said. 'This way.'

'Just a minute,' Blackstone said. 'We don't want every lag in Newgate turning up at the Bank, do we?'

He picked up the key, which had fallen on to the ground, locked the door and pocketed the key. Inside, mayhem continued unabated.

As they made their way down the passage Blackstone drew his pistol. Two minutes after leaving the debtors' yard they had reached the fifteen cells where the condemned men were rioting in a last desperate attempt to save their necks. Two turnkeys had been overpowered, but they never made the mistake of entering the salt-boxes with keys on them, and the prisoners, shouting and screaming and battering at the closed doors, would still be there for Jack Ketch in the morning.

Blackstone said: 'You get the stone out. I'll break into the boy's cell from the outside.'

'But there'll be a turnkey inside.'

'I know it,' Blackstone said. 'But he won't know a skeleton key from an ordinary one.'

He stuck the skeleton key in the lock of the boy's cell and turned it. 'Hey,' said a voice from inside, 'who's that?'

Blackstone said: 'Your relief.'

'But I don't have a relief till morning. Till the job's done,' said the voice.

Blackstone pushed open the door and shoved the barrel of the Manton into the ribs of the turnkey standing on the other side. 'Make any trouble,' Blackstone said, 'and you won't need a relief, now or evermore.'

He stood back, pistol aimed at the turnkey's heart, and gestured to the boy. 'Outside, young 'un. It's time to go.'

The boy ran outside and Blackstone grinned at the turnkey. 'Maybe when they find the lad's gone they'll string you up instead, my covey.' He backed away still pointing the gun, then slammed the door and turned the key on the outside.

Down the passage the Mouse was waiting beside an opening in the wall, holding the flagstone as though it was made of wood. The boy went through first, then Blackstone, then the Mouse, shifting his grip to an iron handle on the reverse side of the stone and pulling it into the aperture behind him.

By 9 p.m. Gold, the boy Tom, George Ruthven, Blackstone, the Mouse and Johnny Bristow were all underground.

But first Ruthven had gone to his rooms, after limping out of the Thames watched by a group of curious mudlarks. There he changed into the oldest clothes he could find and made himself some coffee. One task remained – he had to find out the name under which Gold had been charged when he had been caught with the gold coins in his possession. But this involved going to Bow Street, the last place in London he wanted to visit. Ruthven took a flintlock pistol and one of the new percussions and stuck them in his belt. Then he set out for the Brown Bear, arriving at and the back entrance after making his way through a maze of back alleys.

He let himself into the kitchen and summoned the serving girl who had been out of sorts since Mercy Bristow had moved in with Blackstone. Her great assets were that she was comely, efficient – and she knew what was happening across the road.

Ruthven sat down, explored the various aches in his body and ordered a hot toddy.

'Where's Blackie?' she asked, putting whisky, hot water, sugar and spice in front of him.

'In jail I shouldn't wonder,' Ruthven said, mixing his drink.

'Seriously.'

Ruthven looked at the wall-clock. 'By now he should be in a sewer.' And when she began to get angry he raised his hand and said: 'Don't you worry about him. Blackie can take care of himself.'

'But I do worry about him.'

'The cross you have to bear,' Ruthven said, smacking his lips, feeling the hot medicine blur the edge of pain. 'Now, who's over there and where's Birnie?'

'I don't think there's anyone over there,' the girl said. 'No one that matters, that is. They've all gone to the Bank.' She paused. 'If...if these gypsies do what they've promised, does that mean that Blackie will leave Bow Street?'

And settle down? – her tone implied. Ruthven said: 'Don't you be too sure the Diddiki will do what they've promised.' He held up his glass. 'Some more whisky my dear.' And, when she had brought it: 'Are you sure Birnie's not over there?' He pointed in the direction of the Runners' head-quarters.

'I told you, he's gone to the Bank like everyone else in London.'

Ruthven nodded thoughtfully. Then he swallowed the fresh drink in one abrupt movement and headed for the premises across the road.

The records were kept in a basement, a dark and dusty place stacked with heavy volumes in which murder, rape, robbery, arson, fraud – the heinous and the trivial – were recorded in copperplate writing. The writing had been penned by generations of clerks, and yet it was uniform, neat and impartial. Here passion that had been betrayed, ambition that had spilled over into the abyss of greed, poverty that had spawned thievery – all these plus the dark deeds of those who are born and die bad were collected in these ledgers like pressed flowers, or weeds.

It took Ruthven five minutes to find the month and the year when the young and eager Blackstone had been dispatched to the riverside tavern on the trail of the shofulmen.

Ruthven ran his finger down the charge list until he came to Blackstone's case. There it was, injustice recorded and filed away forever in the same faded ink. So what was Gold's real name? Ruthven found it and closed the ledger thoughtfully. Then he locked up, leaving the dust to settle once more on the albums of crime, tragedy and mischance.

Outside he hailed a cab and told the driver to take him to the baker's in the City.

'You mean the Bank of England, don't you?' the driver inquired. 'Anyone that's anyone's going there. First the Bank then the jail. They say there's going to be eight topping jobs in the morning and the window-seats are selling for three pounds a time. What a week-end, eh?'

'Just take me to the baker's,' Ruthven said wearily.

'Just as you please,' the driver said, whipping up the horse. 'Just as you please. But I'll wager you'll be outside the Old Lady at midnight when the Bow Street Runners gets a roasting. About time too,' the driver added giving the bony mare a flick with his whip.

The baker was less than pleased to see Ruthven. He told him to find his own way to the manhole. Sewers, he seemed to say, were the natural habitat of men like Ruthven. Ruthven took a loaf from a tray and ate half of it, tearing the warm bread to pieces with his fingers. Then he realised that he hadn't got a lamp, and his recent experiences of stumbling through pitch-black sewers without a light would suffice him for the rest of his life.

'I need a lamp,' he told the baker.

'So you need a lamp.'

'You're going to give me one,' Ruthven said.

'Give?'

'Lend.'

'That's better,' said the baker disappearing behind his ovens and returning with an oil-lamp.

'Thanks,' Ruthven said.

'Don't mention it,' the baker said. 'Watch the gases down there. They're liable to explode.'

'And you wouldn't want that to happen to me, would you?'

'Of course not,' the baker said. 'I wouldn't want anything to happen to a fine upstanding man like yourself.'

Ruthven made his way to the yard and lifted the manhole cover. A cold, stinking draught of gas arose. It was dusk and for a moment the gas seemed to ignite as it came into contact with the lamp, and Ruthven was reminded of a ghostly apparition. With a shrug he began his descent; if Birnie sacked him then he could always become a tosherman, or a rat-catcher, or a sewerman, or a corpse.

In the light of the oil-lamp the eyes of the rats shone bright and red, the green weeds were grey and the dripping walls of the tunnel glistened as though covered with ice. Ruthven reached the bottom of the stairs and tried to contract his big body sufficiently to enable him to make his way towards the Bank in relative comfort. All the escapade needed, he thought, was a Bow Street Runner stuck in a sewer.

But his body was too big and he had to get down on his hands and knees, pushing the lamp along in front of him. In fact the tunnel seemed to have become narrower since his last visit. Either that or he was going down the wrong sewer. Or perhaps he had expanded with bruises and hot whisky and bread.

Painfully, Ruthven inched his way along the tunnel, wishing that his friendship with Blackstone had ended years ago with a brawl. Then he remembered that they had brawled and the fight had only strengthened their friendship. Perhaps I should have shot him, Ruthven mused as some slimy weed fell down from the roof of the tunnel and slid down his back.

He cracked his head at the point where he had cracked it before, he grazed his knuckles on the old grazes, he bloodied his knees on the old wounds. He got stuck twice and felt panic threatening to overcome him; he swore and prayed and talked to himself like some crazed mumper begging on the street. The tunnel seemed to become narrower; no sign of the flimsy, freshly-built wall that Blackstone had found.

After ten minutes Ruthven took a rest. Had he turned the wrong way? Should he go back? He took some snuff and sneezed and listened to the explosion rolling down the tunnel. A trapped sneeze! Ruthven almost smiled until he noticed that the flame on the lamp was burning low and it occurred to him that the baker had decided to avenge past

humiliation by dispatching one big bully into the sewers of
London with an oil-lamp almost dry of oil.

By comparison the route taken by Blackstone, Johnny
Bristow and the Mouse could have been chosen for a picnic
outing. But only by comparison.

The drain plunged deep beneath the prison – the first
few hundred yards having been recently cleared of the rubble used to block it – and then crossed a larger sewer which,
in its turn, took a confusing route towards the Walbrook.

At the end of the drain under Newgate they changed
positions: the Mouse in the lead, followed by Johnny Bristow,
with Blackstone bringing up the rear. As they stumbled
along they talked and listened to their voices rumbling away
from them. It was after Johnny Bristow had said 'I knew
you'd come for me' that Blackstone realised that there was
a danger that he might reveal his identity to the Mouse.

'I try and keep my promises,' Blackstone said.

'Known him for long, have you?' the Mouse asked.
They had picked up a lantern inside the tunnel; the
Mouse held it in front of him and his silhouette practically
blocked the tunnel.

'Long enough,' Blackstone replied, fingering the pistol
under his rags.

The Mouse turned his head and looked behind him.
'They try and scrag 'em young these days, don't they,
young 'un?'

Johnny Bristow said: 'I knew I'd be all right when Mr—'

He fell heavily as Blackstone hooked his legs from under
him. Blackstone leaped forward to help him, whispering
that his name was Edmunds and that he wasn't a Bow Street
Runner.

'What are—'

'I know Johnny's sister,' Blackstone told the Mouse. 'A pretty girl is Mercy.'

The boy was silent, snatched from the gallows into mystery.

The Mouse said: 'Johnny might as well know what we're about, eh? He might as well know that he's about to make history.' He turned again. 'Who do you think I am, Johnny Bristow?'

'I heard Mr Edmunds' – Blackstone grinned in the dark – 'call you the Mouse.'

'Aye, that's what they call me because I knows my way around the holes and tunnels of London. Knows them almost as well as Goldie, I does. But I learned everything I know from Goldie. He's the best.' The Mouse paused. 'He's the king.'

'King of the underworld?'

'Underground,' the Mouse corrected him.

The boy said: 'But I don't understand why you're helping me.'

The Mouse laughed his curious, high-pitched laugh. 'Tell him, Edmunds. Tell him what it's all about.'

Blackstone took a deep breath and said: 'It's like this, Johnny. You've heard about the Diddiki?' The boy stopped and turned and said in a breathless voice that he had. 'Right,' Blackstone went on. 'Then this man Gold is their leader. He's the one who's arranged the whole thing. At midnight he and the Mouse will enter the bullion vaults of the Bank of England and make the Bow Street Runners and Blackstone the laughing-stock of England.' Blackstone gently kicked Johnny Bristow.

The boy laughed. 'I reckons Jack Ketch will be the laughing stock, too, when he goes to my salt-box and finds me gone.'

The Mouse stopped and leaned against the wall. 'So, what do you think of that? You're a member of the Diddiki now even if you don't go into the vaults, because if you did the chances are they'd take you back to the gallows.'

The boy shivered.

Blackstone said: 'But don't you worry. We'll have you away from London by dawn. And then—' Blackstone gestured grandly in the dim light. 'And then who knows... New York, Paris... The world's your oyster.'

The Mouse fingered his remaining ear. 'From now on,' he told them, 'the going's not so easy. Edmunds and me will have to keep low. But we should make it within the hour. By ten, I reckon. Then there's a bit of work to do with Goldie. Then a rest. Then up we go into the vaults. Goldie and me, that is,' he corrected himself.

Johnny Bristow said: 'You know, I still can't hardly believe it.' He put his hand to his neck. 'It still feels as if there's a rope there. I don't suppose no one can imagine what it feels like sitting there counting the minutes. You know, you just can't believe it, that they're going to end your life just like that and you'll be dancing on the end of a rope while everyone else's life is going on.'

Suddenly Johnny Bristow began to cry.

The Mouse stretched out an enormous hand, touched the boy's sleeve and said in his soft voice: 'Don't worry, lad. It's all over. You're all right now. You're in good company. Nothing more to worry about.'

They set off again, stooping low, resting every few minutes. During one of these rests Blackstone asked the Mouse how he had managed to retain the physique of a prizefighter – no stoop, no bandy legs. The Mouse told him that he'd once been a butcher and he had taken pride in his build, and now, whenever he surfaced from the underground warrens of London, he exercised and walked around his rooms with a book on his head to fight the hunch that was the hallmark of all toshermen and coalminers. He punched the boy in the ribs. 'And I suppose you want to know what happened to my lug?' The Mouse touched the tattered remains of his ear.

'I wasn't going to ask…'

'They all do eventually.' He grinned and Blackstone saw the flash of his teeth in the lamp-light. 'It was bitten off, young 'un. That's what happened to it.' He sounded proud of the loss.

The boy asked who had bitten it off.

'An Irishman, a big paddy who said something about my voice.'

Blackstone wondered what else was missing besides the ear.

'So we had a go at each other down in Bluegate Fields. Bets were laid, and when my ear came off most of the blunt went on to the mick. But it seemed to frighten him, that did, you know, my ear coming off clean as a whistle, and he just stood there staring at me as though I had no right to be standing there with one ear. But you don't use your ears at milling so I went at him, tapped his claret and laid him out in a couple of ticks.'

'And the ear?'

'Ah, they all asks that,' the Mouse said, reaching into his pocket and producing a shrivelled object wrapped in newspaper. 'There she is, my dear, there's old Mouse's lug. I never goes anywhere without it.'

They stared at the ear for a few moments, then Blackstone asked: 'What's you real name?'

'Ah, that's another question they all asks.' The Mouse put his ear back in his pocket. 'I do believe it was Johnson, but the Mouse is as good a monnicker as any, ain't it?'

227

Blackstone took some snuff. Then asked: 'What's Gold's real name?'

His voice echoed down the tunnel. Silence. Finally the Mouse asked why Blackstone thought he should have any other name. Silence again – suspicion freezing between them.

Blackstone shrugged. 'I always thought he got the name because he found so much gold. But if that's his name, then that's his name.'

'That's his name, all right.' the Mouse said. 'Funny you should think otherwise.'

'I think it's a good name,' Johnny Bristow said. 'I wish I was called Gold.'

'We'll have to call you something,' Blackstone said. 'Can't keep the name Bristow any longer, can you?'

'Call me Gold then.'

Blackstone shook his head. 'One's enough.' He rasped his hand over the stubble on his chin. 'How about Silver?'

The Mouse said: 'Aye, Johnny Silver, I like that.'

'Then Johnny Silver it is,' Blackstone said.

The Mouse, Blackstone and Johnny Silver continued on their way. They arrived under the vaults of the Bank of England at 9.45 p.m.

Which was the time that the flame in George Ruthven's lamp flickered for the last time and died.

Ruthven blundered on, convinced that earlier in the day he had cheated fate and fate was making a come-back. His grave *was* to be a sewer under London and he might as well accept it, lie down and wait for the rats to start gnawing.

He abandoned the lamp and crawled on, repenting his life of sin, until he butted the brickwork with his head. He felt around at the base of the bricks: there were the chips of mortar. He eased himself into a sitting position and stayed still, breathing heavily. Then he took a blunt chisel from his pocket, spread his jacket and began to pick at the mortar between the bricks so that it fell on to the jacket. After five minutes he had one brick free; he pulled it out and placed it gently on the ground. He peered through the hole. He thought he could see a glow far away, but it might have been hallucination – or a ghost. He returned to the brickwork, working with a stealth that surprised him because stealth had never been one of his qualities. Another brick came free; he put his ear to the aperture; he thought he could hear running water. The Walbrook? He felt the surface of the wall and set about removing more bricks at regular intervals so that an observer from the other side would still see the wall without realising that it had been doctored so as to collapse readily with one Ruthven-style shove. An hour later Ruthven had a pile of twenty bricks beside him and the wall was holed like the canvas of a pin-show. He tested the wall with his shoulder and felt it shift. He stopped work and sat back against the wall waiting for the signal, trying to judge the time. If no signal came then he would have to knock down the wall and tackle the Diddiki – Gold, that was, and God knows who else – singlehanded. He relished the opportunity, if only he knew how far he would have to crawl to reach them; a man crawling in a drain isn't a difficult target for the worst marksman in the world … If only he knew what the time was. Ten, eleven? One seemed to lose track of time in a sewer, Ruthven reflected. He took his watch from his pocket and stared at it; he might have been staring at a brick. He found a coin in his pocket and levered the back off the watch; the face and mechanism fell into the palm of his hand; gingerly he tried to feel the hands; but one thick forefinger brushed against the little hand and then all sense of time was lost. He occupied a few minutes planning what he would do to the baker if he ever returned from the grave: he imagined him drowning in a vat of dough and grinned in the darkness. He decided to try and estimate the passing of one hour and then smash down the wall. He began to count the seconds.

At that moment it was 10.15 p.m.

'And now,' Peel said, as a clock in the dining-room chimed eleven, 'I suggest we adjourn to the vaults.'

'Any minute now,' Gold said to the boy Tom. 'He should be here any minute now. Then you do your bit up in the cavity beside the flagstone.'

'The Mouse is taking his time, isn't he?' Tom said.

'Don't you worry about him,' Gold said.

'But he is late, isn't he?'

'He'll be here,' Gold said. He grinned but the boy could sense his unease. 'Just give him a few more minutes. You can rely on the Mouse, we've worked together for a long time.'

'But he should have been here ages ago.'

Gold looked at his watch; it was true – the Mouse *should* have been there ages ago. In a few minutes they'd have to start work without the Mouse, without his muscles. But they could do it, they had to do it, because it had taken all these years. Mouse, Mouse, where are you? Squeak, old mouse, for pity's sake squeak.

The boy said: 'He's not coming. Blackstone's got him.'

Gold bunched his fists. 'Don't say that boy.' He ran his hand through his hair. 'Don't say that.'

'I'm sorry,' the boy said.

'Time to get up into your hole,' Gold said. 'We've got half an hour, just as we planned. All you have to do is get up there and release the supports jamming the flagstone.'

The boy stared upwards. Two layers of stonework had been removed so that one stone was bared; that stone separated them from the bullion vault. The only way up to it was a coffin-shaped hollow in the wall of the tunnel Gold had cut along the course of the Walbrook; he had tried to make it wider but had struck granite instead of blue clay arid only a boy could squeeze up it. Once he was up beside the flagstone all the boy had to do was to remove the supports running parallel with the ground. Then the flagstone would be balanced on a single thick pole with – or so they had planned – the Mouse at the bottom of it. One heave, as though he was tossing the caber, and the flagstone would erupt into the vault. Then Gold on to his shoulders and into the vault. A dangling rope and the Mouse would pull himself up. Except that there was no Mouse in sight.

The boy said: 'But, Mr Gold, you'll never be able to hold the pole with the stone on top of it. Now when I've pulled out the other supports. It'll crush you...'

'Do you think I'm a weakling, young Tom?'

'Not a weakling, Mr Gold. But not as strong as you say the Mouse is. You know, it would be all right with the two of you holding the pole.'

'It'll be all right with one,' Gold snapped. 'It's got to be.' He glanced at his watch again. It was 11.35. Where the hell was the Mouse?

The Mouse would have liked to answer him. But, at that moment, he was sitting on the ground in a tunnel two hundred yards away with his hands clasped behind his neck and the twin-barrels of a Manton percussion pistol rammed in his back.

Chapter Twenty-one

The champagne was ready. Two magnums of it in a silver ice-bucket. If the Diddiki made it, then that's the way the Fancy would like to see their feat acknowledged, and the directors of the Bank of England were very sensitive to public opinion at the present time.

Peel and Birnie and the directors sat together at a table a few feet from more golden wealth than the world's pirates had plundered throughout history.

'Twenty minutes to go,' Peel said. He turned to Birnie. 'Are you sure Blackstone isn't the Diddiki?'

Birnie, who wasn't sure of anything any more, said: 'He's the best Runner we've got,' and was surprised to hear himself say it.

Page and Bentley, standing guard at the massive door to the vaults, grimaced.

'Conspicuous by his absence, wouldn't you say?' commented the director with the glossy voice.

Birnie didn't reply.

At about the same time, not far away, seven men were preparing themselves for the most dramatic event of their lives: they were preparing themselves to die at the end of a rope. The rioting had died away and now they were trying to savour their last hours; surprisingly a couple of them had fallen asleep; the remaining five had drunk enough to intoxicate half the felons in Newgate.

In the eighth condemned cell there was no contrition, no desperate bravado, no attempts to cosset death with alcohol. The occupant was a turnkey and, although he battered at the door for most of the night, no one came to his aid because few relished hearing the last pleas of the damned.

The Mouse said: 'You're Blackstone, aren't you?'

Blackstone said he was.

'Was the young 'un in on this?'

'He just happened to be along,' Blackstone said.

'That's something then. I wouldn't like to think he betrayed me.' He paused. 'What's going to happen to him?'

'To Johnny Silver? I think he'll go to sea. Would you like that. Johnny?'

'Anything you say, Mr Blackstone. But –'

'Yes, Johnny?'

'Isn't there anything we can do about the … the Diddiki? About the Mouse and this man Gold. I mean, they've worked so hard …'

The Mouse said: 'We ain't finished yet, lad'. He jerked his head backwards. 'It would take more than a ball in the back to stop me.'

Blackstone glanced at the most incongruous object concealed in his rags – his gold Breguet. It was 11.50. 'I reckon Gold's about to try it by himself,' he said.

'And he'll make it, I'll wager.'

Blackstone shook his head. 'He won't and you know it. The job needs your strength and you aren't there.'

'Supposing I was to get up now and go and help him?'

'Then I'd shoot you,' Blackstone said. He addressed himself to the boy, conscious that he was disappointing him. The boy was his conscience, the conscience that had haunted him since he had stepped across the border from the wrong to the right side of the law. 'The Diddiki threw down the gauntlet,' he said. 'If you make a challenge then you've got to risk losing. Right now the whole of England is expecting Blackstone to be ridiculed. I can't let that happen, now can I?'

'No, sir,' the boy said.

'Is that all you've got to say?'

'You saved my life,' Johnny said.

'But you think I should let them beat me?'

'I don't know,' the boy said.

The Mouse said: 'You never give up, do you, Blackstone? You sent an innocent man to jail; now you're denying him his revenge. Are you proud of it?'

Blackstone didn't reply. He glanced once more at his watch, then raised his pistol and fired a ball into the roof of the tunnel. The explosion shocked them, pained their eardrums, cannoned around the tunnel as it sought escape.

It reached Ruthven who had been waiting for this signal. He pushed the wall with his shoulder, waiting a second as the bricks tumbled around him. Then he was over them, moving as swiftly as he could on his hands and knees. The glow ahead grew stronger.

The boy crouched in the cavity and shouted to Gold: 'What was that?' The noise of the shot swept past them heading for the source of the Walbrook.

Gold bellowed: 'Knock the supports away.' He grasped the pole and groaned as the weight of the world pressed down on him. He heaved but the flagstone didn't move. 'I can't...' his voice choked in his throat.

The Mouse was running towards them. Blackstone, gun in hand, was close behind him.

Johnny Bristow shouted: 'Don't shoot him Mr Blackstone. Please—'

Ruthven, Blackstone and the Mouse arrived under the flagstone at the same moment – one minute before midnight. The pole was now at an angle and Gold was sinking to the ground.

Blackstone shoved the gun in the Mouse's back. 'Get hold of it, man.' He turned to Ruthven. 'And you, George.'

The pole straightened, the flagstone moved, then shot upwards like a cannon-ball.

Peel ducked, then straightened up, and, with a presence of mind which gave him much satisfaction when he recalled it later, said: 'Here they come.'

And into the bullion vault of the Bank of England climbed Edmund Blackstone.

CHAPTER TWENTY-TWO

That morning seven men died on the scaffold, but their demise was overshadowed by the sensational way in which Blackstone had outwitted the Diddiki and at the same time allowed them their victory.

Blackstone was followed into the vault by Gold, then the Mouse and, lastly, the boy Tom. Ruthven made his way back to the baker's yard with Johnny Bristow.

The champagne corks popped and the envelope stuffed with bank-notes was handed over to Gold. Later Blackstone and the Diddiki appeared before the crowd after a public announcement about the outcome of the vendetta. Publicly they cancelled their side-bets because, after all, neither of them had won – or lost.

Birnie shook Blackstone's hand and said: 'Report to me later. There are one or two things that need an explanation...' But there was a curious lopsided expression on his face which Blackstone interpreted as a smile. He described this phenomenon later in the Brown Bear but no one believed him.

The turnkey found in the condemned cell was severely reprimanded, but the Keeper didn't make too much fuss about the disappearance of the boy. Boys didn't rate very high in the execution stakes, and certainly the prison authorities could do without any more unfavourable publicity with

Elizabeth Fry still snapping at their heels. Lord Hardinge also heard about the boy's disappearance but, for reasons best known to himself, took no action.

Later that morning Blackstone took a cab to the baker's and dispatched Ruthven to his rooms in Paddington to bring back Mercy with her luggage, such as it was. He had booked two passages on a ship bound for America, the New World, and the skipper was waiting impatiently at Wapping.

'Can't I stay?' she asked.

Blackstone shook his head. He couldn't think of anything to say so he kissed her gently and felt the tears on her cheeks.

'Look after the young 'un,' he said.

'I will,' she said and climbed into the cab with Johnny Silver and was gone.

Which left Lawler. According to Page, Lawler had gone to ground somewhere – but the lure of the city would bring him back. Blackstone decided to warn off the punters after Lawler's skin because he now had a more potent hold over him: he could always threaten to reveal his home address to Mrs Rawlinson.

Blackstone waited while Ruthven threatened the baker with the house of correction, the treadmill, the hulks and the convict ships. Then, as they walked back beneath grey skies towards Bow Street, he said: 'By the way, George, what was Gold's real name?'

'Bentley,' Ruthven said. 'Seems our young Bentley was his son. Not surprising Gold got first-hand information about what we were doing, eh, Blackie?'

'Do you think Bentley realised what he was doing?'

Ruthven shook his head. 'Why should he? He didn't know his dad was the Diddiki, did he?'

Absentmindedly Blackstone brushed his cheek as a man deep in thought brushes away a fly. It was a few moments before he realised that he was trying to brush away a snowflake. He glanced at his Breguet: Page owed him a sovereign. He lengthened his stride as the snow began to fall more thickly, covering the city of London – the city, that is, that lay above the ground.

Historical Note

The plot concerning the Bank of England is based on an event which, if it happened at all – and the Old Lady's chroniclers give it little credence – occurred about ten years after the action of my novel. Some sewermen, so it goes, discovered an old drain which ran into the bullion room. They wrote a letter to the directors offering to meet them in the vault 'at a dark and midnight hour'. They were given £800 for their honesty. There is no doubt, however, that Charles Robert Cockerell, architect to the Bank, wrote to the building committee: 'In May 1836, having had reason to apprehend danger from our sewers, it was discovered that an open and unobstructed sewer leads directly from the gold vaults down to Downgate.' What's more, in April of that year, the secretary of the Bank had applied to the Commissioner of Sewers for plans of the area. And in 1837 and 1838 applications were made to George Bailey, curator of the Soane Museum, for the return of plans of the Bank's drains.

So, it would seem, something was up, even if subsequent historians treat the aspirations of the sewermen with some cynicism. Happily, cynicism is not incumbent upon a novelist, although I have been at some pains to establish accuracy, detail and background for the story.

For more than a century after the time of this narrative the battle to repeal the hanging laws continued, round after agonising round. By 1861 capital crimes had been reduced to four: murder, treason, piracy with violence, and setting fire to dockyards and arsenals. The last public hanging took place on 26 May 1868, outside Newgate prison, the grisly distinction falling to an Irishman, Michael Barrett, who was executed for his part in a Fenian bomb conspiracy.